Not Bad for a Girl

ANASTASIA RYAN

sourcebooks
casablanca

Published by Sourcebooks Casablanca, an imprint of Sourcebooks
P.O. Box 4410, Naperville, Illinois 60567-4410
(630) 961-3900
sourcebooks.com

Cataloging-in-Publication Data is on file with the Library of Congress.

Printed and bound in Canada.
MBP 10 9 8 7 6 5 4 3 2 1

For Chance, my son and
bestest friend in the world.

Chapter 1

A LAUGH CAUGHT IN MY THROAT. "YOU'RE JOKING, RIGHT?" NO ONE
said a word. I looked around the crowded meeting room, and everyone
averted their eyes. "Oh, shit, you're not joking," I whispered.

Had I really said that out loud? I clamped my hand over my mouth,
but it was too late. The words were already out there. "I must have heard
you wrong," I said politely, then tried to smile.

Gerald Grass, the managing director who had flown to Denver just for
this meeting, narrowed his eyes at me. "I *said* we should all congratulate
Taggart McCaffrey on his promotion," he repeated.

There was a weak spattering of applause. Taggert, who was sitting right
in front of Grass, pumped his fist into the air and swung his head around
to grin at the rest of us.

My entire body froze. That was supposed to be *my* promotion. I had
worked hard for it. Long hours, no social life—you name it, I'd given
it all to the job. I'd even trained Taggert. He wasn't the absolute worst,
but he wasn't the best either. I'd had to listen to his awful jokes and sit

through his beer pong stories as I showed him the ropes and continually corrected his mistakes as a programmer at Apollo IT. I hadn't even been given the courtesy of a rejection before this very public announcement. And my direct boss didn't even have the balls to show up in person to the meeting.

An ache formed behind my eye. "Taggart hasn't been with the company long enough to qualify," I said. "The rules say at least six months. No offense, Taggart," I threw in his direction, and he beamed at me.

"We made an exception due to Taggart's extreme talent." Grass's eyes narrowed even more. They were practically closed now, daring me to keep talking.

I did worse than that. I laughed. In my defense, it was a fear response. Because, you know, this couldn't actually be happening, right? And now that I'd started, I couldn't stop. The baby gate between my mind and mouth had broken. "Seriously?"

"Are you questioning our judgment, miss?" he asked me sharply.

"No questions, just supreme disappointment," I answered. I looked over at Taggart, then back at Grass. "You know he majored in PE," I said.

Taggart blinked at me. "I majored in physical education."

I sighed and looked up at the ceiling. "Have you ever made an app, Taggart?"

"Yeah, I made one with you, remember?"

"You were more of a spectator there, Taggart." I turned back to the managing director. "This is the guy you chose to run the creative team?" I swallowed, then turned back to Taggart. He was about to outrank me by a *lot*. "No offense. Again," I added.

He grinned. "None taken. I have so much to teach you guys."

Like what? How to do a keg stand? I couldn't wait for the mansplaining of concepts *I* had taught him.

"Will there still be raises for the rest of the employees?" I asked. We'd all been promised incremental increases.

"There's no money left in the budget for raises," Grass said. "Taggert drove a hard bargain." Then he proudly slapped him on the back, and the two of them fist-bumped.

Were they serious? It was hard to tell. Was this whole thing some sort of weird "gotcha" moment?

"What's the incentive for the rest of us to work hard, then?" I asked.

The room was completely still, and I sent a silent *you're welcome* to the other employees for being the one to ask what we were all thinking.

Grass cleared his throat and turned back to the group, dismissing me. "Moving forward we need to change our thinking. These are difficult times; I understand how you all must feel. We're all suffering. I haven't been able to take my yacht out once this past month." He shook his head sadly.

Aw, poor guy. He really *did* seem to understand what we were facing.

He sighed. "It's important to remember that advancement is often overrated. Now that we have a full management team, it's time to uncouple performance from paychecks. Providing a good product to the client is a reward in itself. It builds character." He looked around the room and smiled at everyone but me.

"'Uncouple'? Like a divorce?" I asked. All my anger and frustration bubbled up into my throat. "Could you maybe clarify exactly what that means?" I asked tersely, pushing back my chair and standing. Why was no one else asking questions?

Gerald Grass pinched the bridge of his nose. "Could you please stand?"

"I *am* standing," I grumbled. Being four-eleven had its disadvantages, but I spoke louder to compensate. "Are you saying no more promotions or raises or bonuses?" I asked.

"The reward of *pride* cannot be overstated," he said through gritted teeth.

"It seems like that's exactly what you're doing," I said. "I appreciate that you care about our characters," I added, striving to stay civil, "and we, of course, care about your lonely yacht, but not providing advancement opportunities won't make people *want* to work hard." I'd been with the company for what felt like forever. I was extremely qualified for that job and had accepted the position at Apollo IT *because* they'd promised me the opportunity for advancement during my interview. And they'd given it to a guy practically fresh out of school. How had he had time to prove himself? And now even future promotions were off the table for the rest of us. I felt like I was on the *Titanic* and Taggert had "driven a hard bargain" for the last lifeboat.

I glanced around the meeting room. "We need incentives. Right, everyone?" I looked over at my work besties, Patrick and Heidi, who both stared back at me in horror. "Right? He just said none of us has a future here. You know, except for Taggert."

He gave me a thumbs-up.

"Thank you, miss," Grass said in a way that sucked the warmth out of the room—except for the corner where Taggart sat. He was a bright ball of sunshine. "I appreciate your comments, but the rest of the team understands the power of personal growth in a way you obviously do not. Employees do best when they accept ambiguity in their careers and paychecks."

"'Ambiguity' in our paychecks?" I yelped. "I don't think a financial advisor would agree." I wasn't sure what a financial advisor did—I'd never met one and couldn't imagine ever having enough money to need one—but there was nothing ambiguous about my rent. His eyes hardened again, and part of me wished I could pull the words back out of the air. The rest of me was just over it. Still, I tried to salvage what I could. "I just mean that ambiguity with income usually isn't great." I grunted. "Sir."

"If no one else has anything to add, you can get back to your desks. Everyone except you." He pointed directly at me.

The room emptied in seconds. "Your name?" he asked.

I swallowed hard. "Indiana Aaron," I replied. It felt like I had a ton of lead in my stomach. The same feeling I always had in elementary school. The principal had hated me. I'd always been sure to give him my opinion, too.

Grass wrote it down, nodded, and waved me off.

I took a quick restroom break to dry heave a little as I leaned my back against the cool tiles of the wall. I needed this job. I also needed that promotion. And, okay, maybe I needed a little tact. But I'd always sucked at the dance where coworkers sat around and spoke in euphemisms with deference to their superiors and never said what they actually meant. When you're all adults, does there really need to be a hierarchy where one person can say something but the others have to nod and agree like you're not actually equals (except that some get paid a lot more than others)? That had been what I was most looking forward to about being an adult. Dropping all the *pretense* and finally being respected. I thought back to myself as a kid. That little girl had no idea what was waiting for her.

When my stomach settled a little, I went to the break room and grabbed a cup of coffee. Once I got back to my desk, there was an email from some guy named Shane Dalton in the accounting department. My heart stopped, and not just because of his tiny avatar picture, which looked like the thumbnail of a nerdy romance novel hero. I took a breath and opened it, expecting it to say, *you're fired* in all caps. I had to read it twice before the words sank in.

The funds have been reallocated, and your transfer request to the remote-based New York team has been approved.

My skin felt prickly. I hadn't made any request.

I was so deep in my feels that I didn't even notice when my boss leaned against my cubicle. "Sorry, Ana," he said. "There wasn't anything I could do. I hate to lose you on the team, but you're never going to be able to get a leadership role, especially after that. You just can't keep your mouth shut."

As if. He'd given away my promotion before I'd even opened my mouth.

—————

"This award goes to the employee most likely to say what everyone is thinking," Heidi said brightly as she handed me a little plastic trophy. I twirled it on the bar and shot her a dirty look.

She leaned down close to whisper in my ear. Happy hour at Cisco's was noisy. It was the best hole-in-the-wall bar Denver had to offer. "At least you didn't get fired."

This was my going-away party, courtesy of my big mouth.

"Where are my besties?" our coworker Patrick called from across the bar.

"Over here!" Heidi yelled, waving her arms. "Ana and I haven't ordered yet."

He took the stool next to mine and gave me a quick hug. "Heidi and I thought you needed an award after that performance."

"I think this may be the only award I've ever gotten at work," I said, thinking back. "Should I, like, give a speech or something?"

"I think you've already done that," Patrick said, gesturing for the bartender. "Can we get a pitcher of margs, please?"

"I still think I should be able to give a speech," I muttered.

"That's because you always have so much to say." Patrick grinned.

"I hate that because it's true," I groaned. "But seriously, I just said what everyone else wanted to say. I hate how that job always falls to me." I started to slip the little trophy in my bag when something caught my eye. The homemade label around the base was peeling a little. I tugged on the edge until I could see what was written underneath. "I can count to a hundred!" I read aloud and jerked around to look at Heidi.

"Sorry," she said defensively. "Those were the only trophies they had at the drugstore."

"I appreciate the thought. Sort of," I said. "You know, if I were a guy, I wouldn't be bossy. I'd be assertive." I pushed off my barstool and stood up straight. I was still practically eye level with the bar. "But since I'm not, I'm never going to get promoted. And now, lucky you, thanks to Taggart, no one else will either." I slumped back down and felt my eyes fill up. Damn it. The indignity sucked. It would have been one thing to lose out on the position to someone who was qualified, but to lose it to some kid who probably played golf with the managing director's son was something else entirely.

"Who am I kidding?" I asked. "Who was I *ever* kidding? I can't believe I thought I had a shot at being taken seriously as a coder. They practically demoted me. Nobody wants to work on the New York team." No one had volunteered when we'd been asked, and a lot of it had to do with the guy they'd put in charge of it, Melvin Hammer. The last project he'd worked on failed, but just like so many other higher-ups, they kept giving him chances. "But I don't want to be where I am now either, so…"

"No, don't talk that way," Heidi said forcefully. "I'm not on the tech side of the business since I'm the office manager, but even I know you're the most talented coder at Apollo. So does Patrick. Fuck that dude, seriously."

"You can do anything on a computer; I'm totally in awe of both your skills and your lack of filter," Patrick said. He looked down at his drink. Patrick had been the one to suggest I apply at Apollo IT when I'd hit a brick wall at my last job. We'd gone to college together, and I'd helped him struggle through our statistics class, while he dragged me to all the fun parties and pulled me into his close circle of friends.

Heidi stood and raised her glass to me. "My favorite was when the boss said to embrace paycheck ambiguity, and you told him he wasn't qualified to give financial advice."

"He isn't!" I pushed her glass back down. "And while you're at it, please sit your whole body down." Heidi was like an Amazon: almost six feet, always beautifully dressed, and wearing heels every day. I felt tiny next to her. If I had my way, she would squat-walk next to me every day on our lunch breaks.

She sat obediently and took a drink.

"My favorite was when you yelped, 'Like a divorce?' when he said our job performance and our paychecks needed to uncouple." Patrick laughed, even though just hearing it made me angry again. He poured me a margarita with a salted rim and a little lime.

"Who tells their employees they'll never have a future at the company? Fix it instead. Their system is broken, not my coupling. Rude." I dropped my head onto Patrick's shoulder and sighed.

"Satisfaction in a job well done is the only reward I need," he said solemnly, then downed his drink.

"Did satisfaction pay for those margaritas?" I shot back. I took a big sip and winced.

"I understand the power of *personal growth* better than you." He smirked.

"Because—" I started.

"I learned long ago never to talk in meetings," he said.

I huffed and smacked him on the arm.

"So tiny and so full of rage," he observed.

"That's fair." I kept my face neutral, but the truth was, I was embarrassed. I'd always offered my opinion, even (especially?) when no one had asked for it. I exhaled slowly when I thought of the way I had responded during the meeting. Could I have been more diplomatic and still spoken up? No. Or at least not me personally. The look Grass had given me at the end of the meeting had been clear. I was lucky to still have a job.

"We support you, just not in front of the boss," Heidi added. "That's why we're still employed."

"So am I!" I protested.

"Not for long, sweetie." Patrick winked at me. "Unless you change a few things, especially if you're going to be working for this Melon Hamster guy. Everyone says he's only out for himself."

"Melon Hamster," I said thoughtfully. "I don't think that's his name. I really hope I'm wrong, though. Melon Hamster sounds like a lovely person."

Patrick leaned down and hugged me. He was at least a foot taller than me, but who wasn't? He had a kindness about him that I loved, even when he was snarky. He straightened up and fixed the sleeve of his impeccable suit as he poured himself another glass. He always looked ready for a board meeting, but when he shifted forward, I could see he was wearing his hedgehog socks today. Each day was something equally ridiculous. We all had different ways of rebelling.

"Just don't change *too* much," he said as he tipped the pitcher to my glass.

He smoothed the flyaway hair from the mass of curls down my back. It was auburn, naturally curly, and came down to my waist. "You have so much hair. I could cut it off and make myself a wig."

"You are so weird," I told him. "But you'd look beautiful."

"Quite the meeting, wasn't it?" said a male voice behind us.

The groan slipped out before I could stop it. I knew that voice. Jason Rhodes. He worked in our office, but we weren't in the same division. He was such a guy's guy, but everyone always put up with it. Come to think of it, why had *he* never been transferred?

I turned around and gave him a strained smile. "Can I help you?" I asked.

He grinned at me. Jason was about my age, tall, wearing a navy suit with the tie loosened. He had a Dos Equis beer in one hand, because of course he did. "I think you made an impression on the MD," he said as he leaned against the bar.

"You think?" I asked tartly.

"Not sure he likes you very much," he said after he took a swig.

"So glad you showed up to point out the obvious," I said, feigning relief. "If I had left here without you mansplaining to me, I might never have known. Thank you, Jason. Truly."

His swagger faltered for a second, but he picked it back up pretty quickly. "Why is your name Indiana?" he asked. "Why not Wyoming or, like, Nevada?"

"Why is yours Jason?" I answered.

"Son of Jay," he said, straight-faced.

"Oh." I rolled my eyes. "Ana of Indy then."

Wide-eyed, Patrick sipped his drink, looking back and forth between us, as Heidi put her arm around me. "I think she's had a bad enough day, Jason. Maybe take off?"

He shrugged. "Just wanted to let you all know that after the meeting, I explained to Mr. Grass about how people need an incentive to work hard. Taking away promotions and bonuses lowers morale. He said that I made a good point, and he'd give it some more thought."

"That's what I said!" I burst out. "Are you serious?"

"I guess it's just the way you said it," he said. "Or maybe this whole"—he gestured at me vaguely—"impression doesn't inspire confidence with guys like him," he said. "But don't worry, I told Gerald it wasn't worth firing you."

"What?" I yelped. "He was for sure going to fire me?"

"Yeah, he was," Jason said seriously. "You have to play the game, Indiana. But I didn't know you were going to get transferred to Melvin Hammer's team." He whistled through his teeth. "That's almost as bad.

That division is hanging on by a thread. Melvin got promoted way past his ability, so this is make-or-break for him. He has to turn this assignment into something stellar, or he's out. I guess it's a last shot for both of you." He drained his beer and set his bottle on the bar. "Good luck," he said, then moved off into the darkening crowd.

God damn it. "Is he for real?" I asked Patrick and Heidi.

Heidi shrugged, and Patrick shook his head. "Ignore him. He's just being difficult. What does he know about the New York team? Anyway, I think this whole new chapter will be good for you. It's cool you'll get to work from home," Patrick said and smiled a bit unconvincingly.

"Nobody wants to work on that remote team," I said again. "You heard Jason. Sounds like a sinking ship."

"Every new place is a new opportunity. Maybe you can be the hero who saves the team. At least you'll be one of those people who may or may not be dressed under your desk," Heidi offered.

"I'm keeping my camera *off*," I emphasized. "And my mouth shut. And you're right, maybe this will be a good opportunity for me. I can learn to be chill."

"Not sure that's true," Patrick threw in.

I really could learn, I promised myself. I would install a steel baby gate between my mind and mouth, and I would learn.

Chapter 2

THE WHOLE BIG MESS STARTED A WEEK INTO MY NEW JOB. I'D BEEN learning the ropes quickly and had kept my camera off, saying it was broken, like an OG catfish, and corporate was supposed to be sending me a new computer so I could Zoom with everyone else during meetings. It hadn't really been an issue because most people kept their cameras off anyway, and we were required to have them off during meetings when the boss presented, since all the extra bandwidth caused a lag in the presentation. We just used the chat feature on the side of the screen to share our input.

Everything seemed to be going well, but I couldn't shake what Jason had said. This job didn't have a future. And then there was that other thing he'd implied, that looking the way I do—feminine, short, a little like a cartoon character if I were being honest with myself— was the reason no one could take me seriously. Most of that I had absolutely no control over. Of course, I knew the technology field was male-dominated, but I'd never really considered that I might need to alter myself physically to counter that. I'd always just tried harder than everyone else. Valedictorian. Summa cum laude. Phi Beta Kappa. All the honors.

But when I'd gotten home from the bar after my going-away party, I'd removed all the pink items from my work wardrobe, along with anything that had a bow on it. No more flowers or rose gold or lace in my work accessories or my home office area. No more neon pens or sparkly notebooks. If I wanted to be taken seriously, I was coming to realize, there was more to it than simply being good at what I do. I had to put away the glitter and break out the mattes, so to speak.

This particular morning, I woke up thoroughly confused. I picked my head up from my desk and gasped at the pain in my back. There was a puddle of drool where my head had rested next to the mouse pad. Must have passed out while working on the database. I yawned and stretched and rubbed my eyes on the too-long sleeves of my fleece pajamas. I glanced over at my fish tank—a beautifully planted, but empty aquarium next to my desk—before my eyes focused on what I was really looking for: the coffee maker. I was desperate for caffeine. I started a cup, then ran to the bathroom, and sat back down at the desk to check my email. I must have slept only a few hours at most. That was one thing that truly sucked about working remotely—the day was never truly over, when my desk was in my living room/bedroom/kitchen studio apartment. I couldn't afford a bigger place right now. My savings were running dry even in a studio.

I'd just taken my first sip of coffee when I pulled up the Outlook email tab and saw the message.

From: Melvin Hammer

To: Entire Team

Subject: New Reporting Tool

Team:

I have stressed the importance of providing functioning software to the client by the end of the month. You are nowhere near reaching that goal. I've attached the numbers for you to see below. Performance thus far is dismal. Please consider yourselves on notice. I am beyond disappointed with your failings thus far.

Melvin Hammer

Manager, Artemis Team

I was suddenly very awake and hot all over. My skin flushed. He sounded so angry. I'd only just joined the team, and I was already being lectured about my "dismal" performance? I'd worked my ass off on that software. He *had* to have gotten his data wrong. Is this why he'd been circling the drain at Apollo IT for a while now? I'd spent all night in the spreadsheet tabs, and I knew we were on track, ahead even, of our goal.

I flipped from tab to tab, looking at the programmers' names and output data. Then I would have laughed if I hadn't been so full of adrenaline. We hadn't messed up at all. Melvin just didn't know how to use a spreadsheet. Each programmer had their own tab, and the final page was set up to pull all the totals through a (totally incorrect) formula. Seriously? This dude sent a scathing message before even checking his own work?

I hesitated for a moment, hovering my fingers over the keyboard. I couldn't let this go, not when I'd been putting everything into it. Either I pointed out his mistake and made him look stupid, or I didn't and allowed myself to look stupid. Lose-lose. I took some deep breaths, trying to remember the meditation videos I listened to on YouTube whenever I was particularly anxious. They were usually about letting the calm of the universe wash away my bullshit or something. No dice. Some people ran away from confrontation, and those people baffled me. I had never been one to talk behind someone's back; I would much rather talk directly to their face. In this case, I'd rather just tell my boss straight up that he was wrong. But that was exactly what had gotten me transferred to Melvin's team in the first place.

I fired off a quick text to Heidi. New manager called us all idiots in an email. He said we're all on notice because he can't do simple math.

Uh-oh, she wrote back immediately. Watch your step.

It's not like I have a future on this team either, I texted back.

That's the spirit! she responded. Your positivity is inspiring. Keep your job, k?

I drained my cup of coffee and debated. Maybe it was the sight of my drool puddle on the desk that was the deciding factor. "I wish your name really was Hamster," I muttered, then squared my shoulders and hit the *reply* button. I was careful not to include the entire team.

From: Indiana Aaron

To: Melvin Hammer

Re: New Reporting Tool

Mr. Hammer:

Thank you for your email. I appreciate you reaching out and would like to reassure you that the team's goals have been met, even exceeded. This software is some of the best our company has produced, and I'm very proud of my part in it. The formulas in the database you sent are incomplete, likely due to an Excel error. I have corrected them and attached the new version to this email. Please feel free to follow up if you have any questions or concerns.

Best,

Indiana Aaron

Developer

Remote-Based NY Team

I read it over a few times, making sure not to imply guilt. *Welp, here goes nothing*, I thought, and hit *send*. I'd probably get transferred again or fired, but *someone* had to point out where the real problem was. Right? And, weirdly, again, that job seemed to fall to me.

I half-assed my work and tried to chill for the rest of the morning, waiting for a call. It didn't come.

At about three in the afternoon, a message appeared in my inbox from a Mr. Melvin Hammer, and my heart skipped a beat.

From: Melvin Hammer

To: Entire Team

Re: New Reporting Tool

Hi Team,

I wanted to circle back after my last message to you this morning. It has been brought to my attention that any possible issues with our progress were due to mathematical errors and not on the part of the developers. Indiana Aaron clarified the situation and has also showed me that the team has in fact exceeded its monthly goal. You can all thank Mr. Aaron and log out early this afternoon to get a head start on your weekend.

All best,

Melvin Hammer

Manager, Artemis Team

I blinked. Well, *that* was unexpected. Relief washed over me. He'd called me *Mr.*, but there was no way I was correcting him more than once in one day. I'd let it slide for now. There was still a possibility that Melvin was being shady and would hold it against me privately despite his email, but that was a problem for future me. I grinned at the unexpected extra time and logged out of the database. I grabbed my phone and texted Patrick.

Schools out! "Mr. Aaron" corrected the boss and we got the afternoon off.

Is that you? Haven't you learned not to correct your boss? he wrote back. Also, I can't be friends with someone who talks about themselves in the third person.

Yes it's me. And Ana would like to think our friendship is stronger than third person rhetoric.

Deal-breaker for me, dog, he said.

I fully shut down my computer and cleared off my workspace. I planned to completely unplug for the weekend. I'd booked a pottery class for Patrick and me, starting tonight, to thank him for getting me the job at Apollo IT in the first place. The class was super late in coming, but Patrick had kept rescheduling. It was almost as if he didn't want to go. I hadn't given him a choice this time because I knew he'd love it, even if he didn't. Still coming with me to the pottery class? I texted.

After a few minutes, he wrote back. Do I have to?

I rolled my eyes. Yes. You reschedule every month. Not this time. This is my THANK YOU to you. Accept it, dammit.

Fine. I'll pick you up at 5.

I tamed my hair the best I could and put on jeans for the first time in days. Working from home with no camera had reduced my wardrobe to old concert T-shirts and leggings. My dress clothes were all getting dusty in the closet, but it was awesome being comfortable all the time. I didn't miss physically going to work. There were a lot of unexpected perks to working on my couch. For one, I *loved* seeing so many cat butts during the informal meetings. There was something endearing about seeing people's pets wander by or swat at the screen while they talked about programming. Humanizing somehow. Some of my new coworkers used those weird backgrounds of beaches or city skylines, which made part of their faces disappear if they made any sudden moves. Most of them, however, just kept the camera off, or unflatteringly close to their faces, like shiny forehead shots, or occasionally just showing part of an arm or desk. I hadn't gotten to know any of them personally yet. And, of course, there was no break room or cubicle neighbors. As an introvert, it all went into my "pro" column. There was that one guy, though, who sometimes spoke. His name was Shane something. He wasn't part of the Artemis team, but he joined the meetings now and then, and usually talked about numbers and finances. He kept his camera off, too, but he had the nicest voice. I loved listening to him speak but never caught all the words because his voice was so soothing, it made my mind wander. There was no way he looked as good as he sounded. People rarely got both gifts.

By the time Patrick came to get me, I looked like a normal person who hadn't spent my past week gross and unbathed. Patrick was going to have *so* much fun, whether he wanted to or not.

"Miss me?" I asked as I got in the car.

"I don't play in mud for most people," he said, "so yeah. I guess."

Patrick grumbled all the way to the pottery class, but it was still good to see him. When we arrived, I held the door to the studio open for him. "After you, Mud Master. Oooh, that would make a great reality TV show. You and I could be on a dirt team together with a half hour to construct something impossible. Wouldn't that be awesome?"

Patrick made a sound like a low whine as the instructor, a fellow short pleasant woman named Kelli, waved to us. "Hi, Ana! I love your dedication. Your mom would be so proud of your tenacity. And you brought a friend!" She smiled broadly. "Pick any table you like," she said.

I waved back as Patrick looked around at the pottery wheels, kiln, and stacks of clay. "I pick the table with the wine," he said. "Where's the table with the wine?"

"There's no alcohol here. We're making pottery. I told you."

"But I thought we were doing the Drunken Degas thing. You know, where you get toasty and pretend to do a craft," he protested. "They do it with painting."

"I think you misunderstood," I said. "Besides, you'd get mud in your wine. Especially if we had a time limit and had to race other teams." I grinned at him and raised my eyebrows.

He shot me a betrayed look, settled into the seat closest to the door, and pulled a flask from his jacket pocket.

"What is that?" I hissed.

He shrugged. "If this isn't one of those drink-and-do-pots kind of places, then I'm gonna make it one."

"Excuse you, but no," I answered and gestured to the instructor. "And Kelli might hear you." I swatted his arm because a few other people had begun filing in and settling into the available seats.

"Why does Kelli like your dedication?" Patrick asked as he reluctantly slipped the flask back in his pocket.

"Because I've taken this class a few times. Like maybe more than a few," I confessed.

"Then you must be the goddess of pottery."

I winced. Not quite.

"Today we're going to make pinch pots," Kelli said brightly. "Everyone grab a chunk of clay and start molding it."

"A pinch pot sounds an awful lot like drug paraphernalia," Patrick mumbled, "but whatever."

We molded our clay as he filled me in on everything that had been going on in the office since I left. Jason had been right. The MD had retracted his statement and let everyone know that the idea of advancement was still on the table. Frustration and embarrassment washed through me. He probably didn't mean it, but he'd walked back the statement anyway. Otherwise, there wasn't that much to report. Ever since Patrick had met his husband, Joseph, and settled down, he'd been a lot less concerned about office drama.

As we worked, Patrick abandoned the pinch pot idea almost immediately and was shaping the clay into a little house. "So, Mr. Aaron, tell me about what happened today while I build a hobbit hole out of sticky dirt."

"It was probably just a mistake," I said as I shaped my clay into a wonky bird. "Teachers have mixed up my gender before. People tend to think of Indiana Jones when they hear my name and ask me if I'm an archeologist or if I'm good with a whip." I rolled my eyes. "But the important part is that he didn't fire me for pointing out his mistakes. Or transfer me to the unemployment office." I was trying to shape a beak on the bird when my phone buzzed. I picked it up, smearing clay across the surface.

I stared at the screen, confused, as I opened a message from Venmo. "Bruce Atkins paid you ten dollars."

"Who's Bruce Atkins?" Patrick asked as he looked over my shoulder.

I thought for a moment. "He's a guy on my development team, but

I don't think we've ever talked," I said. I scrolled down to read the message. "Indiana! Bro! You saved us from the Hammer. Have a drink on me tonight."

"Aw, looks like they really appreciate what you did for them, bro." Patrick grinned at me.

"That was really nice of him," I said. "Like, weird, but—"

The phone dinged again, and I again read aloud. "Allen Parks has paid you five dollars." I thumbed the message open. All hail the King! I read, noting the emoji of beer glasses clinking.

"Like, what is happening right now?" I asked myself. "I feel like I'm being initiated into some sort of secret club."

"Maybe you are. Do they all think you're a dude?" Patrick asked. He grabbed my phone and opened the Venmo app. "Well, no wonder," he said. "Your profile pic is Indiana Jones."

My cheeks reddened. "Well, he's the more famous of the two of us, so..." I wiped my hands clean and pulled up my work email on my phone. There were other messages as well, thanking me for the early start to the weekend and for "taking one for the team" by pointing out Hammer's mistake. "So it looks like a lot of people think I'm a man now. Those two little letters in Hammer's email got out of hand quickly."

"So none of your new coworkers have actually seen you? No camera? No conference calls? Nothing?"

I tried not to get defensive. "Well, I'm not exactly a commanding presence, you know? I figured if I kept face time to a minimum, they might respect me a little more. I didn't think they would think I was a guy. I just thought they wouldn't see me as a little girl," I said. "It's going to be so awkward to send out a message Monday morning correcting my gender.

Or should I just add pronouns to my signature? I feel like it's getting to the point where I'm going to have to address it."

"How would you do that? Like a gender-reveal email? 'It's a Girl!' that rains pink confetti when you open the message? I would probably die from secondhand embarrassment if you did that. So maybe you don't."

"Don't tell them?"

"Or don't correct them. You're right—this is a good opportunity to let people see your work instead of you. You're like that blob of clay."

"This one specifically?" I asked, turning back to my bird. It was looking more and more disturbing.

"Yeah, that one. Shape it. Give it wings!"

I turned it over in my hands. "I'm Frankenstein, and you're my monster," I told it.

He nodded approvingly. "Make that monster your bitch."

"I give you the spark of life." The bird listed to the side and fell over.

"It lives!" Patrick cried. "But in all honesty, you suck at pottery. If we really were on TV, you would have gotten us kicked out in the first round. Why are we taking this class?"

"Because my mom used to make pottery," I told him. "I'll never be good like she was, but I think it's fun. I have this one really clear memory of her using the wheel to make this beautiful pot. I think I was about three, and she made it look so easy and so graceful. I still have that pot." I kept my tone light. People always felt bad for me when they found out my mom had died when I was little. I missed her a lot. And I still got sad about it, but the truth was, I'd had a great time growing up with my dad. He'd let me take apart our television when I was eleven, even though it never worked quite right afterward. He'd let me paint his toenails every weekend. And he gave me all the love.

Patrick cleared his throat. "That's so sweet and terribly sad, it almost makes me feel like a jerk for telling you that what you're making looks like third-grade arts and crafts," he said. "Almost. Because it does."

I snorted and turned to check out his hobbit house. "You're one to talk," I began, then stopped. Patrick's little house was adorable. He was adding vines and leaves around a circular doorway and had carved little windows complete with shutters on either side. "Holy cow," I said. "Where have you been hiding this talent?"

He shrugged. "Bilbo deserves the best house in Middle Earth."

Kelli had been walking between the tables and chose this moment to stop by ours. "Oh, my word," she said as she caught sight of Patrick's creation. "This is truly lovely. Have you had classes before? What's your name, dear?"

"Patrick," he mumbled, and I saw the tips of his ears turn pink. I tried not to laugh at his obvious discomfort.

"Everyone, come over and see Patrick's little fairy hut!" Kelli called.

"Everyone don't come over," Patrick muttered under his breath. "And it's not a fairy hut, it's a *hobbit hole*."

The other students crowded around and oohed and aahed at his little house. One of them looked over at my misshapen bird. "What's that?"

"It's going to live in the home Patrick's making for it," I answered.

He drew himself up in his seat. "This is Bag End from the Shire, not a house for your lumpy duck."

I gasped and pretended to clutch my pearls. "Lumpy duck? Take that back," I said. I winked at him as everyone went back to their tables except Kelli, who lingered a moment longer. "What're we making today, Ana?" she asked.

I thought quickly. "Um, I call this piece *Transcendental Incoherence*."

Patrick snorted, but Kelli nodded, tilting her head as if she might see some meaning in the lopsided mess, if she could find the right angle. "Mm-hmm. Are we taking a break from the Emotions series?"

"Yeah. I'll get back to that next week."

"I listed *Suspicion* yesterday on our website," she told me. That one had started as an off-center cat but had ended up partially burned and cracked after firing.

Then she turned back to Patrick and touched his shoulder lightly. "You know, Patrick, our studio relies on donations to stay afloat. When people create pottery they choose not to take home, we list it on our website for people to bid on." Patrick opened his mouth, but she held up her hand quickly. "Now, I'm sure you'll want to keep your elf condo, but if you make anything in the future that you feel like leaving behind, your talent might raise some money for us. Just give it some thought." She smiled hopefully at him, then left for another table.

He dropped his forehead onto the desk. "Elf condo," he muttered.

"I'm almost jealous of your skill," I said, "but your embarrassment evens it out."

"Do they auction off your...er...art here, too?" he asked. "Your *Nonsense Incoherent*?"

I jerked around to look at him. "Are you going to make me say it? She lists them out of pity, okay? I don't think anyone bids. It's fine. It doesn't hurt my feelings. I hate that everyone thinks if you suck at something, you shouldn't do it. Like singing. If you suck at singing but you love it, you should totally sing."

"I agree with the sentiment, but if you suck at singing, please don't."

"Back in the day, when people had nothing to do except stare at each other, they painted and danced and sang even if they sucked. At least they do in Jane Austen. And while that sounds horrible in a lot of ways, it also sounds kinda nice."

"I'd rather have the internet."

I ignored him. "I suck at pottery, but I love it. Occasionally, I make pieces that are legitimately cool; I give those to my dad. I leave the others here. No one can say it's not art if it has an inscrutable name. Even if it's a melted lump. We aren't all able to make beachfront bungalows for hobgoblins."

"Sassy pants is going to be so jelly when my hobbit hole sells for a million dollars," Patrick said.

I couldn't help smiling. I sat back and looked at my duck critically. I had managed to smooth it out and elongate the wings a bit. I'd ended up with a sort of bad-ass robin. I was actually kind of proud of it. "I think I'll give this one to my dad," I announced.

"So this is one of your *better* ones?" Patrick said. "You know, you're not twelve. He's not going to love it just because his daughter made it for him. That stops when you leave elementary school."

"Does not," I said. "It doesn't matter how old I get—he always loves my crap."

"That's fortunate, because you're absolutely full of it."

Chapter 3

WALKING HOME ALONE, LIKE SO MANY THINGS, HAD SEEMED LIKE A good idea at the time. It wasn't fully dark yet, and I listened to a lot of true-crime podcasts, so I knew to keep my guard up. Patrick had offered to drive me, but he had a late dinner date with his husband, so I'd waved him off and started the ten-block trek to my apartment. We'd left our creations so they could get fired in the kiln. Dad was going to love that stupid bird.

I'd gotten about two blocks when I heard someone yell, "Hey!" I slowed my steps and my body tensed, my eyes forward. I'd recently binge-watched *The Walking Dead*, so I was practically a lethal weapon. I walked a little faster until the voice called again, and I spun around with my fists up to find Jason jogging behind me. My body relaxed. Great. My favorite person. All I wanted was to go home and take a bath, watch Netflix, and eat a whole row of Oreos out of the package. I fluffed my hair to hide my fists and tried to look casual. "Oh, hey."

He caught up to me. "Hey. How's the new job going?"

"Fine," I answered. "How's it going being the favorite?"

He grinned. "It's pretty great."

"Ugh, you're the *worst*," I said. It slipped out before I could help myself.

His smile faltered. "If you want the truth, it's not easy," he said.

"It sure seems like it," I answered and started walking again.

"Which way do you live?" Jason asked me.

"In the direction I'm walking," I told him, pointing north.

"Me, too," he said. "I'll walk with you for a bit."

Awesome. "Sure," I said, "thanks." We walked for a few minutes before Jason broke the silence.

"You may not have noticed, Indiana, but I'm Black," he said.

"What?" I cried. "Are you really? I wouldn't have known if you hadn't pointed it out. Thank you."

This time he laughed a genuine laugh that made me smile despite myself.

"What I mean is, things aren't easy for me in the office either."

I paused. "That must be true," I said, "but it doesn't seem that way."

"It's not all that different from what you were saying back at the bar the other night."

"You heard us talking?"

"Some of it. I mean, you're a woman and I'm a man—" he began.

"Jason," I said, stopping and facing him. "I'm so lucky you're here to point these things out."

He grinned at me again, a genuine, almost vulnerable smile, and I decided then that he might not be as insufferable as I'd originally thought.

"It's not just women who have to smile," he said. "It's also Black men. In a culture that sees me as threatening, it takes a lot of effort to shake that stereotype. I take my cues from the person I'm talking to and mirror back their values, even if I don't share them. I didn't climb the ladder because my dad has a membership at the country club. It's work."

"I get it. But doesn't it make you feel, I don't know, inauthentic?" I asked, mulling over his words.

"Is anything about work authentic? Does the best employee get the promotion?"

"No," I admitted. "They get transferred. But even if you and I say the same thing at the meeting, they don't respond the same way."

"That's where you're wrong," he said. "We *didn't* say the same thing. You spoke up *during* an all-team meeting and questioned the MD's leadership. And you did it looking like *that*."

I opened my mouth, but he held up his hand. "Not that you don't look professional, it's just hard to take someone seriously when they're small and cute like you are."

"And female," I added. My cheeks colored, but the darkening sky hid it. "And you went to him, like dude to dude, afterward, and it worked."

"Yeah. I praised his idea, then told him how I thought it could be even better. Compliment sandwich."

"That's hard for me," I admitted. "I have no filter. If I think it, I feel compelled to say it."

He abruptly stopped walking. "Indiana, thank you for this insight into your character. I now see I also need your guidance to understand the obvious."

I snorted. "Sorry. Also, my friends call me 'Ana.'"

"Is that an informative statement, or can I call you that, too?"

"You can be insufferable. But yeah, call me 'Ana.'"

"If you're a golf-playing frat boy, then you can say whatever you want. But that's not you."

I thought for a moment, weighing out how much to tell him. "At the new job, they think I'm a guy."

"What? How'd *that* happen?" He stopped cold and stared at me. "One look—"

"Remote team, remember? No cameras and a weird first name."

"Interesting. Has it changed how you've been treated?"

"Not sure," I said. "I corrected the boss—"

"That's kind of your thing, isn't it?"

"And I didn't get in trouble. Instead, the whole team got the afternoon off."

We started walking again and rounded the corner at Fifth Street.

"Hm. Melvin is a weird dude," he said. "I can't figure out how he's hung on as long as he has. My apartment is just over here, but if you'd like me to walk you the rest of the way home—"

"Nope, I'm good," I said immediately. Night in the city isn't safe with coworkers or strangers. Or even potentially new friends.

"Okay, but let me give you my number," he said, pulling out his iPhone. He air-dropped his contact card to my phone. "Just let me know you got home safely. I have sisters and I worry."

"Thanks," I said. "But I'll be okay. I have someone waiting for me at home." We parted, and I waved as I walked off into the gathering dark. I kept my pace up the rest of the way. I'd taken a self-defense class last year, complete with yelling, "No!" a lot, followed by muffins and juice. It was an illusion of control, though, because at a hundred pounds, I wasn't fighting off a full-grown attacker. I was strong, but even a strong Pomeranian can't take on a German shepherd. It was a matter of perspective.

I popped in an earbud and turned on a podcast as I walked. I knew not to wear both because two earbuds meant not hearing sounds around me.

When I got home, I quickly opened my apartment door, ducked in, closed it, and locked it. I texted *safe* to Jason. Nighttime in the city was not my friend. I followed my usual routine and flipped the garage floodlights on and off twice. That was the signal my landlords, to use the formal term, always waited for when I came home. My basement apartment was below the home of an older couple who tended to think of me as more of a daughter than a tenant. George and Nancy had promised my dad they'd keep an eye on me, and they took their responsibility seriously. They liked to be notified once I'd arrived home safely. I smiled when I got the answering flicker back. It was nice to be cared for, even if it was a little oppressive sometimes. Then I settled in with my television and a wide array of snacks, all chocolate.

Monday came way too early, and I had trouble waking up. By 8:30 I needed a second cup of coffee to shake the cobwebs. I had just taken a sip when my phone blew up.

Omg Ana, where are you?? Heidi. Along with You'll never believe this. And Ana!!!!

I thumbed her text open and hit the *call* button. She picked up, breathless.

"What's wrong?" I asked. "Is everything okay?"

"Sort of," she gasped. "It's about work."

"It's too early for office drama, Heidi," I said, rubbing my eyes.

"No, it isn't! A guy called earlier asking about you."

"Okay?" I said. "Who?"

"I think it was Melon Hamster," she answered. "He sounded old, or older than us, anyway. He called the main line. Lucky, huh?"

A chill went through me. "Melvin? Melvin Hammer?"

"Yep, totally. He asked if he could speak to the person who managed the team that Indiana Aaron had worked on before being transferred to Artemis. I said that was me. Obviously. I wasn't going to put him through to your old boss, you know?"

"But you didn't manage the team—" I broke in.

"I managed the office. Same thing," she said dismissively.

"Totally not, Heidi—"

"Then Melon said he wanted to know a bit about *his* programming background," she said, talking over me. "And I was like, 'Who again?' And he goes, 'You know, Indiana Aaron, who worked on your team. *He* was moved to Artemis, and *his* work is pretty impressive. I went through *his* contributions to our project over the weekend, and I liked what I saw. I wanted to know a bit about *his* past responsibilities.'"

I groaned. "Did you tell him the truth?" I had still been mulling over the best way to handle the situation, and throwing it into Heidi's hands without warning was not it.

"I told him about the apps you worked on and the Java additions you made—"

"God, Heidi." I groaned again. "You weren't my manager."

"I know," she said defensively. "But I know how talented you are. I know way more about your work than the guy you actually worked for."

I softened a little. "Thank you, but did you…?"

"Tell him that you're less Harrison Ford with the fedora and more Strawberry Shortcake with a little puffy hat?"

My insides twisted. "I guess? Yeah?"

"No, of course not. Patrick mentioned something about throwing you a gender-reveal party, so whatever choices you make, I fully support you," she added.

"You're lovely," I told her, "but I don't even—"

"Sooo…" she interrupted again. "He had a few questions about why you transferred. I didn't want to tell him it was because you wouldn't shut up in a meeting, and I was so excited to be helping you along your career path, so I might have maybe mentioned that you were so manly and attractive that people were jealous, and that maybe you and I used to date, and I still wasn't over you, and you thought it was best if we broke it off because it wasn't appropriate to have a relationship in the workplace, especially since I was your supervisor?"

I sucked in a breath. "Heidi, no."

"Isn't this what you wanted?"

"No!" I yelped. "It was a misunderstanding, not a bad movie."

"Well, don't squeak like that when you talk to Melon Hamster-Pants—maybe Hammer-Pants?—or he'll know you have tiny lungs. He's calling you at noon."

"*Shit.*" I almost dropped my cup of coffee. "What am I going to do?" I asked Heidi frantically.

"You have to be Harrison Ford!" she cried. "If you tell him I made everything up, he'll call my actual boss, and they'll totally fire me."

"How did this happen?" I whispered to myself. "I literally just wanted to take the weekend before addressing this gender thing, and now you're my ex-girlfriend and former boss, and everyone is intimidated by my masculinity. We don't date our bosses, Heidi. Even each other."

"I know. I made sure Melon knew it was mostly one-sided. But you're missing the point. You have a virtual penis now," Heidi said.

"Gross, Heidi, I do not!" I yelled.

"You sort of do. Or you might as well have. Maybe he only called and checked on your background because he thought you were a guy. Maybe you have, like, male privilege now! Wouldn't that be cool? Then you could get promoted like you always wanted." She took a breath. "I helped, Ana. I did."

"Heidi, promise me you'll never help me again."

"I can't promise that because I'm still not over you." There was some rustling, followed by a frantic "I gotta go, bye," and then silence.

I sat there, holding the phone, feeling the beginning of a panic attack flood through me. I took a deep breath and held it. How was I going to tell the Hammer that I was a woman after that? They'd throw Heidi out on the street or try to have her committed. But on the other hand, how could I not?

I let my breath out slowly and kept my eyes closed, trying to center myself, until I heard my email ding.

From: Melvin Hammer

To: Indiana Aaron

Subject: Catch-up Call

Hi Indiana,

I hope you don't mind that I took a look into your professional history over the weekend. I'll admit, initially I was skeptical that you were correct in your assessment on Friday. No other team member spoke up. This morning I had quite an interesting chat with your former supervisor, who informed me that not only do you have the technical skills I've been looking for, but also the presence and leadership necessary to command a team. The apps you've created are remarkable.

Would you be able to hop on a call with me at noon today?

All best,

Melvin Hammer

Manager, Artemis Team

Acknowledgment. Appreciation. What I'd always wanted and never been able to get. And it was being offered now because why? Because Heidi had told him I was an assertive guy? My email dinged again, and I saw a meeting invite appear on my calendar.

Catch-up with Melvin Hammer, 12:00 pm–1:00 pm.

An entire hour. If I took that call, he'd hear my tiny lungs. He'd ask if he could speak to my dad. I'd probably get scared and pass out, and end up getting both Heidi and me fired.

I panicked, and my hand shot forward to the keyboard before I could stop it and clicked the *decline* button on the meeting. I didn't even send a reason. I'd never in my life declined a meeting with a supervisor. I tried frantically to think of an excuse. The back of my shirt got sweaty as I hit the *reply* button on the email.

What would Heidi's hypermasculine man say? I thought back to the messages Jason had sent over the time we'd worked together. He tended to be a bit familiar, irreverent but confident, in a way that would totally be seen as unprofessional coming from me. Could I respond in such a way that wouldn't ruin the opportunity completely?

From: Indiana Aaron

To: Melvin Hammer

Re: Invitation Declined—Catch-up Call

Hey Mel—Sorry, no cell reception currently, but I have an internet connection if you're open to talking that way. Thanks—

IA

I sent the message and then closed my eyes. This was probably it. I turned to look at the clock, counting down my last few minutes as an employed person. A few seconds later, my email dinged again. Melvin.

From: Melvin Hammer

To: Indiana Aaron

Re: Re: Invitation Declined—Catch-up Call

Sure—I know you must be busy. Just let me know what works for you.—Mel.

Wow, things were easier when you looked like Harrison Ford. I quickly wrote back.

I have time now.

Immediate response. Great. Where are you that you have no cell reception but a strong internet connection?

What did manly men do? I hike in the mountains while I work. I can triangulate an internet connection in the hills.

I looked down at my pajamas, covered in cartoon corgis. I grabbed a tobacco-and-woodsmoke-scented candle from the end table and lit it, inhaling deeply. It was the most masculine thing I owned. A gift from last year's white elephant party.

Excellent, Melvin emailed back. Would you be open to a Coderpad interview? CoderPad interviews were a common way to test the skills of a coder.

I flexed my fingers, ignoring my bright yellow nail polish. I could absolutely do a CoderPad. It was kind of like a sandbox for coders—you pick your language and code your heart out. One of my favorite things. I have my tablet out here but not sure about audio/visual. Let's give it a shot. I prefer Java.

A moment later I got an invitation for the meeting and connected. Like always, I lost myself in the coding. It was like speaking another language, where the letters and numbers I typed created my own reality. It provided the typical "given this input, produce this output" type of questions. I attacked it like a maze, having to solve many little problems before I was able to take the big one. In interviews like these, it's not *if* you solve the problem but *how*. I ran my code repeatedly, and before I realized it, an hour had gone. But I'd accomplished the task. In the chat window, Melvin typed, I have to run to another meeting. Mind if I run a problem by you later?

I gulped. **Looking forward to it.**

A little while later, an email popped up in my inbox. It had been forwarded to me from Melvin, originally from his own supervisor, which would sort of make him my grandboss, I guessed. He was asking Melvin to explain the ins and outs of our current project, and Melvin's forward included the note, **Can you answer these questions please? Send back to me directly.**

I read through it a few times. Did Melvin not understand what we were doing? Was it beneath him or further evidence that the rumors were true? I fired off a response that outlined all the aspects of our software, how it worked, and how it enhanced the client experience.

I got no response to my email, which was fine. I kept trucking through my workload, until another email came through. **Are you able to bullet point this? ASAP pls.** It was a message discussing a competitor's software and how its highlights differed from the product we were producing. I chewed on my lip. Weird. It wasn't exactly high-concept, so I outlined my response like I was talking to a five-year-old. I hoped he would be grateful and not offended. Or both, so long as he wasn't *just* offended.

If all went well, this could be the beginning of a mutually beneficial relationship. That was probably too much to hope for, though. I knew from every fairy tale Dad had ever read to me that you had to be careful what you wished for.

Chapter 4

I KEPT DIGGING THE HOLE, AND IT KEPT GETTING DEEPER. THE NEXT few weeks flew by with Melvin forwarding messages, often confidential and above my pay grade, and asking me to explain them. It really underscored that his old-white-man-ness or some weird glitch in the system had gotten him promoted above his ability. I mean, he did have a reputation for sinking most projects he was attached to, but one department just moved him to another one, and then another one, and he seemed to squeak by every time. But he trusted me, and it was an amazing feeling. So I broke down each message for him and sent it back. They went into a black hole of no response, but he must have liked what I was doing because the messages kept coming.

Occasionally, I let him know that I wasn't available right away so I didn't look too needy for attention. If he contacted me outside business hours, I was busy brewing my own craft beer, or finishing up my flight training to become a licensed pilot, or I was at Home Depot (which was sort of a masculine equivalent to T.J. Maxx). Always leave them wanting more, right? Granted, I wandered a little into stereotypical manly activities, but he never questioned it. I didn't go overboard, like saying I was wrestling a bear for charity, but I tried to give the impression I led an action-packed life. I wanted him to think the job was a part of my life, but I was so cool that it wasn't my *whole* life, so to speak. Which wasn't true, unfortunately. If I'd actually told him I was too busy to drop everything because I was playing *Animal Crossing* in bed after hours, or building Lego sets, or still working up my nerve to buy a fish for my empty tank, I sincerely doubt he would have responded the same way.

I was digging a hole I'd probably never get out of, but what I did on my own time was none of his business, I rationalized. And then he started to ask my opinion on operational decisions.

Should we take on this business? Should we hire that contractor? What should be on the meeting agenda for next week?

But did he want *my* opinion or a man's opinion? It didn't matter. The ideas I offered were my own, and for the first time at work, someone really wanted to hear them.

He listened to me, thought it over, and often let me take direction on different projects. He made me his real-life Cyrano, presenting my ideas as his own. But he gave me credit often enough, and it was hardly worth quibbling over. This was the most respect I'd ever gotten for my work.

Almost everyone on the team seemed cool with it, but there was this one dude, some guy named Evan Smith, who always had a problem with it. His avatar was a lone wolf (which made me roll my eyes whenever I saw it), and he nitpicked everything he could find. I guess he'd worked on Melvin's teams for a long time, and there seemed to be a little bit of jealousy in his comments. At least that's what my dad would say. Regardless, I refused to let him dull my sparkle. I was doing things I'd never done before, and haters gonna hate.

Melvin eventually asked for my cell number so he could text me when to check my email, if I was unavailable due to all my manly pursuits. I gave it reluctantly, but he hardly ever used it.

Until the kicker. I have a three-day trip planned for the Denver area, arriving Thursday night, he texted. There's an important client in the area that we need to land. I'm going to need your help on this. I'm sure you realize that I've come to think of you as my right-hand man. We'll have an all-team meeting, then I'd like to talk with you one-on-one afterward.

I sat back. Two days. Melvin was arriving in two days. Two. I felt dread wash over me but tried to stay rational. As his right-hand "man," this might be my best opportunity to come clean. What I looked like shouldn't matter. He trusted me with inside information, he relied on me, and maybe he couldn't function without me? He was having way more success with Artemis than he'd had in his previous leadership roles. When he came in person (*OMG, seriously two days?*) I could introduce myself as *me,* and he would be further impressed instead of disappointed. A short opinionated gamer girl was every bit as good as Harrison Ford.

I knew that was true. So why did I have such a feeling of impending doom?

———

If there was a heaven on earth, it was Aspen Skies, I thought as I pulled into the parking lot of the assisted living facility later that evening. I carefully grabbed the package off the passenger seat and hurried inside, away from the chill in the air. The lobby was bright and warm. "Hey, Ana," the woman at the front desk greeted me.

I smiled at her and shivered a little in the warm glow. "How are you, Rita?" I asked. "How're the kids?"

"Everyone's good, thanks for asking," she said. "Chris came in second in the skateboarding competition."

"Awesome!" I exclaimed. "I was rooting for him."

She grinned. "I knew you were. Your dad's been asking when you'd get here. He's not very patient."

I nodded. "One of a few things I wish I hadn't inherited from him."

"He's in the common room, watching the fish." If I lived here, that was where I would spend all my time.

I waved goodbye to Rita and headed toward the common room. Aspen Skies was a beautiful place, and I'd been lucky when they had an opening and had agreed to take my dad. It cost a fortune to keep him here, and the expense had quickly eaten up his savings and mine, but he loved it, and I loved him, so it didn't matter. I turned down the hallway and caught sight of him sitting in front of the stunning saltwater tank that lined the back wall of the room.

I came up behind him and set my package down, then leaned over and gave him a big hug from behind. His arms came up around me. "Indiana!" he cried, swiveling his wheelchair around. "How's my girl?" It was a while before I let go. He smelled like home and so many happy memories rolled into one nostalgic scent.

"I'm okay. How're you?" I asked. I gave him a kiss on the cheek and sat back to look at him. He looked great. He had color in his cheeks and his usual mischievous twinkle about him.

"Doing grand," he said. "This isn't your usual visiting day. Everything okay?"

"Yeah, I just wanted to talk to you about some stuff," I said.

"Always up for a chat. But before we do that, look at all the new seahorses in the tank."

I jumped up and squinted at the water, looking for them. "Oh my god, where? There are a bunch of tangs in there—they're going to eat them! We have to tell Rita!"

Dad sighed and pinched the bridge of his nose. "I forgot what a geek you are about fish." He lowered his voice and pulled me down close. "I'm not actually looking at the tank, Indiana. There aren't any new fish. I'm trying to be discreet, but I forgot that you don't do discreet. I'm looking at the reflection."

"What do—" But then I saw what he meant. Reflected in the glass was an older woman who must have been sitting across the room behind us, reading a book and occasionally glancing over. She had an elegant look about her and great taste in clothes. From the passing smiles she was sending our way, it looked like she had good taste in men, too.

"Are you talking about that lady?" I whispered to him and turned around to look.

He grabbed me as I started to swivel. "Be cool. And don't talk so loud. Just look at the imaginary fish."

I sat next to him and watched the tank. He put his arm around me, and I leaned into him, feeling myself relax. After a few minutes, he squeezed my shoulder. "Did you bring me something?" he asked, gesturing to the box.

I nodded and pulled it into my lap. I took out a few books and handed them over.

Dad was a voracious reader, even more so since his accident. He chortled when he saw the stack and hugged them to his chest. "Thanks, Indiana. I'd be lost without you. I really would."

"And now for your real surprise." I said, "Drumroll…" Then I pulled the lumpy duck from the bottom of the box. It had been fired and glazed and fired again to a blotchy opalescent blue. It was something only a father could love, and Dad took it with reverence, running his fingers down the bumpy curve of the wings.

He seemed to get a little teary. "I love the lumps and bumps."

"I knew you would." I grinned. "Bumps make things more interesting."

"Like life," he said seriously, and I rolled my eyes to keep from misting up. "Wheel me back to my room so we can talk, and I'll find a great place to put my treasure."

I took hold of his chair and wheeled him down the hallway, while he carefully held both the duck and the books as if they were precious. "This guy is going to be named Chuck," he said over his shoulder as we reached the door to his room.

"Chuck, really?" I asked.

"Chuck the Duck," he responded.

"At least you could tell it was a duck." I laughed as I helped shift him from the chair so he was sitting on the bed. The room was full of my pottery creations. Cracked pots and lopsided animals covered every shelf. "Do people ever ask about these?"

He grinned. "They always want to know how old my grandchild is." Then he winked. "Just kidding. They ask who the artist is and if she has a studio somewhere."

"How old do you tell them your grandkid is?"

"About nine or ten." He chuckled. "At least you got all your mother's other talents," he said. "She was the smart one; I was the hot one."

I smiled at him. "Neither one of you was good with technology."

He leaned back and looked at me affectionately. "That's true. You got that all on your own. Our little miracle baby. We never thought we'd be lucky enough to have you, but here you are. Pretty like your dad and brilliant like your mom."

I ducked my head. "Dad, stop."

"We're just proud of you. Your mom sure is, looking down on you. And I am, too, right here."

My eyes welled up, so I quickly looked at the floor.

"You're going to rule the world one day, Indiana," he said. "I mean it."

I sniffled a little. "I doubt that, Dad," I said. "It's hard being in the tech industry. In a lot of industries, actually. Bros promote bros. And then there's me." I let out a hollow laugh. "An outspoken, girl-type person who shops in the juniors' department and doesn't inspire confidence in employers."

"You're normal size," he interjected. "We had you tested."

"That's not the point, Dad."

"You've always worked so hard, Indiana. Way harder than you needed to. I wish you didn't always feel like you had to prove yourself."

"But I do!" I cried. "It never stops. And I'm exhausted."

"Then take a breath and rest. You don't need to meet everyone's expectations all the time. Only your own. But besides that, I don't see how you could not inspire confidence. You're an absolute spitfire, and I wouldn't change anything about you."

"But you're my dad. Let's say you weren't, though. Would you be mad if I deceived you?"

His eyes twinkled. "Deception is part of human nature. I don't know anyone who hasn't lied at some point. Including you. Who are you deceiving, Indiana?"

I blushed. "My boss. We haven't met in person, and he thinks I'm Harrison Ford."

His jaw dropped open. "You told your boss you're a famous actor? That's really, really inappropriate, Indiana."

"No! I didn't!" I protested. "I just…didn't correct him. And besides, it's your fault. You named me Indiana. So now he thinks I'm part of the boys' club, and he's coming to meet me in person, and I had to be tested when I was a kid to see if I had a growth disorder," I pushed out all in one breath.

"So you're worried you might fall a little…*short*…of his expectations."

I humphed, and Dad lowered his head to examine Chuck the Duck, but I could tell he was trying not to laugh. "I knew when you were a baby that *Indiana* was the only name big enough to suit you, no matter how tiny you were. Four pounds, six ounces. Can you believe it? Your mom disagreed at first—she wanted to name you Melanie—but we won her over. Every time she called you 'Melanie,' you cried. But you giggled every time I called you 'Indiana.'"

I'd heard that story so many times, and I'd never believed a word of it.

"If your boss has any sense, he'll realize he's even luckier that you're not—how did you put it?—in the boys' club," he said.

"But he won't. That's not the way it works, Dad. You know it isn't."

"Maybe not, but maybe it should. Just look at this duck right here. There's never been anything like it before, and there won't be again. Like you."

That got an actual smile out of me. "We can agree that the duck should never be repeated. But for real, Dad, should I come clean? Tell him my real size?"

"You won't need to. Eventually, he'll look down and spot you, promise."

"Dad," I groaned.

"Tell him you're a woman. Pretending to be an actor is weird. And he'll love you. Everyone here does. Give him the opportunity to appreciate the real you." He patted my hand. "I bet you can outcode Harrison Ford any day."

Everything always seemed a little better after talking to Dad. "Maybe I overthink things," I said.

"You know, one time when you were six, I checked on you before I went to bed. You were still wide awake, and you looked up at me with your big eyes and said, 'Who is God's mommy? Is it Mother Earth? Was God in her belly? Would that make God our uncle? Is Mother Earth our grandma? I can't sleep until I know who God's mom is, Dad!'"

I inclined my head. "If we're being honest, I still struggle with that a bit. The lack of women in the Holy Trinity confuses me to no end." Dad bobbed up and down like he was gearing up for a debate, so I had to squash it. "I'm too tired to talk religion, Dad. Work's been busy. Besides, now that we're alone"—I leaned forward conspiratorially—"tell me about the lady in the fish tank."

He leaned forward, too, like he was sharing a big secret. "She's new. Her name is Margaret, but she lets me call her 'Mags,' or at least she will one day. She makes me feel like I have seahorses in my stomach."

"Wow, you don't feel that way often."

"Not since your mother."

"Does she know?" I asked.

He shook his head. "We haven't spoken yet. I can't get up my nerve."

A surprised laugh escaped my throat. "You? You're the one who always taught me to say what I think. You have to talk to her."

"I don't have to do anything," he said obstinately. "But don't worry, I'll come up with something."

"You'd better, or I'm going to have to play matchmaker."

"I think you already did, getting me into this place," he said. "I owe you for that." Then he paused. "I didn't want to mention it, but I got a call from Nancy the other day."

I sighed. I really did like George and Nancy, my landlords, but I always hated it when they called my dad.

"She thinks maybe it's time you start dating. She says you stay in a lot and don't have too many visitors."

"Well, you can tell Miss Nancy that it's none of her business if I date or not."

He pulled his cell out of his back pocket. "Got it. I'll call her right now—"

I grabbed the phone out of his hand. "I'm just joking. Please don't tell Miss Nancy that," I said. My dad had taught me manners, even if he'd also taught me not to keep my mouth shut. "She just doesn't need to worry. Or tattle," I muttered to myself.

"I wasn't going to call. I want her to think I raised you better. Just don't forget to have a little excitement in your life, too, okay?"

I leaned forward and squeezed his hand. "You got it. Anything for you, Dad," I said. And I meant it. I would make things work with Artemis. And I would make sure Aspen Skies would be Dad's home for as long as he wanted it to be. As for excitement, Heidi had that part covered.

It would be fine. Totally fine. Unless it all went to hell.

Chapter 5

"I THINK YOU SHOULD RECONSIDER," HEIDI SQUEALED AS WE grabbed our coffee cups from the Starbucks down the street and headed back toward the office building. Her outfit was perfect, as always. The fall air was crisp, and her wool coat matched her sweater and skirt. I'd ordered Patrick his fancy mocha and planned to drop it off before the Artemis team's first in-person meeting. It was Friday morning, and I had just about an hour to go until "Indiana's" death. Or mine. It was kind of a toss-up.

"It's going to be okay," I reassured her. "When Melvin meets me in person, we'll all have a laugh about the silly little prefix that started this whole misunderstanding."

She sipped her iced green tea and made a face. "Or he'll be like, 'Who was that Heidi girl who said you were a sexy dude? We should track her down and destroy her.'"

"That's a bit dramatic. I doubt you're on anyone's 'Track and Destroy' list."

"Well, there's a reason I can't ever go back to the state of Louisiana," Heidi said, averting her eyes.

"Come again?" I stopped walking. "There's a whole state you can't go to?"

"On the advice of my lawyer," she said primly. "*They* probably have a Heidi Cross 'Search and Destroy' order. Melon might, too. All I'm saying is nobody likes being tricked, especially old white dudes."

"I didn't trick him," I insisted. "He did that by himself."

"I helped," Heidi said.

Had she ever.

"Honestly, right now I'm just hoping to avoid Taggart the most. I know it's not entirely his fault I'm in this mess—"

"It's not his fault *at all*," Heidi broke in.

"—but I'd rather not have to hear how he's taken all my old projects and run them into the ground. And I'd rather not see my old boss and have to tell him how things are going on the Artemis team. I can only imagine how he'd react to this whole thing."

"Probably laugh his ass off, then march you straight over to Melvin and formally introduce you."

Definitely needed to avoid that. But this couldn't go on forever, and I had to rip off the Band-Aid. The sooner, the better. Besides, I was confident my skills had won him over. I was *ready*. I'd straightened my hair (which unfortunately made it long enough to sit on) and wound it into a bun. I'd pulled a page from the New York book and dressed in black and white with a black coat and low heels. I'd worn no jewelry, save an understated pair of gold stud earrings. I had on eyeliner and lipstick and a touch of foundation. Covering my freckles always went a long way toward making me look more like my real age, twenty-seven, and less like the teenager I was often mistaken for. There was no glitter anywhere in sight.

"Patrick probably agrees with me," she continued as we walked into the building. "This is a bad idea."

I tried to choose my words carefully since Heidi was a sensitive soul, but like always, they tumbled out before I could stop them. "What's the other solution? Dress like a man? Quit my job? Read more Hemingway? Hire Harrison Ford?"

"I don't think we could afford him, even if we pooled our money. I just wish you could keep it going a little longer," she said, but I could tell I'd made my point. "You could at least have worn a fedora," she muttered.

I saw an old coworker in the lobby and ducked my head. "Maybe a fedora isn't your worst idea." At least the meeting wasn't on my old floor. It would probably be fine.

We reached the elevator, and Heidi leaned down to give me a quick hug before going back to her desk, careful not to bump the coffee caddy I was carrying. "Text me after," she said. "Good luck."

I nodded and got on the elevator, planning to hit Patrick's floor on twenty before heading back down to the meeting on fifteen. I had the elevator to myself until the fourth floor. Then the door slid open, and my heart dropped into my feet. Melvin Hammer got in. I'd recognize him anywhere. He had a tiny picture that showed up in the corner of every email he sent. Permanent frown, slight mustache, and full beard. He reminded me of Theodore Roosevelt, complete with the swagger and slightly too-small clothing (no monocle). It was easy to imagine him having a few pet bears like Teddy was rumored to have. Just because he could.

Just before the door slid closed, a young man joined us. He caught my eye instantly. Tousled brown hair, stubble, and oversize horn-rimmed glasses. Something about him was vaguely familiar. One of the men smelled really good, and I had a suspicion it wasn't Melvin. When the elevator started moving again, I tried to ignore the younger man and grabbed my chance. "Hi," I squeaked at Melvin, then cleared my throat. I'd meant that to come out at least an octave lower.

He turned, as if surprised to see me there, and nodded vaguely. "Where are you headed, miss?"

"Making a quick stop on twenty, then I'm going to the Artemis team meeting on fifteen," I answered, straightening my shoulders.

"Ah," he said and smiled down at me. Then, before I could say anything, he reached out and took one of the coffees out of the caddy and took a long drink. I stared open-mouthed as he drained it and the elevator door opened onto the fifteenth floor. He threw the empty cup in the trash bin. "Next time, make sure it's a little less bitter," he said over his shoulder as he got off.

"That wasn't coffee," I blurted after him furiously as the doors closed. "Those were the tears of my enemies!"

"No wonder it was bitter," someone said from behind me.

I jumped, spilling some of Patrick's mocha onto the floor. I knew that voice. It was the smooth, soft voice of the guy who talked about boring things like budgets in our monthly meetings. My heart rate went up, and I looked over, embarrassed. Why did *he* have to be the one to witness this? My cheeks flushed and I put my hand on my forehead. "Sorry," I muttered, then turned to face him. "Who does that?" I asked, gesturing to the elevator doors.

He shrugged. "Melvin is… I want to say *special*, but that's not the right word. Entitled?"

"Thank you, Melvin, but now my princess is in a different castle," I said grumpily.

He let out a startled laugh. "You play *Super Mario?*"

I shrugged. "Yeah. It's pretty great. The nostalgia almost outweighs the misogyny, you know?"

He grinned at me. "Agreed. You know, you could always drink that one," he said, pointing to the other coffee I was holding.

It was my turn to laugh. "This is a white chocolate mocha with extra whip. Mine was a cold brew."

He held up his hands. "Enough said." He reached into his pocket and handed me a five-dollar bill. "Allow me to buy you a replacement. You'll need the caffeine before our meeting."

"You're on Artemis, aren't you? I think I remember your voice from some of our meetings," I said, stupidly holding the money.

"You remember my voice?"

I nodded and tried to play it cool. "You have a nice voice."

"Um, thanks. I'm actually in the accounting department in the New York office, but I manage the budget for Artemis. I'm here in an escort capacity for Melvin. Uh, *escort* sounds bad." He looked down, flustered, and his embarrassment was cute.

"To make sure he doesn't mess up?" The words were out before I could think, and I tried to bite my tongue to keep from talking more.

"Succinct. Yeah, I mean I'm here making sure his trip goes smoothly. Keep him on track," he finished. "I'm Shane." He held out his hand for me to shake, and I looked down at mine, full of someone else's coffee and someone else's money. He smiled and pulled his hand back. "And you are?"

"Ana," I said.

"It's nice to meet you, Ana."

The elevator doors opened again, this time on the twentieth floor. I stepped into the hallway and looked back. "Aren't you getting off? There aren't any other lit buttons."

"I was supposed to get off on fifteen," he answered. He winked as the doors closed.

I took a deep breath, then headed for Patrick's cubicle. Apparently, it was my turn to be embarrassed.

"Hey, Ana!" he said as I walked up, then stopped, catching my expression. "What's wrong?"

"I think I just met the boss and the surprisingly cute guy with the voice, and he drank my coffee," I said.

"A guy with a voice drank your coffee? Didn't the pandemic teach you anything? Cute or not, don't share drinks."

"No," I said, flustered. "The boss drank my coffee. I didn't get any."

Patrick gasped. "But not mine, though, right?" He quickly took the cup from my hands. He scanned the side, and his face lit up when he saw *Patrick* written on it in Sharpie. "Yes! Patrick's little mocha made it safely," he cooed.

I slumped forward and rested on the side of his cubicle. It was a lot nicer than mine had been. Patrick's was decorated like a living room—he'd wallpapered it, and he had his own rug. There were antique knickknacks, framed artwork, and even a modern little plant display. "He took my coffee from me because he thought I was an intern or something," I said. "Then the cute guy gave me money. The meeting is in half an hour. What do I do?"

He sipped his coffee while he thought. "Don't be yourself. You know what I mean," he added hastily when he saw my expression. "Censor yourself. Save your caustic commentary for me over drinks."

I blew out a breath. "I'll try, but he's already on my last nerve. Who steals another person's drink?"

"And the other guy gave you money? What for?"

"For more coffee. He said I needed caffeine before the meeting."

Patrick nodded. "Sounds like a good guy. Like me. And Joseph." That was Patrick's husband. "I want to say that if you follow your original plan, it'll work out fine. But honestly, after that, it probably won't. But don't make it worse. Just go down there and tell him you're you. Respectfully. Then it's up to him to be the good guy or not. Try not to talk too much and remember that adding *sir* to the end of an insult doesn't make it respectful."

I nodded. "Okay. I'm doing it." I straightened my back and walked toward the elevator.

"You got this!" he called after me.

Easy for him to say. He already had his male privilege, and he had gotten his coffee intact. That put him way ahead of me.

I approached the elevator cautiously. Knowing my luck, it would be filled with everyone I *didn't* want to see. Fortunately, my second elevator ride was much less eventful than the first. When I got back on fifteen, I clung to the strap of my messenger bag as I made my way to the Artemis meeting room. Outside the door, I counted to ten to get my nerves together, then walked in. It was a big room, with the seats arranged in a horseshoe configuration with a big screen and podium near the front. It was mostly empty, except for Melvin, who was fiddling with his phone, and another guy I didn't recognize. He was rail thin, a bit sallow, and wore a sour expression. And of course, Shane, who was surrounded by wires. Melvin and the skinny guy didn't look up, but Shane smiled and nodded, though he looked annoyed.

"You can collect coffee orders from the team in about fifteen minutes," Melvin said, still not glancing my way.

I closed my eyes briefly and hung on to what Patrick had said. I cleared my throat. "I'm part of the team—"

Shane swore under his breath and dropped the cable he'd been fiddling with.

"You need to get that working ASAP," Melvin told him.

"I'm trying," he said in a tight voice, "but this equipment is outdated, and the online system…" He trailed off as I dropped my bag to the floor and went over to help. I had worked with this system's maddening inconsistencies before my transfer, so within a few minutes, I had the computer hooked up and the presentation ready to go.

"I can't wait to see your presentation, Melvin," the thin guy said. "It's going to be epic."

"Sure, Evan, if I can get any of this tech to work."

Wait. That was Evan? The hater who always seemed so jealous of Indiana? He looked a lot like I'd imagined.

Evan made no move to help Shane and me fix the equipment. Instead, he stayed focused on Melvin. "The Artemis team is shaping up well, don't you think?" he asked.

Melvin ignored him. "Now can you hook this up to my phone so I don't have to use the pointer?" he said, handing his phone over—not to Evan or me but to Shane.

Shane looked at me, then wordlessly handed the phone over. I adjusted the settings, added the network, and synced the Bluetooth.

"You should be good," I said to Melvin as I handed the phone back.

He took it and turned to Shane. "Thanks." Finally, Melvin turned to me. "Miss, if you're not here to take coffee orders, then you need to see yourself out. I don't have the energy or the patience to take on an intern right now."

"I'll take a Grande Frappuccino with extra whip," Evan said.

"Seriously?" I turned to Melvin. "I just set up your presentation and synced your phone, two things you didn't seem able to do—" I said before I could stop myself. None of this was going according to plan.

"Good for you," he said. "Go back to class. Maybe you can get a job here when you grow up. I have an important meeting after this."

A couple of Artemis team members came in at this point, nodded, and sat in the farthest chairs.

"With Indiana Aaron?" I asked slyly. I had just about reached my limit with him. He'd stolen my coffee, and I had no filter at the best of times. Uncaffeinated, I was downright dangerous. Out of the corner of my eye, I caught Shane watching us with interest.

Melvin blinked in surprise. "Yes. Do you know him?"

An evil smile broke free. "I do. You could say we're in constant contact."

Shane and Evan both looked over at me with new interest.

"Is he your dad?" Melvin asked me. He looked over at the other team members who were sitting and others who were slowly trickling in to start the meeting. He lowered his voice. "If so, make sure he gets here for this meeting soon. We have a potential client we need to land. If we don't, Artemis gets shelved. And anyone who lands that client will be well-suited for a position at the head of the creative department. So, as you can see, this is a big deal. He *needs* to come through on this."

That wiped the evil grin right off my face. I'd been about to out myself and let him have it until he dropped *that* little bomb. A promotion or losing the job altogether. All I could do was blink.

"Run along," he said, gesturing to the door. "Let the big boys talk." The rest of the team members began filing in.

I swallowed and grabbed my bag.

"Don't forget my coffee order," Evan called after me.

What should I do? I couldn't say who I was, but Indiana couldn't miss this meeting, meaning *I* couldn't miss this meeting. So this potential client meant life or death for Artemis, and I hadn't met any of these people in person before. I didn't want to go. But I had to. I needed a new plan, and fast. I gulped in a breath and practically ran out of the conference room. The second I was outside, I sent an SOS.

What do I do??? I texted Heidi and Patrick. We have to keep this monster we created alive. I can't be in that meeting but I can't not be. Help!

This whole mess belongs to you and Heidi, but I got you. Patrick.

I backed up against the wall outside the conference room and waited. I had about ten minutes before the meeting started. Should I go back in? But what would I say? Should I stay outside? Both options sucked. The minutes ticked down, taking all my hope with them. I was about to text Patrick again when suddenly there was an earsplitting shriek of a fire alarm over the sound system. The noise was at such a decibel that people immediately got up from their desks and scrambled for the exits. The Artemis meeting room emptied, everyone shoving their laptops back into their bags as they pushed past me with Melvin stomping after them.

Patrick? I texted.

Someone tried to make popcorn in the break room. Looks like they put it in the microwave for ten minutes. Idiot.

Be nice, Heidi wrote. We have a lot of remote workers in today who don't know how to use microwaves.

Pssst—Heidi, it was me. Patrick. I created a diversion.

So I don't need to run? Heidi.

Exit in a calm and orderly manner, Patrick responded. Don't you know anything about fire safety, Heidi?

But if it's not an actual fire, Imma take my time, she wrote back.

It might be by now, I threw in. He legit set the break room on fire.

Allegedly, Patrick answered. What's the boss's name, Ana?

Melon Hamster-pants I think, Heidi texted.

I frowned. Are you Ana? His name is MELVIN HAMMER.

I jammed my phone in my back pocket, feeling a weird mixture of intense relief and dread, as I sprinted up the five flights of stairs to the twentieth floor, against the crowd heading downward. No one seemed to pay me any attention. I was sweaty and breathless by the time I arrived at the break room. Sure enough, there was a smoking bag of popcorn placed on top of the refrigerator, which was directly under the smoke alarm. Why did he have to put it up so high? I grabbed a chair and pulled it over to the kitchenette and, balancing carefully, grabbed the smoking bag. I threw it in the sink and turned on the water. There was some hissing but no flames. I was thoroughly soaking the bag when someone touched my shoulder. I almost jumped out of my skin.

"Oh, hey, Taggart," I said, leaning against the sink and trying to look casual despite the smoke hissing behind me.

He flipped the blond hair out of his eyes and grinned at me. "Hey, how you been? Are you setting the fire or putting it out?"

I stared at him. What kind of question was that? "I'm putting it out, Taggart. I'm saving your life right now."

We both looked back over at the pathetic-looking wet bag in the sink and then at each other.

"Thanks," he said. "I guess I owe you one."

Um. Okay. "So great to catch-up, but we should probably vacate the building, don't you think? And, you know, maybe keep this whole thing a secret? Whoever microwaved this bag is totally embarrassed and doesn't want to get in trouble."

"For sure," he said. "Evacuation time!"

I fled the break room too quickly for him to follow, to head back down to the main lobby. I blended into the crowd in the stairwell, trudging down floor after floor. Most people were booking it, but I took a little more time. There wasn't a real fire, at least not anymore, and my shoes didn't mix with the cramped steps. After a few flights, Patrick caught up to me, breathless.

"I should have thought this through better," he said between gasps. "I forgot they don't let you use the elevators in a fire. We work way too high up for this kind of bullshit."

"Thanks for helping," I told him. "Melvin said we, or basically, *I*, have to land some new client or lose my job. Or, you know, Mr. Aaron does. The guy who plays rugby and barbecues or skydives or whatever men do." I sighed. "Not Ana, the intern who eats Oreos and drinks bitter coffee." At this point, the waning adrenaline had me winded, too. "I hate lying, Patrick."

He nodded. "I know. I love that about you."

We had let pretty much everyone go ahead of us, and I waved to a woman who was rounding the landing below us. I used to see her in the break room sometimes before my transfer. I thought her name was Molly. She was struggling with the stairs, and she stumbled starting down the next flight. I picked up the pace and grabbed her arm. "You okay?" I asked.

She was breathing heavily. "I never use the stairs."

"Let me help you," I told her, "and slow down. It'll be all right, promise."

She held on to my arm as she limped down the last few flights. I felt awful putting her in this position. Once we got outside, she thanked me and headed for the parking lot.

I found Patrick again in the crowd. "I didn't know Molly was pregnant," he whispered to me. "I feel bad we made her go down twenty flights of stairs in her condition."

I made a slicing gesture with my hand at my neck. "I don't think she's pregnant," I whispered back. He winced and looked around to see if she had heard us.

"My bad," he stage-whispered. "Just carries her weight low. Glad I didn't congratulate her."

"Never, ever do that," I said. I heard the sirens through all the other noise in the courtyard. It sounded like the whole fire department had come. It was the perfect amount of chaos to blend into and would hopefully give me enough time to escape.

Patrick looked around, then squeezed my hand. "I've got one more thing to do. Meet you by the fire trucks in a bit." Before I could respond, he took off. I looked around until I found Heidi, who waved from the parking lot, where she was leaning against the hood of her car. "Isn't this exciting?" she asked once I made my way over.

"No," I answered distractedly. I moved behind her for cover and glanced around for Melvin, but I couldn't find him. I did, however, catch sight of Patrick. He was talking to someone, then made a beeline across the grass. I turned to see where he was headed and gasped.

"Are you Melvin?" Patrick asked, still a little breathless, to Melvin

Hammer, who looked annoyed and out of place on the lawn. We moved close enough to hear their conversation but stayed far enough away not to be easily spotted in the crowd.

"I'm Melvin Hammer," he replied. "Why?"

"I have a message from Indiana Aaron," Patrick replied.

I yelped, then got up on my tiptoes to grab Heidi's back and peer over her shoulder.

Melvin's stance changed. "Yes?" he said. "It's unfortunate that this foolishness has gotten in the way of our meeting. I'm on a tight schedule and can't stay after this."

"He wanted me to let you know he's also sorry he won't be able to make the meeting. You see, the noise and confusion caused a woman from the sixteenth floor to go into labor. Indiana managed to carry her out of the building before"—and here Patrick paused dramatically—"he delivered her baby."

"He delivered a baby?" Melvin asked, looking stunned.

Heidi guffawed, and I quickly smacked my hand over her mouth.

"You should have seen him, Melvin," Patrick went on. "He was incredible. Both mother and baby are going to be fine. She's going to name the baby Indiana," he added.

"Oh my god, please shut up, Patrick," I whispered under my breath.

Melvin's mouth hung open in astonishment. "But he's a programmer. He's not a doctor."

Patrick shrugged. "Maybe they cover basic labor and delivery in Navy SEAL training. I don't know. There are probably a bunch of babies named after him. He's a good person to have around in a crisis, you know?"

Melvin nodded vaguely. "Where are they now? Can I see him?"

"I'm afraid not." Patrick shook his head sadly. "The mother was taken by ambulance and begged for Indiana to go with her so she'd feel safe. He said he'd contact you when he has a moment."

"Yes, yes, of course," Melvin murmured. "No, of course, I understand."

Patrick nodded and patted his arm sympathetically, then turned to go.

Melvin reached out and touched his shoulder. "But he was in the meeting? Before the fire alarm went off?"

"Yep," Patrick answered. "The tall one with the piercing eyes."

"Oh," Melvin said, seeming to think back. "That sounds kind of familiar."

Patrick nodded. "It does."

"Black hair?" Melvin asked.

"I'd say salt-and-pepper, really."

Melvin nodded distractedly. "Yeah, that's what I meant."

No one had salt-and-pepper hair in that meeting. I was sure of it.

"Have a great afternoon, sir," Patrick said. Then he went back toward the building and, at the last second, turned and winked at me.

Heidi sighed. "I'm definitely not over Indiana. I'm still in love with him."

I nodded. "I'm starting to fall in love with him, too."

"Speaking of falling in love, who's that?" Heidi gestured with her chin to where Shane stood at the side of the building scanning the crowd.

"He's the guy with the voice!" I said. "His name is Shane, from New York. I think he's Melvin's babysitter."

She bumped her hip into mine. "Lucky you, voice guy isn't a troll. Aren't you supposed to have a team happy hour thing this evening to get to know each other?"

"Yeah, but I can't go."

"Why not?" she cried.

"Because I just delivered a baby, Heidi!" I exclaimed. "I'm needed at the hospital."

"Indiana is, but not Ana. Ana would never have made it through SEAL training. She can go get drinks with coworkers."

"First of all, excuse you," I said indignantly, "but *neither* me was in SEAL training. And we shouldn't even joke about that. It's super hard and prestigious. And stuff."

"It is. My brother washed out of it. You have to be cold. And wet. And like, sit in swamps and crawl through mud. But Patrick didn't say he'd been a SEAL, just that maybe they cover obstetrics in training."

"Why would they do that?" I cried. "Is the battlefield full of people giving birth? Whatever. I can't go. It's the worst idea. I'm two people now, Heidi! I'm this," I said, gesturing down at myself, "and I'm also a man who can do anything. Not that I don't *like* being this"—I gestured vaguely at myself again—"but it's not doing me any favors right now. And the man me is the one who's gotten all the accolades and recognition. It's not fair. I want to meet my team. I want to get to know them, and I want to get promoted on my own."

"I bet Indiana can't code like you can," she said.

I blinked at her. "Heidi. *We're the same person.* Of course he can code like I can. I mean, *I* am the coder. This isn't *Inception.*" I rubbed my temples. What was wrong with everybody?

"I know. That's what I meant," she said. "I get it. But you have to work within the system you're given. And this system has given you piercing eyes and, you know, male privilege."

Kill me now. I turned away, but she grabbed my arm. "We're going tonight. You're right, you *do* deserve to meet your team. Just show up and talk to them as Ana. And take it from there."

"We?" I asked.

She averted her eyes. "Well, I just learned that your team has a babysitter named Shane, and I bet he has so many fun Melvin stories…"

I sighed, warring with myself before making up my mind. I wasn't going to let Melvin Hammer's love-hate relationship with the two of me stand in the way of experiences with my team and living my own life. I was ambitious, sure, but I also *really* loved to talk about coding. That normally got you kicked *out* of parties, not invited *to* them.

"All right," I relented. "We're going. But no talk about how you and Other Me used to date. Got it?"

She stood up straight and saluted me. "I'll do my best. Patrick is going to be so excited."

Patrick would be there, too? Awesome.

Chapter 6

CISCO'S BAR FELT LIKE A MINEFIELD. HEIDI AND I MET AT THE entrance. The bar had been Indiana's, or rather, *my* suggestion for where to meet. Everyone there knew me as Ana, and I was comfortable there, so it was as good a place as any. I'd dressed more like myself, choosing a black shirt and jeans, and let my hair dry naturally, curls everywhere. Dressing to impress as Ana clearly hadn't worked.

It was kind of dark, and the rock music was a little loud, but both of those worked in my favor. I saw a few of the Artemis people sitting at the bar and was scanning the crowd for other familiar faces when I heard, "There they are!" Patrick. Of course.

He gestured wildly from his seat at the bar, where he appeared to be in deep conversation with a man whose back was turned. As Heidi and I made our way over, my heart stopped. Patrick grabbed me and pulled me into his side. "Ana! I hear you've met my bestie Shane."

I grimaced as Patrick squeezed me, refusing to let go. "I thought *I* was your bestie," I said. Patrick chortled a little drunkenly and finally released me. Did Patrick really have to find Shane, of all people? And when he was a little tipsy?

"Shane here was just telling me about how you two met in the elevator bringing me my bougie coffee, and then we got to bitching about the Melon—"

I winced and smacked Patrick in the chest, glancing around quickly.

"I don't think he's going to show," Shane said, leaning forward to be heard over the music. "This kind of 'fraternizing' isn't usually his thing."

"I'm glad it's yours," Heidi interjected, blinking at Shane in an exaggerated way.

He smiled politely. "Are you a friend of Ana's?"

"No." She tittered. "Ana is a friend of mine."

"I think we need drinks!" Patrick said brightly. He waved the bartender over. "Margs, please!"

When the drinks arrived, Patrick turned to Heidi and grabbed her hand. "Heidi, there's a bunch of stuff I need to show you."

"Here? At Cisco's? I've seen every dirty thing here a million—"

"Let's let Shane and Ana geek out over computers," he whispered loudly.

"Before you go." I leaned in close so only Patrick could hear me over the music. "A baby? Are you freaking kidding me?"

"Well, I thought Molly was pregnant! And now she's not. And you delivered me of the notion." He grinned at me in a devilish way, which looked totally out of place on his kind face. "Get it?"

I groaned and shoved him lightly into Heidi. "Go."

"Yeah, we should probably go say hi to Indiana, anyway. I heard he's the one who actually put out the fire. Did you hear that, too?" Patrick asked Heidi loudly as he dragged her away. I shushed him loudly before I could stop myself. Taggart had seen me—Patrick needed to stay quiet. He ignored me, and I hid my face behind my hand as I settled onto the barstool next to Shane.

"Sorry about them," I said.

He grinned. "They're a delight. Would you like to meet the rest of the team? With the fire and the chaos, I don't think we all had proper introductions."

I swallowed. "Um, sure," I said. "Sounds great."

We walked down the bar a few seats, and Shane cleared his throat. "Everybody, this is Ana. She's on Artemis, but I don't think you've met her. That's Bruce," he said, pointing to a man in his forties who offered a friendly salute. "Over there is Allen, and there's Evan, and that's Mike. Obviously not everybody, but a good group."

My eyes settled on Evan. He had on black jeans and a black T-shirt, and I realized, a little uncomfortably, that we were dressed exactly the same. I immediately wanted to change.

Evan squinted at me as if trying to place where he might have seen me before. "I didn't know we had any girls on the team. What do you do exactly?"

I paused. There were only a few coders on the team, so the vaguer my answer, the better. Maybe I could ride the coffee intern thing. I already stood out as a female, and someone like Evan was just enough of a jerk to cause trouble. I gave him a bright smile and played the helpless girl card. I shrugged. "Whatever they tell me to."

"Well, if you ever want to learn about programming, one of us guys would be glad to teach you sometime."

Wonderful. I took a long drink from my margarita and counted to ten. *Keep your mouth shut*, I told myself. *Don't give them a reason to think you could create a secret identity that could put out a fire or jump out of a plane.*

"So I guess everyone's here except the golden boy," Evan said, his voice a little slurred. He lifted his beer in a toast. "I guess he's too busy kissing Melvin's ass to show up and hang out with us little guys."

I tensed and used all my will to keep my thoughts inside.

"You're just jealous because Indiana doesn't *have* to kiss his ass to be the favorite," Mike threw in.

"I put in my time, I've manned every sinking ship, and then some dude comes along and steals my spot. Fuck that."

"Maybe you just called it—you've manned every sinking ship," Mike said. "Maybe the Hammer wants to stay afloat this time."

"Wouldn't it be cool if Indiana found Noah's ark?" Allen asked. His eyes didn't seem to be focused. He burped. "I really hope he does. I bet *it* floats," he said. "If it doesn't, I bet he can *make* it float."

"I think you have your Indianas and maybe also your arks confused," Shane said.

"Who cares, so long as *this* Indiana stays lost," Evan said.

"We'll probably see him at the brunch tomorrow," Mike said. "I'm looking forward to meeting him."

"Why do we have to go to that again?" Allen asked.

"Mandatory bonding. The bosses are even supposed to serve us, cosplaying as peons," Evan said and rolled his eyes.

"Did you guys hear the Hammer is thinking about promoting Indiana to, like, head our team?" Mike asked.

Evan shook his head violently, nearly slipping off his barstool. "No, the rumor is we'll *all* be unemployed unless he can get us that one account."

My ears perked up. "What do you mean?"

Evan rolled his eyes. "So Melvin is on his way out, right? He needs a big get. He told the higher-ups that he could land this impossible account. They don't usually send people from our team. But now he thinks he's got some sort of ace in the hole, some James Bond hacker who can throw a football or whatever, so he convinced his bosses to let him try to land S.J. Sporting. S.J. wants to up their online presence to outsell Browne Sporting Goods. I guess Indiana likes to go spearfishing and cave diving and do triathlons and, I don't fucking know, model underwear for Calvin Klein or some shit. So the Hammer thinks he and Indiana together can win over a sports CEO."

Wait. So now I was a spearfisher and a cave diver? And what was the *tri* in *triathlon*? Yikes on bikes. Seemed like maybe more than Patrick and Heidi (and, I guess, I) added to Indiana's mystique.

Evan took another swig of his beer. "I told him I could do it, but he said I'm too much of a computer geek."

"You *are* a computer geek," Bruce said. "And you didn't save anyone from a fire, so…"

"I could win that account better than some knockoff Indiana Jones," Evan grumbled.

"That 'knockoff Indiana Jones' is a better coder than you'll ever be," I said angrily, "and a better obstetrician," I added. Oh my god, where had that come from?

"Indiana's been a great addition to our team, and you know it.

Besides"—and here Mike lowered his voice—"I heard he's her dad, so maybe be nice."

"That's where I know you from! The coffee girl at the meeting! So, Dora the Explorer," Evan sneered at me, "do you and your dad go on rescue missions together?"

"He's not my freaking dad," I said, exasperated. The "Dora the Explorer" comment had stung, probably because of its accuracy. I was way more qualified to lead a group of small cartoon children through a forest than do the things Indiana was supposed to be able to do.

"Are you sure?" Mike asked. "Because—"

I had to get out of here before I told them I knew exactly who my father was, and it wasn't me. I cleared my throat. "Nice to meet you all," I said in a hoarse voice, then turned to Shane. He was giving me an unreadable look that made me extremely nervous. "Want to find a table?" I asked, hoping to distract him.

It seemed to work. He gave me a smooth grin, and I noticed again how handsome he was. "Sure. Follow me."

Once we were seated, he leaned in. "I have to ask. Did Indiana really deliver a baby before he put out the fire?"

I shrugged, trying to choose my words carefully. "Hard to believe, don't you think?" I asked hesitantly.

He took a sip of his drink, watching me. "Almost impossible. And he's not your dad?"

"No." I scoffed. "Absolutely not. Now enough about him. What do you do back in New York?"

He smiled again and launched into a rundown of what his daily responsibilities were and how he'd been volunteered for the job of accompanying

Melvin to Denver. He had a warm smile. He also had a bit of a New York accent and nice eyes. I wondered what he would think of this whole mess.

When he'd finished, he turned it around. "What about you? What made you get into coding?"

I couldn't help it; my face lit up. "There's always a right answer, but there are a million ways to get there. It transcends cultures, and you can make anything if you figure out the right order." I fished my phone from my bag. "Like this." I scrolled through some of the apps I'd built, showing him how they worked. I was immensely proud of them, and it was always a bonus to share them with someone who understood how it went together.

"These are incredible, Ana. You're very talented," he told me.

My cheeks colored as my modesty finally kicked back in. "Maybe at this, but not at everything. You should see my pottery."

"I would love to see your pottery."

I opened and closed my mouth. I hadn't meant that to be an invitation. "On second thought, maybe not. Let's just have you go on thinking I'm super talented."

He watched my face. "I have to ask, is it hard being a woman in your industry?"

I looked up at him and felt my shoulders drop. "You have no idea."

"Then tell me," he said.

"When I was younger, I was the only girl in Computer Club. I was the only girl in Mathletes. I got teased a lot. I was head of my class, and guys were *still* mansplaining to me how electronics worked. Or saying they could kick my ass at *Mario Kart. Which they cannot,*" I said fiercely, rising a little in my seat.

He held up his hands. "I would never presume to say I could kick your ass at *Mario Kart*. Unless we're talking Baby Park, in which case your ass is toast," he said.

"Um, I am *amazing* at Baby Park, I'll have you know," I retorted. "It's not as fun as Excite Bike, but I'm unstoppable at Baby Park."

He grinned and ran a hand through his hair. "Good to know," he said.

I couldn't help smiling. It was nice to be asked, and it felt good to get some of the feelings off my chest. "College was worse. It wasn't Imposter Syndrome; it was Wrong Room Syndrome. Like, 'Poetry class is down the hall.'" I rolled my eyes. "I wish it were different now, in the work world, but I'm still always in the wrong room." Or the wrong gender, I thought bitterly.

He nodded. "I'm sorry about the way Melvin treated you today. I can't imagine how frustrating that must have been."

I thought for a second, unsure how to respond. I hadn't told him my official role on the team, and I didn't know if he'd realized yet that there wasn't an Ana on the Artemis roster. Before I could think of what to say, he touched my hand lightly.

"Speaking of…" His eyes focused on some point above my head.

I whipped around to see Melvin standing in the door of Cisco's bar, looking around. When he saw us, he headed our way.

"Damn it, damn it," I said under my breath. "Left my fedora at home." I could feel my lower back start to sweat. I let my curls fall over my face and shifted slightly, doing my best impression of Cousin It.

"Shane," Melvin said brusquely. "I carved out a few minutes to come here before I'm out of pocket for the next little bit. I'm looking for Indiana Aaron. Have you seen him?"

I held my breath, hoping the change in hair would disguise me, but he barely looked my way.

"I keep missing him," Melvin said.

"No, you don't," I said loudly. I was suddenly so tired of the whole thing. "Indiana was at the meeting this morning. And Indiana is here now." I kept my face turned partly away from Melvin but couldn't keep the annoyance out of my voice.

"Indi*ana?*" Shane repeated, then glanced over at me. He looked back over at the guys, then again at me. "Indi-ana," he repeated, and my body went cold. Shane looked directly into my eyes, and that same unreadable expression passed over his face. He glanced up at Melvin, then back at me. After a beat, he straightened his shoulders and gave Melvin his full attention. "He was here just a minute ago. We played a game of pool, and he kicked my ass," Shane said, then ducked his head. "He said he might fit in another game. Or he may have taken off already. He's...he's the emergency backup goalie for the Colorado Avalanche. They have a game tonight."

I choked and almost swallowed my tongue. What were these words coming out of his mouth? Now Indiana was on a professional hockey team? When did he have time to do anything work-related? Behind the curtain of hair, I held my breath, and my eyes watered. For a brief second, I wondered who Indiana was and if I was ever going to meet him myself.

Melvin sighed and leaned against the bar. "Whiskey straight," he told the bartender. He stayed focused on Shane, oblivious of my identity crisis or choke fest. He paid for his drink and took a long swallow. I noticed he didn't tip. "I wish I could catch him."

"But you said hello to him before the managing directors' meeting," Shane said. "Remember?" He turned to me and caught my eye. "You remember, too, don't you, Ana." It wasn't a question.

Melvin squinted and nodded while I tried hard to keep my stomach contents down. "Of course, I remember," he said. "I just mean…never mind. You said he might still be playing pool?"

When Shane nodded, Melvin drained his drink and took off toward the pool tables.

I stared at Shane. "Did you…actually play pool with Indiana this evening?" I asked tentatively.

He shook his head. "I haven't yet, but I will later if she wants to."

I swallowed hard and tried to calm the sudden puddle of dread in my stomach.

"You were going to tell him who you were back at the meeting before he made an ass of himself, weren't you?" he said.

I nodded. "Why did you cover for me?" I asked, my throat raw.

"Why not? Melvin's the worst. But I *am* a little confused." His cheeks colored, and it looked like it was his turn to be nervous. "I don't want to make any assumptions, but there seems to be a discrepancy, and… I'm from New York City, and we hate all people equally, and I have—" He stopped himself. "I don't want to be insensitive." He ran his hand through his hair, tousling it in an adorable way. "I sound so stupid. Let me restart."

I decided to take pity on him. "It was just a misunderstanding at first. He assumed I was male because of my name when I corrected his work in an email. But there's a context to all this. When I corrected my supervisor at the main office in person, it didn't go well, and I got transferred to Artemis. With Melvin, he seemed to think I was brilliant. And then I realized maybe his gender assumption was the reason." I swallowed. I didn't want Shane to think the worst of me, so I tried to pick my words carefully. "I was going to tell him the truth, but Heidi—you've met Heidi, you know how she is—got hold of him first. She said I was full of charisma and talent and masculinity."

"I agree with the first two," Shane broke in.

I smiled and looked down at my drink. "After talking with her, he started trusting me with more leadership and bigger responsibilities. He never would have done that if he didn't think I was a rugged Hemingway dude-bro; you saw the way he treated me in person. And I'm not that person. As much as it hurts to admit, Evan's right—I'm more Dora the Explorer than Indiana Jones. I watch *Bridgerton* and eat ice cream in my pajamas," I confessed, then took a breath. "And I'm not normally a risk-taker. For example, I love fish but not *to* fish. I have a fully cycled twenty-gallon tank at home. But I worry about the responsibility of caring for a life that depends solely on me, so I haven't gotten a fish yet."

His eyes widened as he looked at me in disbelief. "There's a lot to unpack there."

"Trust me, I know how it sounds. But when it comes to work, I can be a badass. I want to be treated fairly, and I want a promotion I deserve, and I don't want to be seen as a little girl who needs help all the time. Men are always asking if they can just speak to my husband instead of me."

"Do you have one of those? A husband?"

"Nope, and if I did, I'd never admit it to those assholes. Do you?"

"Do I what?"

"Have a husband?"

He held my gaze. "No, I'm single. And I think I get it. Maybe work-from-home positions are providing a lot more opportunities for people than I realized. If you've earned a promotion, it shouldn't matter what you look like. Though you *do* look very nice. Beautiful, even."

I swallowed several times before I could speak again and quickly changed the subject. "So Indiana plays for the Avalanche?"

Shane chuckled. "Yep, when needed. He's one of Colorado's best."

"And…he's…the backup goalie? I don't think he can skate."

"That's unfortunate. But an *emergency* backup goalie is not the actual backup goalie. They're not technically part of the team; they just help out in a crisis." Shane shrugged. "I was thinking on my feet. I hope I didn't make things worse. If what Evan was saying is true, I thought it might help with him trusting you with S.J. Sporting. Too far?"

"Thank you. Really. And no, not compared to the crap Patrick and Heidi have come up with."

"Do you have a plan for how you're going to keep this up? What about the company brunch tomorrow?"

Tomorrow's brunch. In all the excitement, I'd almost forgotten about it. Leave it to the higher-ups to think having a mandatory work event on a Saturday morning would be a treat for the employees. Even if there was food. The information I'd let slip past earlier reared back up. "Are the bosses really going to be serving us?" I asked.

"That's what we were told." Shane shrugged.

I put my forehead down on the bar. "Are you kidding me?" I groaned. "Why can't they read the room? Like, they think it's a cute role reversal, but it's actually super degrading and upsetting." I lifted my head, instantly regretting having put it on the bar. My forehead was sticky. "To answer your question, I don't really have a plan," I admitted. "My plan went up in smoke today. Literally. But I have to tell the truth, so I guess I find another opportunity to do that."

At that moment, I heard a loud laugh coming from the pool tables. Definitely Patrick. "But not today. I think I need to follow Melvin. Not sure my friends should be talking to him, especially when they're tipsy."

I got up and took off for the pool tables, arriving just in time to see Heidi throw her arms around Melvin's neck, sniffling into his shoulder.

"He broke my heart, Melon." She sobbed. "And then he broke my winning streak, and then he left!" Thank god. Heidi had gotten rid of Indiana the same way Shane had. "Did you see him on your way over? He's so handsome, he's not even real. I could drown in those blue eyes." She saw me over his shoulder and gave me a thumbs-up. Her eye makeup was perfectly intact.

"He had to get to the Avs game," Shane said, coming up behind me. "Don't take it personally."

Patrick popped up, a look of ecstatic glee on his face. He threw his arm around Shane's neck. "Yes! He had to get to the Avs game because..." He looked at Shane.

"Because he's the emergency backup goalie," Shane supplied.

"Of course he is." Patrick nodded, barely keeping the grin off his face.

"He goes to all the sports rehearsals," Heidi interjected.

"Practices," Shane corrected.

"Right. He's great with a ball," she said.

"Puck," Shane muttered.

Melvin awkwardly patted Heidi's shoulder as he pushed her away. "Right. Okay. I'll just text him. Thanks, everyone." He looked around, then took off for the door.

"He might have gone out the back way," Heidi shouted after him. "I couldn't see through my tears."

A few seconds later, my phone vibrated in my pocket, and I squeezed my eyes shut. No doubt a check-in from Melvin. How had this imaginary version of myself completed more in his week of life than I had in all of mine?

"Can you give us a second?" I asked Shane as I grabbed Patrick and Heidi and dragged them toward the women's restroom. Shane waved at us as I forcibly jammed them through the door.

"We can walk on our own," Heidi said irritably but stopped moving when she saw my face.

"*He knows*," I said breathlessly, bugging my eyes out at them.

Patrick squinted at me. "Who, Melon? Me?"

I took a deep breath to steady myself and leaned against the sinks.

Patrick checked for feet under the stalls. "I don't think I should be in here," he said. "It's nicer than the men's, though. I like it." He turned to Heidi. "I'm not the 'he,' am I?"

"No," I groaned. "Shane. Shane *knows*."

"Duh," Heidi said. "He backed you up out there with Melon."

"He's practically a stranger! He's here babysitting Melvin, and now he knows I'm not who I've let everybody believe I am."

"Wait, you didn't tell him?" Heidi asked.

"No!" I cried. "He figured it out on his own and then just backed me up. Like, seamlessly."

Patrick touched my arm. "Ana, Artemis isn't a large team. Props to Shane for figuring it out, but honestly, how is he the only one? This isn't exactly rocket science, you know? It's like a third-grade word problem."

"It's the *ease* with which he figured it out that scares me. Plus…"

"Plus he's hot?" Patrick asked.

"Exactly. Like burn-your-hands hot. And kind. And a good listener. He talks to me like an equal…" I trailed off again when I saw the expressions on their faces.

"You have a crush," Heidi announced.

I winced. "Kinda. But I can't like this guy!"

"Just because he's Melon's nanny?" Heidi asked.

"Not just that. He knows my secret. What if it doesn't work out? What if he makes things worse for me? Plus, we work together. *And* he lives in New York, which is like a million miles away. Plus, maybe he doesn't even like me."

"First, slow your roll," Patrick said soothingly. "You're already talking divorce after a rocky marriage. You just shared a drink. That's all. There's no reason to assume he's going to betray you or that he has any ulterior motives. Take it a day at a time. Personally, I think he seems like a nice guy."

"Me, too," Heidi said. "He should narrate sleep stories for that meditation app, don't you think?"

"He does have a nice voice," I admitted. Then I squeezed my eyes tight. "Which I've already told him a few times."

"Deep breaths, Ana," Patrick said. "I know it's been a long emotional day. I mean, saving our lives and witnessing the birth of a child—" I reached out to smack him, but he ducked it easily. "Stop borrowing trouble. All is good. Okay?"

I closed my eyes and willed myself to believe him. "Okay. But I still have to tell Melvin who I really am. And I still have to go to that stupid work brunch tomorrow."

"Then just combine the two. Find a quiet moment tomorrow when the vibes are good and confess. Then you don't have to worry about your embarrassingly large crush on Shane—"

"Patrick!" I growled.

"Sorry. But it fixes both problems." He looked at both of us and raised his eyebrows. "Did you hear the bosses are supposed to be serving us food?"

I sighed. "I really hope that's a rumor. Besides, that makes forcing us to go to an unpaid weekend event even worse. It's just mean."

"I bet Melon licks his fingers while he makes pancakes." Heidi shuddered.

"Gross," I said. I stared at my reflection in the mirror. I kind of looked like a scared rabbit. I lowered my shoulders and rolled my head from side to side. Then I checked my eyeliner. Still on point. Shake it off. Patrick was right. Future Ana could deal with the potential fallout from a nasty divorce with Shane. Present Ana could just enjoy a drink and see where things took her.

Right now, I just had to focus on the brunch. I had a new plan, and with good vibes, it should work out fine. *Should* being the key word.

Chapter 7

APOLLO IT HAD RENTED OUT THE ENTIRE TOP FLOOR OF A BUILDING in downtown Denver for this stupid event. The official word was that it wasn't "mandatory," but we were expected to attend. It was all I could do not to send a gift-wrapped dictionary to the CEO with the definition of *mandatory* marked. Changing what you called something didn't change what it was. It amazed me how many adults struggled with that concept.

The event dress code was labeled as business attire, so I'd gone with a long-sleeved black dress that hit below the knee and boots with four-inch heels. I didn't want to look up at anyone I didn't have to. Thank goodness the event was limited to a few remote teams and didn't include the people I had worked with previously. The last thing I needed was chitchat with Taggert or even Gerald Grass.

Heidi had organized the event, so she and I had come together, and we stopped in the entrance to take it all in. There were different breakfast food stations, waiters in suits, and, of course, the bosses each manning a station—one was at the pancakes, another was sloppily making omelets, one cutting quiche, and of course, Melvin was making waffles. There was batter all over the floor.

I must have tensed because Heidi grabbed my arm. "Keep your mouth shut," she whispered.

"They don't have money for promotions, Heidi," I said, turning to look up at her. "We had to decouple, but they've found money in the budget for this place." I gestured around the expansive floor before my eyes lit on a station in the corner. "And the rumors are true—there's even an open bar. And look at all this food! The excess is sickening," I grumbled. "This must have cost a fortune."

Heidi nodded, her eyes fixed on Melvin. "It did. I was mainly in charge of organizing the guest list, which is why Patrick and Joseph are here, and I threw Jason on the list, too, just because. But I definitely didn't have control of the budget. The brunch just started, and most of the food is already on the floor, too," she murmured before suddenly jumping up and down. "Look! Melvin just licked his hand! I called it!" She spun around, doing a bad impression of the Running Man in her heels and floral dress.

"So gross." I'd come here to find the perfect moment to tell Melvin the truth. I heard about the bar, so I thought maybe I could catch him a few whiskeys in. He'd be in a good mood, and we could both have a laugh about the Big Misunderstanding. But seeing it all in person... Melvin and the other bosses were serving the most condescending grins along with badly cooked food, enjoying their "cute" little role reversal, serving their servants. *Barf.* If I were being completely honest with myself, this was never a club I would want to belong to, whether they'd have me as a member or not. Maybe it was just the sight of so many health-code violations in one place that was getting to me. If they cut back on events like these, they could easily afford to pay their workers more.

I turned to Heidi and grabbed her arm to stop the dance. "I need more time. I don't think I can tell anyone who I really am today. I'm already up way too early for a Saturday, and I might never eat again."

She nodded. "Totally. This isn't the best atmosphere for confessing anything." She scanned the room, then pointed to a table in the distance, where Patrick was sitting with his husband, Joseph. "Let's tell Patrick; then we can sit through the speeches and take off, okay?"

"Perfect."

We made our way across the room.

When Patrick saw us, he waved widely and grinned. "Come say hi to Joseph."

It was always great to see Joseph. He was at least six-four, with a body-builder's physique and jet-black hair. He towered over me and always gave the gentlest hugs.

"It's nice to see you again," I said.

"You, too, Ana. Patrick's been telling me about all the shenanigans."

Patrick shrugged. "We have the best adventures, don't we?"

"Great, so you're up to speed," I said as I slid into the seat next to Joseph. "I don't think I can come clean today. Too many people are making me mad, and I haven't even talked to anyone yet."

"Whatever you're comfortable with," he said. He looked up, and I followed his gaze. Jason Rhodes was coming toward us, dressed impeccably as always with (you guessed it) a Dos Equis in one hand. I hadn't talked to him since he walked me home from my pottery class, and it was actually nice to see him. I'd told him then, a bit casually, about being mistaken for a man at work, but things had exploded since then.

"Do you mind if I join you?" he asked.

"Please," I said. Jason sat next to Heidi, and she murmured a quick hello in his direction.

"Good to see you, Jason," Patrick said. "Joseph and I were waiting, but now that you all are here, anyone up for a mimosa?"

"I think we'll need them if we have to listen to the self-indulgent lectures about how great management is," I grumbled. "I'll go grab them."

I hurried over to the bar, careful not to make eye contact with anyone as a couple of employees tested the microphone that had been set up on a makeshift podium. I smiled at the bartender. "Can I get a pitcher of mimosas, please?"

"Sure," he said as he pulled up a shaker and began mixing ingredients. "That'll be fifty-five dollars."

I almost choked. "I'm sorry, I thought this was an open bar."

"It is, for the VIPs. You have to be a managing director or higher to get free drinks. Do you have one of the badges? They gave them out this morning."

"No, I don't. They're the ones who have the money, so they shouldn't be the ones getting free drinks," I explained.

He shrugged. "I don't make the rules."

"For real, fifty-five dollars?"

"Tips appreciated."

I backed away as he tapped the tip jar. "Actually, I'm good, thanks," I said. I looked over at our table and made eye contact with Patrick. "No open bar," I mouthed. "Cruel joke."

Patrick knit his brow and opened his mouth to answer but was cut off by the sound of the microphone squealing.

"Hello, everyone," a man said, his voice echoing through the room.

He looked vaguely familiar, probably from one of those manager spotlight pieces they did on the website. "Thank you all for coming today. We appreciate that you're spending your Saturday with us…"

I didn't want to draw attention to myself by walking back to the table, so I stayed at the edge of the room near the "open" bar, staring longingly at the mimosas the bartender was mixing for someone else. No liquid courage for me.

And I zoned out. Maybe my body had to be here, but my mind certainly didn't. I scanned the room for Shane. I finally found him sitting at a table with the Artemis team, and I noticed that he was scanning the room, too. Our eyes met, and I gave a little wave. He held the eye contact a second longer, then gave me a sexy little half smile. My stomach flipped over, and I thought about how nice it had been to talk with him the night before. But I'd told him too much and made myself vulnerable. On the other hand, he seemed like a centered, genuinely caring person, and maybe—

"Indiana Aaron, would you please come to the stage?" Melvin's voice boomed out of the microphone, pulling me out of my reverie. My attention snapped back to the podium. When had *he* gotten up there? He still wore his dirty apron from the waffle station. My body filled with dread and froze in place—for a second too long. I watched in disbelief as Heidi made her way to the stage and grabbed for the microphone. She and Melvin struggled for a bit before he let go. Bits of waffle batter were flying.

She held the mic between two fingers to avoid getting more of the sticky batter on her hands. "I have some bad news," she said breathlessly, ignoring the reverberation. "Indiana Aaron would have wanted to be here to accept your appreciation for his baby-delivering skills. It's very kind of you to want him to say a few words." She glanced over at Melvin, who narrowed his eyes at her. It was hard to take him seriously, though, as he ran a batter-covered hand down the front of his apron.

What had I missed? There was a smattering of applause and murmuring from the crowd, and when I looked around the room, everyone seemed confused. Except Patrick, who looked horrified.

I tried to make eye contact with Heidi, but she avoided looking in my direction. She was too busy playing to the audience. "Indiana has always been an accomplished pilot, and early this morning, he was kindly teaching others how to fly as well. Unfortunately"—she paused dramatically, screwing up her eyes to start the tears—"there has been a crash. He swerved to avoid hitting a bird. We all know how much he respected nature. He managed to save everyone on board but lost his own life in this last heroic act." She sniffed. "He was so looking forward to attending this brunch."

Melvin gasped and clutched his chest, but Heidi plowed on. "His masculine sexiness—and excellent technical abilities—will be greatly missed. Let us have a moment of silence." She bowed her head as the audience broke out in murmurs.

"No!" I yelled in horror and leaned against the bar, breathing hard. I felt my legs weaken, and I slid down until I was crouched behind it.

The bartender looked at me distastefully but still muttered, "I'm sorry for your loss," before scooting over so I wasn't hyperventilating on his leg.

But before anyone could gather themselves enough to ask questions, Jason was on the stage. He gave Melvin a casual smile as he grabbed the microphone from Heidi and gently nudged her to the edge of the podium. She teetered on her heels before falling over the side. He winced but turned back to the audience. "That's our office manager, Heidi Cross," he said amicably. "She keeps us on our toes. Don't you, Heidi?"

She was struggling to right herself on her heels. "Ummm," she said, pulling her skirt down. He held his hand down to her, and she took it, climbing back up onto the podium. She looked annoyed, but I noticed, even through my fear blinders, that she didn't let go right away.

Jason turned back to the crowd. "Heidi loves to joke. We're just messing with you. You all right, Melvin? You don't look so good," he said over his shoulder. Jason's irreverence seemed to let some of the air back into the room, and Melvin lowered his hand from his chest and nodded.

"Besides, we all know Indiana, don't we?" Jason continued. "He would never swerve. He studied under the famous Captain Sully Sullenberger, who landed his plane in the Hudson River when he, too, was attacked by birds. So don't worry, everyone, Indiana is fine. He's being attended by medics, but he'll be cleared shortly to come and have some whiskey with us."

I shrank even farther behind the bar. Jason, too? I squeezed my eyes shut. And I was going to have to murder Heidi when I got to her later. I stopped listening as Jason handed the microphone to someone else and was intensely focused on how to make myself fully disappear when I felt a hand on my shoulder.

I let out a yelp and turned around, ready to fight off my attacker, when I realized it was only Shane. He frantically shushed me, then crouched behind the bar with me. The bartender snorted at us and went back to making drinks.

"I came over to see if you were okay," he said.

"I'm not. Definitely not," I said.

Shane craned his head around the corner of the bar, then turned back to me. "There's a clear path to the terrace door. If we book it now, I think we can make it."

"Say no more."

He put his suit jacket over my shoulders, and I ducked my head as he led me out the back doors and onto the terrace. I shivered and pulled the jacket more tightly around me. It smelled like him. I wanted to breathe it in and relax, but I may or may not have swerved to avoid a bird while *driving a fucking plane*. I grabbed my phone and texted Heidi. Out on the terrace. Now.

Shane put his arm around me. "It's okay," he assured me. "That got a little out of hand, but I'm sure—"

"I'm so sorry!" Heidi squealed as she ran over to me on the terrace. Jason and Patrick trailed behind her.

"What were you thinking?" I cried. "I know I zoned out, but you told everyone I *died*?"

"I'm sorry!" she said again. "They called you up to talk about the baby birthing or whatever, which is totally Patrick's fault, by the way, not mine, and you already made it clear you weren't ready to tell the truth, but somebody *had* to say something, so it came to me in a rush—you had to die."

"What?" I yelled.

"You had to die," she repeated. "It was the only way out. If you were dead, everyone would feel bad, and you'd never have to confess anything. Problem solved."

I grabbed her shoulders. "Heidi. I'm a real person. *Indiana* is a real person. We are the same person. I can't *die* my way out of this. I'd lose my job for sure!"

Jason reached out a hand and gently pulled Heidi out of my grip. "I can see where she was coming from," he said, and she beamed at him. "I imagine this whole situation you've got going on gets complicated. It's certainly grown since you and I talked a couple of weeks ago, Ana."

"I mean…yeah, it has, but Heidi didn't have to kill me! If Indiana dies, Ana dies. All my credentials and education and work history go away. And they'll stop paying me!"

Heidi pressed her lips together. "I see your point. I didn't have time to think it through. I made an executive decision in the moment."

"*Points*, Heidi! Many, many points!"

"I brought you back to life," Jason added. "So no harm, no foul."

"You!" I said, turning on him. "I studied under the 'we're landing in the Hudson River' guy? Why?"

To his credit, he kept his cool. "Because I also made an executive decision in the heat of the moment. Heidi made a mess trying to save you, so I had to save her. And everything's copacetic now." He turned to Heidi. "Can I get you a drink?"

She smiled at him. "Sure." She looked back at me as she walked away. "I was only trying to help, Ana."

I sighed. "I know." I took a deep breath and forced the scream back down my throat. Everyone was so helpful. They were so helpful, they'd almost killed me. And probably Melvin. He'd looked on the verge of a heart attack.

When I finally looked up, I saw Patrick and Shane looking at me as if they were trying very hard not to laugh.

"You all think this is funny?" I asked them tartly.

They both shook their heads, but they deliberately didn't make eye contact with each other.

"So glad you're amused," I grouched.

I huddled down, planning to stay put until the brunch was over. I felt myself starting to relax a little, as each minute took me farther and farther away from that horrible moment where Heidi killed me, then flopped off the stage.

A little while later, I'm not sure how long, I heard Joseph call out, his voice deep and bearing a slight Minnesotan accent. "Patrick? Are you out here?"

Patrick waved, and Joseph jogged over. "I did my part, so we're good to go," Joseph said.

"Great," Patrick said. He took Joseph's hand, but I immediately stood between them. "What was your part, Joseph?" I asked as steadily as I could.

"I helped," he said and smiled at me, reminding me way too much of Heidi. "I placed a few half-finished whiskeys, all neat, throughout the room. That's the manliest way to drink it, in my opinion. Plus, I don't order anything 'straight.'" He and Patrick grinned at each other. "And did you see there's a bird's nest right above the terrace door? Probably not, because even I could barely reach it, but I grabbed a bunch of feathers and sprinkled them throughout the room. With the whiskeys. I think we have our bases covered."

I didn't say anything, which Joseph took to mean I didn't understand.

"You know, like you came back from the plane covered in bird and had some drinks with people, with bird still on you," he explained slowly.

"I get it," I said, then pulled my head and arms into Shane's oversize jacket as if it were a turtle shell and hid, ignoring the sound of their retreating footsteps and Shane's quiet, infectious laughter.

Chapter 8

AFTER LAST NIGHT, I WANTED TO STAY IN BED ALL DAY WITH THE covers pulled up over my head. I wasn't even hungry; I couldn't shake the image of little bits of batter flying as Heidi tussled with Melvin before announcing I had died. It took a few texts from Shane to get me out of bed. He wanted to go somewhere fun to distract me, and since he was leaving Denver soon, I didn't want to waste an opportunity to get to know him better. So I cleaned myself up and had an extra coffee to shake off the bad mood.

"Good morning, sunshine," he said brightly when he came to pick me up. "You're looking pretty spry for—"

"Say it and I'll kill you," I growled.

He tried to look serious. "Too soon for jokes?"

"Give it a year or two; then we can laugh and laugh about my crash landing because of a *freaking bird*."

Shane gave me that sexy half smile, and I shook myself. None of this was Shane's fault. He'd been nothing but nice to me and kept my secret, at least for now. It was in my best interest to be nice to him. Plus, he looked so handsome in his dark jeans and black crewneck sweater.

"Sorry," I said. "I still have a little extra adrenaline from yesterday. Where are we going?"

"Brace yourself—we're going to the pet store."

"What? Why?"

"Because it's time for you to become a pet parent."

———

Shane and I arrived at the pet store just south of my apartment. "I'm still not sure about this," I grumbled.

Shane chuckled as he cut the engine and turned to give me a smile. "You overthink things. You've memorized the nitrogen cycle, right?"

"Of course!"

"See? And I'm confident you've tested all the water parameters quite a few times. You're ready for a fish. Trust me. I mean, you delivered a ba—"

"Not one more word about the baby I didn't deliver."

Shane grinned. "Right. Onward. We have a fish to save."

I smacked him on the shoulder but allowed him to lead me into the store and, despite myself, couldn't hold in a gasp of delight. There was a koi pond that stretched the length of the front windows, with lily pads and turtles sunning on rocks. The fish flopped on top of each other to greet me, and I felt ridiculously special until I realized I was standing next to the gumball machine filled with fish food.

There were tanks everywhere with different types of freshwater fish, and even though I was nervous, I was stoked that Shane had made me come. Not many people understood why I loved fish so much, especially since I couldn't swim and didn't like the water, but I just did. Fish were the coolest little creatures on the planet. Looking into a planted tank or a nano reef was a window into an entirely different world.

Meanwhile, Shane had gone straight to the front desk, where a woman in her late teens or early twenties was working. She had sky-blue hair, and almost every part of her face was pierced. "What brings you in?" she asked.

"My friend here is looking for a fish. Easy to care for, hard to kill."

I walked up behind Shane and gave her a little wave. "I have a cycled tank at home, and I take this responsibility very seriously." Adopting a dog or a cat from a rescue was almost as hard as adopting a child, but I guessed a pet store would give you anything you could pay for. "You don't do home visits, do you?"

She looked at me for a beat and then laughed. "Owning fish will make you a murderer," she said. "Happens to all of us. If you're not comfortable with that…"

"What?" I yelped, then turned to Shane, who looking at the attendant and frantically slashing at his neck in a "be quiet" sort of way.

She ignored him. "I have four tanks at home, so I guess you could say I'm a mass murderer." She snorted.

I backed away from the counter. "I don't think I'm ready to be a murderer."

"Come back," she said, still laughing. "I'm only partly joking. Actually, I'm totally serious. You have to be prepared for them to die at any time, for no reason. They're fish. And they freaking *love* to carpet surf."

"Do what?" I asked.

"Jump out of tanks and dry up on your carpet. Crispy little guys when you find them in the morning. Make sure your tank has a lid. But some of them will find a way out regardless."

Shane put his head in his hands, and she turned and gestured to the left. "Since you're looking for something that'll take you a little longer to kill, I recommend a betta. They're pretty and they breathe air, so they can live in nasty water. They don't swim a lot, though, and they can be total dicks."

I looked over at the wall of bettas. They really were beautiful. Some looked like blooming flowers; others, like badass dragons. I knew they had a labyrinth organ and didn't need to use their gills, but the bettas also looked like they were struggling to swim while wearing tiny wet ball gowns. Commercial breeding hadn't done them any favors.

"Anything else you might recommend?" I asked.

"How about a guppy?" she suggested. "They're smaller but hardy and a lot of fun to watch."

She led us over to the guppy tank.

"I've heard they have babies, though," I said. "I don't think I'm ready for that."

"No babies if you get a male," she answered.

I looked into the tank, and one immediately caught my eye. Blue, my favorite color, with a spotted tail and a chubby little belly. "I like that one," I said. "Is that one male or female?"

She squinted into the tank. "That's a dude," she said. "And he looks well fed, so I think you'll be okay with him for a while."

"Can you not?" Shane muttered under his breath. Then, more loudly, he said, "Let's take that one. How much?"

"Three dollars and seventy-five cents," she said. So cheap for an entire life that would depend on me.

She netted him quickly, and Shane said, "Allow me to treat you to this little guy, since this was my idea." He also grabbed a net and the fish food the woman recommended.

"Thank you," I said to him.

We walked back out to the car, with Shane carrying the food and me cradling the bag with my new fish in it.

"What're you going to name him?" he asked as I gingerly got into the car so as not to bump the bag. My heart was beating a little faster than normal. I'd bought a fish. I could care for a fish, right?

"Police Chief Jim Hopper, from *Stranger Things*. Fits him, don't you think?"

Shane sputtered as he got back on the highway. "I don't think anything has ever looked less like a Jim Hopper, and I doubt his abilities as a police chief. His mobility is severely limited. And I don't think fish are exactly bright."

"Are you kidding? They can teach fish to drive cars. We don't give the animal kingdom nearly enough credit."

"I maintain that driving a car would raise suspicion and blow his cover pretty quickly. Also, I'm going to need supporting evidence on that," he said. "Who is '*they*'?"

"For-real scientists. Also, done and done." I pulled out my phone and did a quick Google search, then air-dropped him the link to a peer-reviewed scientific study I'd read about how scientists taught goldfish to drive. But I could understand his suspicion.

We chattered back and forth about the alternate worlds of *Stranger Things*, our childhoods, and pets we had when we were younger. I frequently checked the bag in my lap to make sure Hopper wasn't jostled. Then something caught my eye.

"Hey, Shane, it looks like we have a hitchhiker," I said.

"Huh?"

"There's a tiny little thing in here with Hopper. Looks like a tadpole. Did you see her net another fish by accident?"

His forehead creased. "No, just the one."

"Weird." We'd gotten about a mile closer to my house when I glanced down again. "Shane! There's another tadpole in here! There are two tadpoles in this bag! Did you see any frogs in that tank? I didn't."

He glanced over before deliberately keeping his eyes on the road.

"Shane?"

"I don't think those are tadpoles, Ana. I think Hopper is giving birth."

"No. That's not possible. He's a dude, she said that. I signed on for slowly killing *one* fish. One."

We pulled into the lot next to my apartment complex. "Maybe I'm wrong," he suggested.

I got out of the car and held the bag up to the light and gasped. "He just had two more! Hopper's in labor!"

Shane winced. "I feel like this is partly my fault."

"It's totally your fault," I muttered distractedly, staring at the bag. While I watched, another couple of tadpoles squeezed out of Hopper and swam around the bag. "Jesus Christ," I whispered.

"Well, it's not *totally* my fault. I didn't impregnate that fish."

Touché. I guess.

"We should probably get them inside and start acclimating," he said, a little more loudly. "Because, you know, guppies eat their young."

"They do *what?*" I screeched as I followed him to the door.

"They don't eat them right away," he assured me. "Hopper'll be too busy for a while to notice them."

"Too busy doing what?" I asked.

He just stared at me until I understood.

"You mean he's not done? How many more are in there?"

He shrugged. "Hard to say. My sister had guppies growing up. They breed constantly. Like all the time. They never stop. It occurred to me briefly that Hopper might be a girl. But how would I know? I'm not a fish expert."

"Neither was the woman at the store," I observed.

Just then, George and Nancy came ambling around the side of the house, dressed for gardening. "What's all this yelling?" George said in a naturally gruff voice.

"This guy"—I gestured to Shane—"suggested I get a fish. Now I have like five because there's birth happening in this bag!"

George ambled over to Shane and removed one of his gloves before giving Shane a firm handshake. "I'm George. This is Nancy," he said, pointing to her. She lifted her little sun hat and gave a wave. They were both in their sixties, with white hair and usually some form of matching clothing. Today, they were both in plaid capris.

"It's nice to meet you," Shane said.

"You have a nice voice, young man," Nancy said. "Are you Ana's new friend?"

"We live upstairs in the house," George explained, "but we tend to think of her as part of the family."

I ran over and gave Nancy a brief hug, then scurried to my front door. "It's good to see you, but *birth* in a *bag*!"

Shane didn't seem to feel my urgency. "Doing some gardening?"

George leaned back and wiped sweat from his forehead. "Yup. First frost is coming soon, so we have to get our more delicate annuals inside."

I unlocked the door and waved for Shane to follow me into the apartment, not even caring what his first impression might be.

He followed me, but Nancy put a hand on his arm. "Have you met Ana's dad, honey?" she asked.

Shane looked over at me, and I bugged out my eyes at him, gesturing frantically to the bag in my hand. Then he looked back at her. "No, ma'am, I haven't."

"Oooh," she said. "I'm sure he'd love to meet you."

"I'm sure he would, too," I said and grabbed Shane by the shirtsleeve, "but again, new life!"

I pulled him inside and shut the door firmly. Then I floated the bag in the tank and stared at it in wonder as I tried to calm my racing heart. "What have I done?" I whispered.

"Well, for starters, we got a supergood deal on that fish, don't you think? What, twenty for the price of one?"

"They just keep coming," I said in awe.

I took a few deep breaths. There wasn't anything more I could do for Hopper at the moment, so I left him and his babies floating in the tank and led Shane into the main area of the apartment.

"Your neighbors seem nice," he said.

"Yeah, I love them, but they're going to call my dad and tell him all about you, and then he's going to call and insist on meeting you, because they all still treat me like a kid. Which is super embarrassing for me. But that's a problem for future Ana. Right now, I can't believe I let you talk me into this," I said, pointing at the tank. I blew out a breath. "Want some coffee?"

"Honestly, I can't either," he answered. "And sure."

I made us each a cup from my single-serve brewer and sat next to him on the couch. "I like your apartment," he said conversationally.

I blushed. "Thanks."

"You know I *have* to stay now to see what happens, don't you?"

"You'd better. You can't leave Hopper and me alone in this vulnerable state."

He nodded toward my Nintendo Switch setup and raised his eyebrows. "Ready to have your butt kicked at *Mario Kart*?"

I bumped his arm playfully. "If I had a nickel for every time someone said that and then were *decimated* by me, I would never need to work again."

I hooked up the game and tossed him the extra pair of controllers. The first course he picked was Baby Park. We were actually pretty evenly matched. There was a lot of laughter and pillow tossing as we deliberately ran each other off the track and threw cartoon bananas. I was breathless by the time the match ended. I'd won, but just by a couple of points.

I did a sort of chicken-beak victory dance when Shane tossed a pillow straight at my head.

I threw it back and settled next to him on the couch. "Why did you push me so hard to get a fish?" I asked.

"Because I have a dog," he answered. "No matter how bad my day's been, he's great to come home to. I don't feel the way you do about fish, obviously, but maybe Hopper can do that for you, too."

"What's his name?" I asked.

"Odin. I got him at the shelter. He's missing an eye, so it seemed to fit."

"Good call not naming him Cyclops," I agreed. "What's his breed?"

He shrugged. "It said, 'GSD' on his kennel. I think he looks more like a husky, but I've never had him tested."

"That always weirds me out. They're so careful to specify German shepherd *dog*. Like people actually go to the shelter to pick up shepherds who happen to be German."

"Is *that* why they do that?"

"There are two types of German shepherds—dogs and German people who tend to their flocks. Somebody somewhere is really worried about picking the wrong one. Can I see a picture?"

His smile lit up his face, and he pulled out his phone. "Here he is at day care, in this one he's at the park, oh, and sometimes he hogs the bed, like here…" He flipped through a ton of photos, all showing an adorable gray dog with ears too big for its head.

"He's perfect," I said.

Shane nodded. "Just like Hopper. Speaking of, we should probably check on him."

I gasped and ran to the tank. Hopper was still acclimating in his plastic bag, but not alone.

Shane came up behind me and whistled. "I think that bag is over capacity."

"I have a box that I float new plants in." I grabbed it from the cabinet, and once it was inside the tank, we carefully dumped Hopper and the babies in it to keep them contained. It had slats on the sides to allow water flow.

"You should probably leave him in there until he's done birthing or whatever," Shane said. "Then let him loose into the tank. But leave the littles in the box."

"I can't believe this is happening." I tried to count the babies, but they wiggled too much, and they all looked exactly the same: like clear little tadpoles with tiny black eyes and pink intestines. I teared up a little. "It's like the miracle of life in my own apartment." I quickly wiped my eyes. "Or some such shit."

"Hey." He put his hand on my shoulder and gently turned me toward him. "You got this. And selfishly, I'm happy that this is such a moving experience because that means you'll always remember today."

He stepped close to me, and my whole body tensed. "How could I forget?"

His nearness was distracting. "We've witnessed a miracle of nature, and you've finally met your equal at *Mario Kart*. And I found out you have some amazing dance moves."

I smiled despite myself, but my nerves were on fire. "Too bad you live in New York. Now I have to raise these babies alone." I'd meant it as a joke, but as soon as the words were out, I wished I could pull them back. "What I mean is, I don't know how to be a fish's midwife."

"I don't think this is Hopper's first reproductive rodeo." Then he snorted. "And Indiana helped to deliver a baby after all. Like I said, you've got this."

"Tadpoles don't count," I protested. He was still standing very close.

"So…" I stared at his mouth, willing my nerves to relax.

He leaned in and tucked a strand of hair behind my ear. "If you didn't want to seduce me, you shouldn't have done that chicken dance," he whispered.

I started to laugh even as he lowered his face and kissed me. I thought my heart would jump out of my chest, but it felt so good, I wanted the moment to last forever.

Finally, he pulled away. "It's getting late. I should head out."

I walked him to the door, and he leaned down and looked into my eyes a beat longer than normal. "Text me and let me know how it's going, okay?"

Nancy and George were still outside, though they immediately stopped what they were doing and watched us. "Sounded like you were having fun in there," Nancy said and waved.

Heat traveled all the way up my body to my forehead as Shane waved to them and to me before he pulled away in his rental car. Once he was gone, I closed and locked my door, then changed into pajamas and grabbed a blanket. I cuddled up next to the aquarium, playing *Animal Crossing*. It took a while for my pulse to go back to normal. Hopper continued to expel babies for the next hour or so.

When my phone vibrated, I picked it up quickly, hoping to see a message from Shane. Instead, it was Melvin. Damn. Are you busy?

I'm playing the most dangerous game, I wrote back. Anyone who'd been on a villager hunt in *Animal Crossing* would understand.

Like hunting wild game? Not people, right? Haha, he wrote back, and I rolled my eyes. Once again, spending my evening in fuzzy pajamas, watching a fish give birth, wouldn't be Melvin's idea of how a leader spent his time.

In this business you're always hunting people, I texted. I tried to pick my words carefully so as not to outright lie to Melvin. I guess it didn't matter anymore after what had happened yesterday, but I still wanted to keep it to a minimum as much as possible. There was a moral difference between allowing a misconception to continue and outright lying. Or at least I told myself that so I could sleep at night.

So true. Unfortunate we haven't been able to connect over the last two days. Are you injured?

No, but I appreciate you asking. Awkward.

Everything okay with that woman and the baby?

She's no longer pregnant, seems to be doing fine. I winced. I mean, what do you say?

Also wanted to speak with you at the brunch this morning, but we both kept getting sidetracked.

What a nice way to put it. Because of Heidi, I had nearly died. I thought quickly. Yeah, I tried to catch your attention, too.

So many speeches, am I right? he wrote.

I almost typed *totally* but caught myself. Affirmative.

They almost had me when they said you died lol.

My stomach heaved. Everyone's a comedian.

Impressive landing. Jason said you'd just stepped out when I came to have a drink. There were feathers in your whiskey. How big was that bird?

I tried not to squeal and burrowed farther under the blanket. There were feathers in the whiskey? Subtlety, thy name was not Joseph. Or Heidi. Or Jason. Or even Patrick. I winced again, imagining Big Bird from *Sesame Street* attacking a commuter plane. Nightmare fuel. Nothing I couldn't handle, I typed, then squeezed my eyes shut.

No doubt. I know you're busy so I'll keep this brief. I don't know what you've heard. Artemis needs a win. That's where you and I come in. We need to land the website revamp and app creation for S.J. Sporting. I heard you were an EBUG for the Avs.

A what now? I quickly googled the term. Oh yeah. I was a goaltender. I'd forgotten about that.

I picked my words carefully. I don't get called on to play very often, I responded.

Doesn't matter. S.J. is looking to partner with the Avs to expand the brand. We need to get a meeting with the CEO at the Avs practice arena. Put together a kick-ass pitch. Explain our software and what we can do. You can tell them about your hang gliding and your connections to the team. Can you get them season tickets? I'm going to email you a packet of info and we'll connect tomorrow. We need this account, Indiana.

Understood, I texted, even as I felt the panic start to set in again. I was the least athletic person in the world. When I'd been in kindergarten, they'd sat me up on the piano while the other kids played because I'd been so much smaller than everyone else. There was no way I could bullshit someone into thinking I was a modern-day Viking.

I took a cleansing breath and tamped back the panic. I could panic tomorrow. I wanted to sit with my memories of my day with Shane and marvel at the variety of emotions I'd experienced that day. I looked back over at Hopper. He was still at it.

When the phone dinged again, it was Shane. What's the current count?

I pressed my face to the glass and did my best to count every tiny pair of eyes. There were so many that my vision crossed, and I finally had to give up. Too many, I wrote back. I think there are at least seventy.

I hate to tell you this, but when I got back to the hotel, I googled it. They can have up to 200 babies at a time.

I sat back in shock.

I really am sorry about all the grandfish, he wrote. It's a lot for your first day of fish ownership.

It is, I agreed. I hope that girl at the shop stubs her toe every morning for a month.

Damn. I don't want to get on your bad side.

I grinned. I really was growing to love my grandfish. I'd deal with the Melvin thing, I promised myself. Tomorrow.

Chapter 9

When I woke the next morning, it took me a few minutes to remember that I was now responsible for, like, a zillion creatures with no arms or hands that were helpless without me. I wanted to lie in bed for a few extra minutes, savoring my day with Shane and pushing off thoughts of Melvin, how I was going to support my dad, and the hole I'd dug with my alter ego.

I jumped out of bed to check on Hopper. He happily swam up to the glass to greet me. From what I could tell, he'd finally finished ejecting his young. He looked much thinner. No wonder he'd seemed so well-fed at the store. I netted him and released him into the full tank, where he began exploring the plants. Then I looked at the babies. I sprinkled a little crushed fish food over their box so I could count them better. From what I could tell, the final count was…eighty-two. I was now responsible for approximately eighty-three tiny lives.

I picked up my phone to text Shane but sat back for a moment, again savoring the memory of the day we'd had together. Why did he have to live in

New York? I hadn't really dated a lot in my life (not that yesterday had been a date) because for the most part, I didn't like people all that much. As an introvert, meeting people and forcing myself to go to parties was excruciating. It was easier to marathon Netflix, and make ugly pots out of clay, and (now) stare at my new aquatic fan club. But easy came at a cost, and I wondered if Shane might be worth more than the little life I'd carved out for myself.

Even though it was a Monday morning, today was a holiday. Still, I made a cup of coffee and settled in reluctantly to check my work email. When a large file took forever to come in, I felt the familiar wash of dread in my stomach. Melvin. I'd forgotten. He and I were going to be like Batman and Robin, or Mario and Luigi, or Bert and Ernie, or whatever. Some valiant, if ridiculous, male duo on our way to win an account and save the day. God damn it.

So instead of texting Shane, I sent a group message to Patrick and Heidi. Are you two free today? I need help.

Does it involve Melon? Heidi.

Yeah. We're going on an adventure together, I wrote back.

I am THERE, Patrick interjected.

Are you still mad at me? Heidi asked.

I softened. No, of course not. Just please don't kill me before I'm ready.

Yay! I won't. Patrick, come pick me up, Heidi wrote.

K. See you in 20.

When they showed up a half an hour later, I'd showered and was neck-deep in the information Melvin had sent over.

"So you said you were hanging out with Shane yesterday. What did you guys do?" Patrick asked as soon as he walked in the door.

I hung my head and gestured to the tank. Patrick and Heidi pressed their noses to the glass. "You bought over a million tadpoles!" Heidi gasped. She looked over and cleared her throat. "What I mean to say is, that's not the journey I expected for you. I didn't even know you liked frogs."

"Shane got you fish! They're so cute!" Patrick cried as he made fish faces at them.

"I don't like frogs. They totally look like tadpoles, but they're baby guppies," I said. "Hopper gave birth on the way home from the store. I'm trying to come to terms with it."

"Guppies cost like ten cents," Patrick said. "So if you do the math, you practically made a fortune with that purchase."

I blinked. "No. No, I didn't."

"Why Hopper and not Joyce?" Heidi asked.

I waved off her question. "I need help with this Melvin thing. We've got a situation that a fire in the break room can't solve."

Patrick and Heidi pried their attention away from the tank. Patrick sat on the love seat and leaned his elbows on his knees while Heidi sprawled out on the beanbag chair.

"Was there kissing?" Patrick asked.

"Ew, gross, Patrick. No kissing Melvin," I said.

He raised an eyebrow. "I mean with Shane."

"Oh." Color rose in my cheeks. "No comment."

Patrick and Heidi exchanged a smug glance.

"Is he coming over today?" Heidi asked.

"No, he said they had him booked up, even though it's a holiday. But we're talking about Melvin now. I need some advice."

"Okay, I'm focusing," he said. "So this isn't something that can be fixed with fire. I contend that pretty much anything can be fixed with fire. Bedbugs, sharks, alien attacks…"

Heidi flipped upside down on the beanbag chair, her blond hair on the floor and her heart-shaped face looking up at me. "The destruction of company records… I agree with Patrick."

I smiled politely at them both. "Thank you for your contributions." I had to remind myself that inviting them over had been my idea. "Melvin wants me to go with him to meet with the CEO of S.J. Sporting. The Artemis team was talking about it last night. Seems Indiana has a reputation for being really buff and into physical activities." I glanced down helplessly at myself. "Sports stuff like cave diving or rock climbing. Things you need sporting equipment for. I don't know how he got those ridiculous ideas, except from the two of you and Shane. And Jason, and I guess, me. Okay, so bottom line is if he and I can land the account, it sounds like he might give me, or rather Indiana, the promotion. Otherwise, the Artemis team gets cut."

"The entire team?" Heidi gasped. "You hold the lives of like a hundred people in your big strong hands."

"There are only like twelve of us altogether. If you count the non-IT people, too."

Patrick whistled. "That's still a lot of pressure."

"So if this were a game of chess, Melvin moved his bishop, and we need to counter," Heidi said.

"I recommend the rook," Patrick said.

I pulled my feet up underneath me on the couch. "Do either of you know anything about chess?" I asked.

"Not a thing," Heidi answered.

Patrick shook his head. "But I watched *The Queen's Gambit*."

"This is the last time I suggest it, but maybe a fedora—" Heidi started.

"No." I shook my head. "This isn't Shakespeare. I'm not dressing as a man. Or having a man impersonate me. Ever. *I'm* Indiana. If I win or lose the account, I'm doing it as *me*."

"But we definitely don't want Melon having a fit during an important meeting," Patrick concluded. He nodded at Heidi. "This is also the last time I'm going to suggest it, but I do think this is something fire could easily fix—"

I grabbed the throw pillows from the couch and threw one at each of them. Patrick caught his, but the other pillow bounced off Heidi's face.

She grabbed it to toss it back to me when we heard Patrick gasp. I looked over at him, and he quickly slipped his phone into his pocket and looked at me innocently.

"Can you find out what he's been doing?" Heidi asked. "He's been checking his phone incessantly all morning. He won't tell me what he's been looking at."

"Patrick?" I asked.

He chewed his lip for a moment before finally relenting. "Okay, so remember how we took that pottery class together? Well, I told Kelli she could list Bag End from the Shire on their auction site. I wrote the name down for her and explained the basic plot of *The Hobbit* and then *The Lord of the Rings* arc even though she clearly wasn't giving me her full attention."

"That's really kind of you," I said. Poor Kelli was probably bored to tears. "I'm sure she was thrilled for the opportunity."

"Well, at first there weren't any bids, so I sort of, maybe, might've created an Instagram for the pottery studio and tried to advertise a little."

Heidi smacked his arm. "Nobody wanted your pixie palace, so you had to advertise it?"

Patrick shuffled his hands defensively. "It's a great piece, okay? It just needed to be found by the right audience. It should go to a *fan*."

"I know your motives aren't pure, but it really is a great piece. This kind of thing could really help Kelli. Thank you, Patrick."

"But that's not the weird part."

"Is, too," Heidi said.

"Take a look at this, Ana."

He turned his phone screen toward me, and Heidi scrambled off the floor to see. On the page was my melted almost-a-cat, titled *Suspicion* by Indiana Aaron. It actually had some bids. I squinted closer. "Holy crispy cracker," I whispered. "The price is up to five hundred dollars."

"What?" Heidi yelped in my ear. "For *that*? It looks like someone mutilated a lump of dirt, then set it on fire."

"Are we in the Upside Down?" I asked Patrick.

"My hobbit hole is only up to fifteen bucks," he muttered.

I grabbed my laptop from the coffee table and pulled up a search engine. For practically the first time in my life, I googled myself.

APOLLO IT's EMPLOYEE SPOTLIGHT SERIES was the first link in the long list that Google brought back. It was an offshoot page of the company's main website.

"Uh-oh," I breathed as I clicked the link.

Patrick squished himself onto the couch on the other side of me, so I was the filling in a Patrick/Heidi sandwich as the page loaded.

Meet Indiana Aaron, Featured Employee was splashed across the top of the page. Next to my name was a generic silhouette with the words *photo not available*.

We all leaned in closer to the screen as I read aloud. "Indiana Aaron has been with Apollo IT for over a year and has recently begun work with the Artemis team as a coder. When Indiana is not changing the interface of today's world, you can find him crash-landing planes, running with the bulls, or playing hockey with the pros. You might even find him saving lives in a burning building. Indiana also expresses his complexity through art. An accomplished potter, Indiana's Emotions series reflects some of the darker aspects of our society, likely a result of his time in a war."

I froze, too shocked to move. "Who wrote that?" I asked in a whisper.

"I would put my money on Melvin," Patrick said.

"A war? Just like, *a* war?" I groaned.

"To be fair, it doesn't specify which one," Patrick offered. "If that helps."

"It doesn't. You don't think that guy Evan could have written it, do you?"

Patrick thought for a moment, then seemed to remember. "The angry little dude at the bar? Why would you think that?"

"Well, he's always questioning my work, and he seems to hate Indiana."

"But this is a glowing bio, Ana. You sound like a rock star."

"You don't think it's sarcastic?" I argued. "Surely nobody thinks Indiana *runs with the freaking bulls*," I said pointedly.

"I don't think it's sarcastic either," Patrick said. "I think you have a fan."

I covered my face with my hands. "All I wanted was a job I'm qualified for and a big enough salary to keep me, my dad, and my new tadpoles comfortable."

"And look what happened. You're an emerging star in the art world," Patrick said.

"You're so jealous." Heidi snickered at him.

"I am. I thought I was better than that, but it appears I'm not."

My phone buzzed from the coffee table, and I grabbed it. A text from Melvin Hammer flashed across the screen.

"Shhh, Patrick. It's Hammer time," Heidi said.

"How long have you been waiting to say that?" I asked.

She looked away. "Quite a while."

I thumbed the message open. Indiana. Did you get the materials I sent over?

"We get to watch the magic happen, Patrick," Heidi whispered.

I concentrated on the phone with Heidi hanging over one shoulder. Received. Looking forward to the opportunity to meet with S.J.

A few dots, then: I have a very tight schedule and need to be back in NYC tomorrow morning—

"I'm Melon, and I'm the most interesting man in the whole world," Heidi mimicked in a raspy voice.

I shushed her and kept reading. So I need you to get to work on the pitch by yourself right away. Make sure to highlight any inside knowledge you have about the Avs. Location is the training center for the Avalanche. I'm sure you're familiar with it.

Patrick, who was also reading over my shoulder, bumped me. "On account of all the professional ice golf you do."

"Hockey is not ice golf—" I started. "Actually, it totally is. My bad."

This was even worse than I'd thought it would be. I knew Shane had been trying to help, but my "insider" knowledge didn't include the basic names of players. Or even how to play. He clearly had some hockey knowledge—I brushed away the thought before it even fully formed. I wasn't going to involve him in this. It was risky enough with him knowing who I was.

Heidi read the panic on my face. "This is good. This is fine," she said. "You're their fake goalie. You stand in front of a lace cage to block projectiles, right? That's all a goalie does."

I let out a breath. "There's got to be a little more to it. Have either of you ever been to an Avs game? I thought I was the only one in Denver who hadn't."

Heidi and Patrick exchanged glances. "It's difficult to avoid but totally doable," Heidi confessed.

"I, for one, am not ashamed that I don't support my city's cold stick battles," Patrick announced.

"God, I don't know if I can do this," I said.

"Sure, you can," Heidi said. "You tell Melon that you'll already be there practicing in the morning, and he can just meet you there for the appointment, whenever it is. Then you'll have all the time you need to win them over before he even gets there. Have you ever been to the Family Sports Center? That's where the Avs practice. I only know that because my brother used to go to camp there. It's massive, like Disneyland for the sportsball crowd. Super easy to lose people in a place that big."

"Even if I were as cool as the real Indiana, I don't know if I could do this. I don't know anything about sports."

"Hey," she said softly and put her arm around me. "You don't need to. You just need to understand the tech part." She shook my shoulder a little. "Don't you see, Ana? This is it! This is your chance. If you win this account, which you *will*, then you'll not only be getting the promotion you deserve, but you'll be saving Melon's job! There's no way he won't love you or at least be forever grateful. You said it yourself; you *are* the real Indiana. You can do this in your sleep. I have full confidence in you."

Patrick put his arm around me on the other side. "And if they hate it and Melvin fires you, you didn't want to keep this up forever, right? Go big *and* go home, that's what I always say."

Heidi swatted him. "Just put together an amazing pitch, and the rest will follow."

I relaxed into them. "Thanks. I don't know what I'd do without you two, even if you lie to make me feel better."

"Okay." Heidi sat up and clapped her hands. "Now I want to hear a little bit more about this troll town house and why Patrick wants people to buy it."

"I also want every detail about this," I said. Bless Patrick's heart for helping Kelli's studio, even if it was for selfish reasons. I really did have the best friends.

Chapter 10

Early the next morning, my doorbell rang. It was Shane.

"Hey," he said, smiling. "Your apartment is on the way to the airport, so I thought I'd stop by." It absolutely wasn't. "And, you know, catch a look at the new fam."

I let him in, still wearing my leggings and an old concert T-shirt. At least I'd run a comb through my hair and added mascara. He leaned in for a quick hug, then went to the tank. "You weren't kidding. Tadpole Town is hopping."

"Yep," I said, coming up behind him. "I got to witness their births, and the whole thing was actually pretty cool. So thanks for pushing me out of my comfort zone."

"Anytime. Actually, I have another push for you, if you're up for it?"

"What do you mean?"

"Next time I come to Denver, maybe you can show me around a bit."

Hope blossomed in my chest. "Do you have plans to come back soon?"

"Well, Melvin is going to need to come back to Denver quite a few times to get this deal through, right? And, for reasons I'm starting to understand, Apollo doesn't want him traveling without someone to show him around."

"An escort."

"Gross. No. Like a..."

"Warden?" I suggested.

"Like a guide, okay? A *guide*. And pretty much no one wants to do it except, now, me. So I can come visit. Visit Denver, I mean. And I'll brush up on my *Mario Kart* to give you some real competition."

I rolled my eyes and grinned. "Prepare to be beaten again."

He grinned. "Deal." Then he leaned down and rested his forehead on mine for a few seconds. My breath hitched, and I closed my eyes. Then I felt the softest kiss on my lips, and my heartbeat tripled. Suddenly, he pulled back, and when I looked up, he was grinning. Then he started to sing John Denver's "Leaving on a Jet Plane."

I pushed him, laughing. "Go. Don't keep Melvin waiting. And text me when you land. Just so I know you got in okay."

He touched my hand as he walked out the door. "See you soon, Ana."

I waved as he drove away, then shut the door, giddy and ready to work on my pitch.

A short while later, I looked up from my work and stretched, checking my phone. I had a text from my dad. I shot up into a sitting position. Dad didn't text. Ever. It wasn't that he didn't know how (sort of), but he didn't like learning new things, and learning email had been enough to annoy the hell out of him.

I hear of new man, he had written.

I rolled my eyes. For one, thank you, Nancy. For two, he sounded like something out of *Twin Peaks*.

A friend came over to my apartment yesterday, I wrote back.

Nancy mentioned pregnancy.

I had just taken a sip of coffee when that came through, and I choked hard. Damn it, Nancy. I couldn't tell which one of them was being difficult.

Unrelated. I am not pregnant. Neither is anyone I know. I glanced over at Hopper. At least not now.

If not ashamed of dad, bring new friend for a visit.

Of course I'm not ashamed of you. We can figure something out. I threw the phone back on the couch. I added that to the list of things of fun, awkward things to do.

———

Heidi came over later that evening. I'd been working all day, studying S.J. Sporting's inventory and current web design, and it was nice to have a break. We ordered some pizza, watched the fish, and talked about work for a bit before Heidi turned to me with a serious look. "You know I love you as you are, Ana, but Indiana really is the ideal man. I wish he were real. But I would keep you, too," Heidi said hastily, seeing my expression.

"'Indiana' would be insufferable, Heidi. You know that," I said. "He's exactly the type of guy we hate. Spearfishing? Cliff diving? Craft beer? He's such a macho hipster dude that it actually makes my stomach hurt."

"Not true," Heidi insisted. "He has a sensitive side. He expresses his feelings through art. He's working through stuff he had to experience in a war."

"*He was not in a war,*" I said, staring at the ceiling. She could be incredibly exasperating. "God, why am I even talking to you like this? None of this is real. You, of all people, should know that."

"I do," she said and flopped back onto the couch. "I'm just saying, it's kind of like we created the perfect guy."

"We definitely didn't. We created a stereotype of over-the-top masculinity. I prefer bright, talented, nerdy guys. If they're smart but also kind, that's way better than someone who can wrestle a tiger."

"Now that we're not cavemen anyway. Back in the day, the tiger wrestling might have been higher on the list."

"Can you imagine how unbearable those cavemen must have been?"

"'I'm so strong and eat raw meat with my hands,'" Heidi mimicked. "'Go home-make, woman.' But still," she murmured, almost to herself, "it'd be nice to feel petite, or whatever, for once."

I made a face. "Trust me, it's overrated. I'd kill to be tall and willowy like you are."

She looked away. "I wouldn't mind being tall, except guys don't like girls who are taller than them."

"You have twice the cupboard space I do," I argued, "because you can reach all your cabinets. You could also kick someone's ass in a fight. I wish I could do that."

A slow smile spread across her face. "I could. I guess there are a few perks."

"You have presence. Shorties like me are rarely 'beautiful.' We're 'cute.'" I thought of Shane calling me beautiful that night at the bar, and warmth spread through my chest. "You know, ever since I got into this mess, I've been thinking about all the women through the years pretending to be men just to get a bit of respect. Like our girl Joan." I sighed.

She squinted at me from her spot on the couch. "Who now? Joan Rivers? Joan of Arc? There are so many."

"But only one *Pope* Joan, the female pope. Middle Ages."

"Pretty sure there wasn't a female pope, Ana. We were like even more backward in the Middle Ages than we are now."

"Barely," I muttered. "You haven't heard the story of Pope Joan? You're Catholic."

She shrugged. "I assure you, all our popes have been dudes."

"Pope Joan dressed as a man. She was, like, the smartest and most talented scholar; I think she went by John or something. She was so well respected that they picked her to be pope. So the story goes."

Heidi sat up now, looking at me with interest. "What happened to her?"

"Well, *allegedly* one time she was getting on a horse, and a baby fell out of her, and they stoned her to death on the road. But that part isn't important."

"I bet it was super important to her!" Heidi exclaimed.

I rushed on. "The important part is that she dressed as a man and was even better than the men."

"And they didn't find out she was female until she literally ejected a baby onto the street?"

"*Allegedly.* That's like the one thing men can't do," I said. "And they killed her for it. Those old priests must have been terrified of her."

"Like I told you before, nobody likes being tricked."

"I bet if she'd been tall like you, she could have delivered a killer right cross and knocked them all out. And run off to live a nice life with her street baby. I wonder if she knew she was pregnant. Can you imagine not knowing? I know there's a whole TV show about it, but I still can't—"

Heidi waved her hand in the air. "It freaks me out to think about it, especially with all the margaritas I drink. But this story…her posing as a dude, but being better than the dudes? Sounds like you."

"Thanks, I guess." Then I grinned. "Want to hear the best/worst part of the whole thing?"

"I already did. She punted out a baby and was immediately stoned. No one stopped to see if maybe she'd just hidden the little guy in her robes. Like, 'Oh, maybe our pope found a baby on the ground and tucked them in there because he's nice and nice people do that.' It doesn't sound like they even asked."

"No, it doesn't sound like they asked. But the wackiest part is"—I lowered my voice—"some scholars think that's why we have the Pope potty seat."

"Ex-fucking-scuse me?" Heidi squeaked.

"I took art history in college, and I thought I was going to pee my pants when I first saw a picture of it," I said. "There's even more than one. It's a carved wooden chair except instead of having a seat, it has a hole in the middle."

Heidi's face turned a little green. "Did they put a special chamber pot under it so he could poo in style? Because I don't like where this is headed."

I shrugged. "Possibly. But *maybe*, if the legend is true, it was because they felt they needed some dude to reach up under there and check for testicles. Because of how they'd been humiliated by Joan. Then the dude would stand up and say, '*Duos habet et bene pendentes*,' or 'He has two and they dangle nicely.'"

She threw a pillow at my face. "I went to Sunday school every week for *years*, and nobody ever said anything about dangling!"

"Well, it's not exactly a Sunday school topic, don't you think?"

"I dunno, it's way more interesting than a lot of the stuff we talked about. How come I've never heard of this before?"

"The Catholic Church doesn't acknowledge Joan. They say she's a myth. And that the pope chair is more about 'dung' than about balls, which, personally, I don't think sounds a lot better. But there's no proof she *didn't* exist, and she was first mentioned in the ten hundreds, so..."

"I'm gonna have to spend some time on Wikipedia later. This whole story is *nuts*. And way more relevant to today's world than I'm comfortable with. Like, even now—look at you. We have a girl dressing up as a man just to get some freaking respect."

I drew myself up. "I've *never* dressed up like a man. And we agreed I'm going to come clean as soon as I've won this account for Melvin. He'll love me because I'll have saved his job and the team, and everyone will be super happy."

"Yeah, that's totally how it worked out for Joan, huh? Sounds like she was a kick-ass pope, but one unexpected baby, and it all goes south."

That twisted my stomach. I'd been thinking about the story a lot, but I hadn't made the connection with the *end* of the story like Heidi had. Would the Artemis team stone me in the street?

I wandered over to the tank to examine Hopper and his babies. They were starting to get some color and looked like fish now instead of baby frogs. I watched them swim for a moment before I turned back to Heidi. "Like, why have men always been so threatened by women? To the point that they erased this woman and even now refuse to acknowledge that she might have been real? We've come so far, and yet we haven't at all. We still don't have a female pope, even if we did, or a female president, even if she got the most votes."

"It boggles the mind," Heidi agreed. "But we know way more good guys than we do bad ones."

"I know," I said. "It's systemic, not individual. Unless you're Melvin. But hashtag not all men." I immediately thought of Patrick. And my dad. And Shane. "Out of curiosity, since Indiana is no one's prince, how would you describe your perfect guy, Heidi?"

"He's still a little bit *my* prince. But I guess I would say…tall, smart, confident. Has swagger but also a sensitive side. An artist but also suave. Knows how to talk to people. Extroverted. Cute. Takes the lead but respects me and my opinion. Did I say 'tall'?"

"You did." I blinked. "Do you know who you just described?"

"No, who?"

"Jason."

She sat up and turned to look at me. "I did?"

"You did."

She lay back down slowly, deep in thought. "I guess I did," she murmured.

I discreetly pulled out my phone and air-dropped Jason's contact info to Heidi's phone. When it buzzed, she looked down and blushed. I couldn't help but smile.

———

After Heidi went home, I stretched out on the couch and flipped through the channels. There was a hockey game on, so I tried to watch it, scanning the crowd to see the types of fan apparel that were most popular. But after a few minutes, I had to change the channel. I knew so many people loved sports, but I couldn't get past how boring they were. I reached over and grabbed my phone off the coffee table. Shane had texted me to let me know he'd landed, so it wasn't weird to text back now that the game was on, right?

Do you see me on TV? I'm blocking all the projectiles, I texted to Shane.

I'm watching you right now. But it's weird, I don't see a phone in your hand, he wrote back. And your jersey doesn't say Aaron on the back.

I wrote back immediately. I keep the phone in my big glove. And you know how it is in the locker room, we all throw our jerseys in the air before a game and then wear the one we catch first. It's part of the pregame dance we do.

Choreographed? he texted back.

Of course. Freestyle is for postgame.

I have the weirdest picture in my head right now. Thanks for that.

I'm sure it's accurate, I wrote, then put the phone back on the coffee table. Once again, I couldn't help feeling a little bummed that he lived in New York and wasn't here in person so I could narrate the game for him. I was sure he would have loved to hear all my insider knowledge on the team.

Tomorrow I was going to be putting the finishing touches on one of the most important things I'd ever done, but I'd make sure to leave the secret dancing rituals of the Avs out of it.

Chapter 11

THE NEXT MORNING, I GRABBED MY LAPTOP AND HEADED TO A LOCAL coffee shop that I hadn't been to in forever. They usually weren't too busy and always had a few corner booths free. I grabbed one, and after I ordered a cold brew, I settled in to add some slides to the PowerPoint presentation I was polishing for SJ.

I was proud of what I'd done so far. If a fan pointed their phone at a shirt, jersey, hat, etc., the app would easily take them to the S.J. Sporting website, where they could order that product or the closest equivalent S.J. made. It would also tell them what aisle and bin number the item was in at the nearest S.J. store. Since the Avs had agreed to partner, I had added a special feature where the user could rewatch game highlights, keep a current score, and get little bios of all the players. If they took my idea, we could eventually expand it to include other teams and other sports entirely. I was sure it could give S.J. Sporting the edge they were looking for.

I practiced snapping a few pictures of products "in the wild," so to speak, and running them through my code to see if it recognized the right part of the image and ignored the rest. I felt like I had an innovative approach to enhancing SJ's app and web presence, and if I could just tweak a few of the glitches, I would be golden. The rest of the glitches, I'd turn into features. It was all about how you looked at it.

I was stoked to show my final project to Melvin. He'd checked in here and there but hadn't offered any of his own ideas. That was good, though—we both knew he sucked at this stuff, and it was nice not having anyone around questioning the aesthetic of what I'd put together. He could give me feedback after it was finished, but for now, it was my vision that was coming to life.

I almost lost track of time and forgot to log in to the catch-up meeting Melvin had put on our calendar. The invitation flashed on the screen, so I quickly checked to make sure my camera was off before logging in. Melvin was already speaking.

"As you already know, the S.J. account is of the utmost importance. If and when we win the business, all our team resources will be allocated to executing the vision we've sold to the company. That means all other accounts will be transferred to other teams, and our main focus will be S.J. Sporting."

I took a long drink of my cold brew and felt a caffeine buzz kick in. *Thanks, Melvin. Just keep upping the pressure; awesome, you're the best*, I thought.

Then something unexpected happened. Evan Smith's camera clicked on. His shiny forehead filled the screen, and I could see a mass of equipment and wires in the background. "Mr. Hammer, sir," he said.

Melvin blinked and the computer lagged, leaving him frozen with his eyes closed for a second. "What is it, Evan? I was speaking."

"Well, I'm currently the one who is sort of, unofficially, of course, the team lead when it comes to our client Cake Bakes. What's going to happen to that account? How will the team lead thing work with S.J. Sporting?"

Melvin waved his hand dismissively, but the lag made it look like he was hitting himself. "Cake Bakes is a nothing account compared to SJ. That project can be passed to another group at Apollo IT. Once we win SJ, that will be our only focus. And I'll choose the lead accordingly."

"But—"

Melvin reached down off-screen, and immediately Evan's camera and microphone were cut off. "Rest assured, I am hard at work on this pitch. Many sleepless nights. I'll update you all once the meeting has occurred. Then the real work begins. Be ready."

He signed off, and I rolled my eyes while taking another sip. Sure, *he* was hard at work. Well, lucky for him and all his "sleepless nights," I was getting close to having a finished product to present.

I closed out of the meeting and had pulled back up the PowerPoint when my phone buzzed.

How's it coming? Melvin.

I thought for a minute. In the work world, men tended to self-promote, whereas women tended to be humble. This is some of my best work, I texted back.

When can you get it to me?

I wanted to take my time, and the meeting wasn't for another week, but I understood he would want to look things over.

I should be able to have it to you by tomorrow evening.

Perfect, he texted back.

And if we arrived at the meeting separately (because, you know, I'd already be there due to practice, ha ha), he wouldn't be able to say anything when he walked in. He could confront me after I'd given the whole speech and won the account, but by then it wouldn't matter. My nerves were high, but things were coming together so nicely that this was the only way it could go down: Melvin would love it and love me, and I could come clean and go back to being myself with a newfound respect in my field.

I spent the next few hours rounding out my ideas before it was time to see my dad. I closed the laptop with a click and drained the last of my (second) cold brew. Seeing dad was always the highlight of my week. And he didn't even know about his great-grandguppies yet.

———————

Aspen Skies was quieter than usual when I pulled into the parking lot. Like always, I marveled at the beauty of the mountains and the sunset. I knew dad liked to hang out in the gardens and read in the afternoons, and today was the perfect day for it. I would have loved to have him live with me, but given the care he needed and how much he valued his independence, we'd done the right thing moving him here. I scanned the yard but didn't see him.

When I walked inside, Rita was on the phone at the front desk, but she waved at me and gestured toward the common room. I nodded in acknowledgment and headed in that direction. When I got there, I stopped in the doorway, captivated by what I saw.

Dad and that lovely woman Margaret were sitting at a table near the back of the room. They were bent toward each other, and as I watched, Dad reached out and ran his thumb down her cheek. She blushed and looked at her lap before looking back up and smiling shyly at him. My heart caught in my throat. Dad hadn't dated after Mom died. He'd put everything into being both a mother and father to me, despite my protests. I'd never witnessed something like the scene in front of me before.

I cleared my throat as I walked over, and the two of them jumped apart awkwardly, just like Jay McGuire and I had when Dad caught us kissing on the porch after senior prom. Dad turned and gave me a huge grin. "Indiana! Please come over and join Margaret and me."

"You must be the artist," Margaret said in a rich, low voice, and she smiled warmly at me.

I couldn't help but laugh. "You mean the pottery?"

She nodded. "It's very expressive."

My dad and I shared a look. "That's very kind," I told her, "but I already like you. You don't have to pretend my pottery is good. I just do it for fun."

"Indiana always liked to play in the mud. Just like her mother." Dad winked at me.

I leaned over to him but didn't bother to lower my voice much. "So you got up the nerve to talk to her. I'm so proud of you! Looks like it's going well?" We both glanced over at Margaret, who averted her eyes.

"Yep," Dad stage-whispered back. "Told her I thought she was beautiful. Asked if she wanted to get coffee in the garden. She said yes. I'm trying to wait a few days before I ask her if she'll be my girlfriend. Timing is important."

Margaret, who had been pretending not to listen, tried to hide her chuckle. "Russell, for goodness' sake."

He gave her the softest look, and I thought I might cry right there. "Just trying to be considerate, Maggie." He turned back to me. "Mags here was a lawyer before she retired. No kids. Moved in here just a little bit ago. Married twice; they both died, but she says she didn't do it."

She leaned in closer to me. "Though I watch so much *Dateline*, they've almost convinced me I *am* somehow responsible."

I let out a surprised laugh. "Keith Morrison will do that to ya. He's very compelling."

She nodded. "But I like the way he leans on things."

"Like his legs can't support the weight of his coolness." I asked, "So you were a lawyer? What was that like?"

"Not as exciting as it sounds," she said, and I again appreciated the rich, low authority in her voice. "I was in environmental law. Your dad says you're a technology person? He's so proud of you, making your way in the working world. He brags on you all the time. I hope it's easier for you than when I had to do it. When I was in law school, I tutored men who got jobs at better law firms than I did when we graduated. I had to work my way up from the lowest-tier firm. But that was over forty years ago."

I looked down. "We still have a ways to go." A thought occurred to me, and as usual it was out of my mouth before I could reconsider. "Do you ever wish you'd been born a man?"

"Please say no," my dad whispered, but Margaret appeared to take the question seriously.

"Not for a minute. Women make the best friends and the best supporters. Our empathy is part of what makes us strong, despite the stereotype."

"You think so? Culturally, the whole idea of being female is equated with weakness. If you do anything 'like a girl,' it's an insult. And, of course, the ultimate insult, being called a pussy. Sorry, Dad," I said and ducked my head. I never said words like that in front of him.

"On the contrary, I would argue that men's emotions make *them* weaker than they do us. Take the old-fashioned art of dueling for example." She put her elbows on the table, bright-eyed. "Men used to set a date for a formal get-together to shoot each other if someone got their feelings hurt. Can you imagine women doing that? Janet said that Sharon called you a tramp over dinner the other night, so you're going to meet her at dawn with your guns. Which somehow proves you're not a tramp?" She shook her head in disgust. "And almost all murderers are men, which should also tell you something about who's more emotional," she muttered.

"I guess I hadn't thought about it too deeply," I said. "We kind of just accept the fact women are more emotional. We make fun of periods and how women cry all the time, and men are seen as stoic."

"I'd like to see how stoic they'd be during labor and delivery. History books are full of men who couldn't handle their feelings and did something stupid. So yes, we make those connections culturally, but they don't stand up to any sort of examination. But I digress. No, I wouldn't want to be male. They may have more power, but look what they've done with it. Oh, and we live longer." She shot me a wink.

I stopped to consider that. Not that I wanted to be male myself, but lately it seemed like everything would be so much easier if I were. I'd be where I wanted to be professionally, but Margaret was right; there was a lot to lose in exchange for that power.

"Mags is smart, you know," my dad said. "Men are great, but we'd be lost without you women. At least I would be."

"Thank you, Margaret," I said sincerely. "I would love to get coffee with you sometime and talk more."

"Anytime, Indiana."

I smiled at her and my dad. "How's it been going for the two of you?"

Dad brightened. "Every morning, Mags takes me out to the garden, where we have our coffee and watch the mountains. You know how much I love this view. Mags isn't from here; she moved from the East Coast. She loves it, too. But now I have an even better view to look at when I have my coffee, sitting right next to me." Dad raised his eyebrows at her.

"Russell," she said and swatted his arm, "stop it." She turned to me. "Has he always been this sentimental?"

"No," I said. "You must be very special."

"She is, Indiana," he said. "Even if she kills me, too, it'll be worth it."

I shook my head. "Margaret, don't kill my dad."

"Wasn't planning to, but you have my promise."

"Then you have my blessing."

Dad turned to me. "So what's this about a guy coming over for the afternoon? Nancy said there was a lot of giggling and you couldn't wait to get him inside."

I blew my hair out of my face with an exasperated breath. "It's not what it sounds like."

"Regardless of what it sounds like, I'd like to meet him."

"Nancy misunderstood. I was excited because, well, guess what? I finally did it. I finally got fish for my tank."

"That's a big step, Indiana," he said seriously. "A lot of women your age are having children, and you've just gotten up the courage to get a single fish."

I ignored that. "Not just *a* fish, Dad, but, like…feeeeesh."

"What does *that* mean?"

"I now have eighty-three fish, Dad. Maybe more. There's definitely going to be inbreeding. Unfortunate but unavoidable. Aren't you proud of me? I'm the matriarch of a whole inbred fish family now."

He whistled through his teeth as Margaret looked back and forth between us. "How inbred is this colony going to get? Will they grow legs and hang out on your countertops? Are they going to sleep in bed with you?"

"Most likely they'll just develop spinal deformities, but by all means, if they grow lungs and want to sleep with me, there'll be fish sleepovers with tropical snack flakes and Animal Planet on TV—the whole deal."

"You go all in, don't you?" Dad asked, shaking his head.

I nodded proudly. "I knew you'd want to see pictures, so I brought a photo of each one. Just kidding," I added hastily when I saw his shoulders droop. "Just top forty."

After torturing my dad with fish pics, I went home to finish the last of my pitch. I knew the idea was good, and the execution was even better.

When the package was complete, I sent it off to Melvin as a zip file, which I followed with a text. I reminded myself to overplay, not underplay the accomplishment. Check your email. This account is as good as ours.

Then I snuggled into bed, yelled good night to my fish, and fell into a happy, dreamless sleep.

———

When I woke the next morning, I checked my message for feedback from Melvin. I knew he would love it, but there hadn't been any response. Maybe Melvin had a personal life? Nah.

Then a text from Shane came in, and my heart skipped a beat. What're you doing today?

Same thing I do every day. Not taking over the world. Just workin' a job.

Would you have time for a visitor?

I sat upright. Today? You?

Yeah. I felt Denver calling, so I thought I'd come and we could hang out for the day. Can you take the day off?

Excitement rushed through me. I thought about how hard I'd been working to get everything ready. The pitch was now in Melvin's hands for review, so my part was done, for now. There wasn't anything I'd rather do than spend the day with Shane. Yep, consider my schedule open.

Great. I'll come by and get you at noon.

I threw the phone down on the bed and ran to the coffee maker. I started a cup, yelled good morning to Hopper, then hurried to the shower. That gave me just a few hours to get super cute before an unexpected date.

Chapter 12

When Shane knocked on my door a few hours later, I was ready with flawless eyeliner, a sweater and skirt, and wedged boots that brought my head just under his chin. I'd left my curls natural but used a diffuser and had put a little cover-up over the freckles on my cheeks to tone them down. When I was done, I'd looked myself over critically and had decided that was as good as it got. The whole time I had gotten ready, my thoughts kept wandering back to why I hadn't heard anything from Melvin. I was pretty sure he would have looked at the proposal immediately, so why hadn't he texted? I didn't want it to spoil the date, though, so I tried to shelve the thoughts until later.

When I opened the door, the look Shane gave me reminded me of the look my dad had given Margaret, and I suddenly felt flushed.

"You take my breath away, Ana," he said softly.

I touched my hair self-consciously. "Thanks," I said shyly. Then I noticed movement behind him. I grabbed his hand and pulled him inside, breathing hard.

"What's wrong?" he asked, alarmed.

"I think I saw Nancy behind you," I whispered. "I don't want her to see you."

"Why not?" he asked, sounding a little offended.

I softened and looked up at him. "Because she's already told my dad about you, and she mentioned pregnancy—but don't worry, I clarified that—and he wants to meet you. If he knows you're here and I didn't bring you by, he'll be so annoyed with me."

Shane raised an eyebrow. "Then why not bring me by?"

I sputtered for a second and thought about how to word my thoughts as diplomatically as possible. "Um, because this is a new thing here, right? We don't know each other that well, and usually, introducing families happens a bit more organically. Later on. You know?"

He leaned against the doorframe and crossed his arms. "You don't strike me as a rule follower."

"I'm not. In fact, my dad was convinced I had oppositional defiant disorder when I was six. If you tell me to do something, I usually do the opposite."

"So why are you letting cultural norms get in the way of making your dad happy? I'd like to meet him, too."

Well, he'd backed me into a corner with that one. "But didn't you say you had made plans already?"

He shook his head. "They're flexible."

Well, that left me with little choice. "Okay, I'll just text him and see if he's free."

No longer ashamed of Dad, I said. Ready for new friend to come over?

I got an answer quickly. Dad in garden and wants to see new friend.

"He says he's free," I muttered.

"Great! Now," Shane said briskly, "are you ready?"

I nodded, and he took my hand and led me to the car. He opened the door for me, and once we were settled in, he turned in the driver's seat to face me. "Where to?"

I gave him directions to Aspen Skies, and when we got on the highway, I figured I'd better fill him in on a few details. "Dad had an accident a few years back. He's in a wheelchair, but he's not sensitive about it. Also, my mom died when I was little. Dad never dated, but he's found a woman he really likes at Aspen Skies. I've never seen him happy like this before, so I'm stoked about it."

"Wow, Ana, I'm sorry," Shane said as he shifted lanes. "That must have been hard for you when you were younger."

"It was," I said, "but it's okay. Dad and I talk about Mom a lot, and he's the best dad in the world. So you don't need to feel sorry for me or anything like that."

He shook his head. "I don't. I'm just sad that you experienced something so heartbreaking when you were young. My parents are divorced and hate each other, but they both love me, so I can't complain."

"Well, you do seem pretty loveable," I said before I could stop myself.

He looked over and grinned while I did my best to swallow my tongue. In just a few minutes, we were pulling into the parking lot.

"This place is beautiful," Shane said.

"Right? Sometimes living in Denver, I forget to notice how gorgeous the mountains are, especially in the fall. Dad has a great view from his room, too."

We headed around back to the garden. As he'd said, Dad was sitting there with his back to us, staring at the skyline, a mug of coffee in one hand. There was another mug beside him on the table with steam rising off the top. Margaret must have just stepped inside.

"Hey, Dad!" I called as we crossed over to the table. He turned in his wheelchair, and his eyes lit up when he saw us.

"Indiana! New friend! Come join me." His blue eyes twinkled as I leaned down to give him a hug. "My goodness, you look nice. I can't remember the last time you were so dolled up. New friend must be pretty cool," he said, not quietly enough, and I looked away, embarrassed.

"Mr. Aaron, it's so nice to meet you," Shane said, shaking Dad's hand firmly. "I'm Shane Dalton. I work with your daughter."

"Isn't she great?" Dad asked earnestly. He had no chill when it came to me, which was one of the things I loved and hated about him.

"She is. One of a kind," Shane said.

"I tell her that all the time. She usually just ignores me," Dad confided. "Would you like something to drink?"

"We can't stay too long," Shane said, and I felt relief course through me. "I live in New York, and I flew to Denver today to hang out with Indiana. We have some reservations we can't miss, but I really wanted to meet you, and I heard the feeling was mutual."

"Sure is," Dad said and grinned. "That's so nice, coming all the way from New York to take her out. Such a gentleman. Since you can't stay long, would you like to come back to my room and see some of her artwork before you go?"

"No!" I cried at the same time as Shane said, "Absolutely."

Dad chortled. "Bring Margaret's coffee inside for her, will you, Ana? She'll be back in a bit. Let's show him Chuck the Duck!"

I groaned and did as he told me, and Shane walked next to Dad's chair as they headed toward the building.

"There's a saltwater tank in here," Dad said to Shane as they passed through the door. "She loses her mind over that thing whenever she comes by."

Shane leaned down to whisper something in my dad's ear, and Dad grinned broadly. "Spot on, sir! That's the way to her heart."

"Wait, what are you two talking about?" I asked as I set Margaret's coffee on the counter by Rita's desk.

"Oh, nothing," Dad said, twinkling at me again.

I heard Shane's gasp when we finally got to Dad's room. He turned to me, his eyes bright, a quiver in his voice. "Are all these your…creations?" he asked.

I narrowed my eyes. He was trying not to laugh, I could tell.

"Indiana mentioned that she likes pottery," he told my dad, and his voice sounded a little strained.

"I think she likes it a little more than it likes her." Dad chuckled.

"All right," I said loudly, "we can't all be good at everything."

"Even landing planes?" Shane asked innocently.

I narrowed my eyes at him. "I'm every bit as good at landing a plane as you are," I said, poking my finger against his chest.

"Touché," he said, laughing, and my dad looked at us, amused.

"I wouldn't trust my Indiana with a plane," Dad said jovially. "I didn't even want her to get a driver's license."

I whirled around, and he put his hands up. "Not that you're not a good driver! I'm just saying, you're my baby girl. Kids driving cars are scary."

"They would be, but I was *sixteen*." So much fun when they ganged up on me at once. I turned back to Shane. "My mom was a potter. She made beautiful things, and most of the memories I have of her involve the wheel, and the kiln, and her humming in our kitchen. I feel closer to her when I make things, even if they're awful." There. Try to laugh at someone's art after a statement like that.

"Those are beautiful memories to have," Shane said somberly. Still, he turned and ran a finger over a cracked triangular shape that had been fired in two different colors. "What's this?"

I looked at it for a minute. "I honestly have no idea."

"I think we knew at one point, but it escapes me now, too," my dad added.

I fought the urge to smack my head against the door. "Dad, we should probably be going."

"We do have to run," Shane said. "But I'd love to come back for longer next time and look at more pottery." I swatted at him. "And also meet Margaret."

Dad knew not to push it. "That sounds great. Thank you very much for coming." He reached out and grabbed my hand, and I softened. "Love you, Indiana."

"I love you, too, Dad."

———

Once we were back in the car, Shane turned to me. "Your dad is great. Thank you for including me. Now, I have a couple of things in mind. Even though I'm the guest here, I thought I could take you somewhere you might enjoy."

"I thought you wanted *me* to show *you* around. If I'd had some more time, I could have come up with something. I don't usually do the touristy stuff. I don't even really notice the attractions anymore."

"It's the same with me and New York. I make it a point to see the shows, but beyond that, all I see is the subway."

I nodded, a little intrigued. "So where are we going?"

He shook his head and gave me an adorable grin. "Not telling. But I think you'll guess soon enough." He focused back on the road, and I took a moment to appreciate his square jawline and tried to calm the butterflies in my stomach. The embarrassment of introducing him to my dad was starting to fade.

Shane was right; once the car slowed and we pulled into a brightly painted parking lot, I could barely contain my excitement. "You brought me to the aquarium! I don't think I've been here since I was a kid."

"I thought that might be the case. But I figured even if you had, you'd probably still like to see some fish."

"Yes!" I bounded out of the car and ran around to his side, where I grabbed his hand. He laughed as I dragged him into the building. Inside, the walls and lights were all blue, giving an underwater effect. "So cool," I breathed.

Right inside the lobby, jellyfish tanks were built into the wall, pulsing under color-changing lights. I walked over to one and stared at it until I heard Shane come up behind me. He put a hand on the side of my waist, and my breath hitched. Then he leaned down to my ear. "I have to know, what is it about fish that's so appealing to you?"

"They're aliens," I said immediately. "Or as close as I'll ever get in my lifetime." I gestured to the domed, tendrilled creatures floating in front of us. "Look at them. Have you ever seen anything more otherworldly? This isn't something we were meant to see. The entire underwater world isn't meant for us—it's beautiful and strange, and we know next to nothing about it. I mean, look at the way they float! Isn't it wild?"

"I've never thought of it that way," he said and dropped a kiss onto my neck. I shivered.

We wandered from exhibit to exhibit, and I had trouble keeping my excitement in check. It was just so cool of him to think of this and to plan for us to do something so fun together.

At the next display, I stopped to marvel at a pair of clown fish hosting a bubble-tip anemone.

"They're pretty cute," Shane said.

"They're some of my favorite fish," I said softly, watching the little orange fish nestle into the anemone's arms.

Shane peered over my shoulder. "It's amazing that they don't get stung when they do that."

"It's symbiotic. The anemone eats their waste," I explained, "and in return it protects them. Also, wanna know a fun fact?" I plowed on, not waiting for an answer. "All clown fish are born male. The biggest one in the hierarchy becomes female. If you remove that one, the next biggest one becomes female."

"Imagine if people were like that," Shane commented, squinting down at the pair of fish swimming in and out of the glowing anemone. "You're, like, a forty-year-old man, and suddenly it's your turn to be the matriarch."

"I'm not sure they have as much trouble adjusting emotionally as *you* apparently would, but it would definitely make *Finding Nemo* a different movie."

Shane whistled under his breath. "So Nemo's dad becomes his mom."

"And probably his lover," I said, just to make Shane uncomfortable. He made a face at me, and I couldn't help laughing.

"What other horrifying facts do you know?"

I bounded up on my toes. "So many. I've been learning about guppies, too, since I play benevolent god to like a hundred of them. Did you know the females can store sperm in their bodies for, like, two years? And can continue to have babies without a male around every thirty days?"

"Wait, so does this mean Hopper could have more?"

I nodded. "He probably has enough sperm to go for at least a year making babies on his own, but he'll likely start reproducing with his own offspring soon enough."

He tilted his head at me. "What're you going to do when that happens?"

"That's a problem for future Ana."

"Hm. Guppy facts are quite disturbing, but not as good as clown fish facts. Try again?"

"I love this game. How about this: dolphins have been known to use puffer fish to get high. They pass the puffer back and forth, and it releases a toxin because it's like super scared, so the dolphins get trashed and veg out staring at their own reflections in the water."

"That's... disturbing. Don't they know it goes against their magical reputation?"

I shuddered. "Dolphins are straight-up terrifying. They're violent and mean, just like us. And they don't go on dates. But seahorses do. They're so romantic. They dance together in the mornings, too."

Shane put his hands up, laughing. "You got me." He walked a few feet over to the next exhibit.

"Seahorses even hold tails!" I called after him. "They form a little heart with their bodies, but I'm sure that's coincidental. I doubt that symbol has any romantic significance to them. But who knows, am I right?"

He turned back around and took my hand in both of his own. "How do you fit so much in that head of yours?"

I shrugged. "It's a steel trap."

"It would have to be." He checked his watch. "Hungry?"

"Always," I said.

"Would you like to grab an early dinner? You can tell me some of the less disturbing things you know while we eat. I reserved the private dining room in the shark tunnel."

I squealed and threw my arms around his neck. Laughing, he led me by the hand toward the restaurant portion of the aquarium. Once the waiter had settled us at a table and brought a bottle of wine, I put my forearms on the table and focused on Shane. "I'm sorry, I've been so caught up in this experience that I haven't asked you anything. How was your flight? Did you really come all this way just to hang out with me?" I blushed, feeling light and happy, as if the weight of my alter ego had lifted somehow over the past hour. "So how are things?"

He took a sip of wine and pointed upward as a large hammerhead swam directly above us. He grinned at my gasp. "As much as I would love to say I did, I'm here for work again. I figured I'd take a day off and get here before Melvin does. That way I can see you, and I also don't have to sit next to him on the plane. He always takes off his shoes." He made a face.

I paused, my wineglass halfway to my lips. "Melvin's coming?" So Shane hadn't flown in just to see me.

"I assumed he told you. He's supposed to be arriving tomorrow night.

Some big meeting, I think. Anyway, I assumed he could manage that part of the trip without a babysitter."

"He didn't mention anything to me," I murmured. "That's not like him." I reached into my bag and pulled out my phone. I checked my texts and email just to make sure I wasn't mistaken. Then I fired off a quick text. Haven't heard back about the S.J. pitch. Thoughts? When are you next due in Denver?

Something wasn't right. I took a big sip of wine while I waited for his response.

"Everything okay?" Shane asked.

My phone buzzed and I looked down, reading the message. "No, it's not okay," I said softly.

Got the pitch. It could use some work. I'll have to spend some time on it. I'm not headed to Denver until next week.

I looked up. "Melvin said he's not coming to Denver until next week."

Shane tilted his head. "He's flying in tomorrow. I wonder why he wouldn't tell the team, or at least 'Indiana.'"

A bad feeling formed in the pit of my stomach. "I think I might know why, but I really hope I'm wrong."

I tried to take another sip of wine, but it tasted sour and turned my stomach. I set the glass down and tried to focus. Maybe it was another meeting. Maybe something else was going on. Maybe Melvin was back in town for an encore performance as waffle chef and didn't want the rest of us to feel left out. He'd even had batter in his hair when I'd last seen him. One could hope, but it was unlikely. Melon Hamster might be back for a romp in waffle dough, but Melvin Hammer most likely had a far less fun motive for his secrecy.

The waiter chose that moment to come in carrying a full tray. He laid out the appetizers, and my stomach turned over. Seafood. I looked up to see if the fish had noticed. Seemed kind of rude. But so was I because there was no way I could eat. "I'm sorry, Shane," I said, turning my face away. "This was so thoughtful of you, but I need to go home. I'm not feeling well."

"Are you okay?" he asked.

I shook my head. I didn't have to fake the green tinge to my cheeks. "I hate to do this, but I have to go home. Like, now. I'm so sorry."

His face was tight, but he turned to the waiter. "Would you mind boxing this up, along with the next three courses? We have to take off a bit early."

The waiter nodded, put the food back on the tray, and left. I couldn't meet Shane's eyes.

"I already paid for it," he said, "so it might as well not go to waste."

I nodded. Once we had the food, we got in the car and drove back to my apartment mostly in silence. God damn Melvin for not only messing with my career but for ruining what could have been the best date I was ever going to have.

Shane dropped me at my door but didn't get out of the car. "Would you like some of the food?"

"No, thanks." I shook my head and started to close the passenger door.

At the last second, he grabbed it, holding it open. "I hope this isn't because of something I did," he said.

I'd been a bundle of nerves ever since the Melvin thing, but I softened at the thought that he might feel responsible. "No, Shane, it's not you. I'm really not feeling well. And I probably couldn't have eaten seafood in front of living seafood, even on a good day. Though I appreciate the thought," I said hastily. "There's just something I have to deal with."

"I don't think they'd be able to tell what cooked fish look like, but I understand your point." He shrugged. "If you feel like confiding in me, I'd love to help."

"Thanks," I said again.

He let me close the door and pulled out of the parking lot without looking back.

I shut the apartment door and took a few deep breaths. Maybe I was wrong. I decided to give Melvin one last shot to clarify things before I flew off the deep end.

Want to tell me your issues with the pitch? Maybe I can help. Was it possible that Melvin didn't understand it? His tech knowledge wasn't where it should be for someone on his level, and I knew it was some of my best work.

I have to turn my phone off in a minute, so I apologize for the brevity. I think we only need one person in the S.J. Sporting meeting. I can take things from here.

Excuse me? I reread the message a few times. There was no way this was for real. There was no way he could make the presentation and answer questions alone.

You're cutting me out of the meeting altogether?

Maybe that's for the best, since you feel that way. I can look after the potential contract with S.J. from now on. You can help Evan on Cake Bakes.

Like hell, I thought. He gets my completed project, then cuts me out altogether? No. Just no.

I think you need me with you on this pitch.

The message sat in *send* mode for a moment before being marked as undeliverable. Bastard had turned his phone off.

Deep breaths. I had a few options here, but all of them sucked. I tried to channel Patrick's calm before doing something rash. I couldn't work for Melvin anymore, that was clear. Once he won the account, and I created and finalized the interface, he'd fire me. At least I would if I were him. Then no one could counter any of his claims. Or he'd try to make it himself and fail miserably, and all the work would have been for nothing. There was no way I was getting out of this with my job intact. Melvin would be lucky if I didn't drown him in waffle batter or worse. But this website and app interface was a career-making proposal. I couldn't just let Melvin take it.

I sat in front of the fish tank in my living room and watched Hopper thrash up to the surface of the tank, begging for food. Sometimes he acted like a dog. I stared at him for a few minutes, thinking. What would Hopper do? My gut said he would eat Melvin, or at least try. According to Google, he'd even eat his own children like an apathetic Medea, if given the opportunity. That wasn't an option for me. I usually hated the idea of the circle of life, but for a split second, Hopper's approach seemed so much easier: eat everything.

I knew one thing. I wasn't going to end up in another dead-end job doing responsibilities over my pay grade without any benefit. Fuck that. And if I was able to pull off getting the S.J. account and making an incredible product, then I could write my ticket as far as jobs went. As long as Melvin didn't get the credit.

There was one surefire way to find out. I grabbed my cell and dialed the number before pulling out my girliest voice. "Hi, I'm looking for the office of S.J. Sporting," I said brightly.

The woman at the other end of the line cleared her throat. "This is S.J. Sporting. How can I help you?"

"Well, my boss, Melvin Hammer, has a meeting with S.J. Sharpe scheduled for next Wednesday? I just wanted to confirm that time and date?" Nothing said *incompetent* like making a question out of a statement.

"Certainly. Just give me a moment to check the calendar." There was a pause of about thirty seconds while my heart was in my throat. Then she came back on the line. "It's a good thing you called. That meeting has been moved up a week. It's now on the schedule for ten a.m. this Wednesday instead."

Of course it was. That freaking bastard. "That's what I was afraid of," I said sweetly and forced a laugh. "His schedule has been all over the place. Would it be possible to bump that up to tomorrow morning? He has this conflict that, you know, he's just not going to be able to change, so he's asked Indiana Aaron to go in his place? I'm sure you've heard of Indiana." I squeezed my eyes shut.

"Let me see what I can do..." I heard her tapping keys. "Looks like I can squeeze him in tomorrow, Tuesday, at eleven. Will that work for Mr. Aaron?"

"That's perfect."

"Certainly. I've adjusted the schedule. Is there anything else I can help you with?"

"Just to clarify, this meeting is going to take place at the Family Sports Center, where the Avs practice?"

"That's right, we're in Centennial. Anything else?"

"Nope, that should take care of it," I said in my best receptionist voice. "Thanks so much."

I hung up and tried to let calm replace the anger and panic. That little twit. He'd bumped the meeting up without telling me because he'd always planned to present my idea to S.J. Sporting and leave me out of the loop entirely. There was absolutely no way I was going to let that happen. I was *not* losing that addition to my résumé.

I thought briefly of my dad, and of Margaret, and of how much easier the promotion would have made supporting him. But again, fuck it. There was no way my dad would want me to let this go by. I'd get a job somewhere else and start all over, maybe even better than before, if I could pull this off, which made me no worse off than I was right now. Except that I *was* worse off. Melvin Hammer had not only messed with my career, he'd quite possibly ruined my personal life as well. I doubted I'd ever have an opportunity for a romantic dinner under the sharks again.

As soon as my heart rate had returned to normal, I texted Heidi and asked her to come over. It was almost the end of the workday, so she cut out a bit early and headed over.

I opened the door when she arrived, ready to unload all over her, when I noticed she had a dopey, sweet smile that transformed her face. She was glowing. It looked like love. Or a virus.

"You okay?" I asked.

She looked down at her phone screen and back up at me. "I'm great," she said happily. She turned the screen in my direction. It was a series of text messages, to and from someone labeled ♥ Jason♥. I'll come and pick you up for a date tonight. Can't wait. I'm really glad you texted me.

"That's wonderful, Heidi, really," I said. Under other circumstances I would have jumped up and down and hugged her, then demanded details. Not this time. *Vengeance, thy name is Ana Aaron. Melon Hamster, prepare to feel my wrath,* I thought to myself. *Stay focused.*

"Heidi," I said and cupped her face with my hands, "I need you back on earth. Melvin is trying to screw over Indiana. Indi-ana, both of us. He's taking my pitch to SJ, and he's cutting me out."

Her eyes narrowed as they focused intently on me. "Are you freaking kidding me? After all the stressing we did about how you were going to tell him you're not an archaeologist and how this was your big shot to prove it to him? That bastard!"

"Right? So much worry about how to have the meeting with him not knowing what I look like, and turns out he was planning to have the meeting without me all along."

"I always thought he was a jerk," she murmured, but she'd turned back to her phone.

"Heidi, I need you," I pleaded. Heidi was amazing at presenting herself. Everything was always on point, from her clothing to her apartment to her color-coded notes. Her concentration, not so much.

"I'm sorry, I don't mean to be distracted." She chewed on her lip. "What's the plan?"

"I'm going to scoop him. He's flying into Denver, but I moved the meeting at S.J. up a day. I'm going to do it alone. I mean, if I'm going to lose my job, I might as well go out with a bang."

She nodded. "You just go and make a kick-ass pitch. It really makes things easier if he's not going to be there. But he's totally going to fire you for doing this."

"Yeah, and I'm not leaving without this in my portfolio. What is it that Patrick likes to say? Go big *and* go home? That's going to be me."

"Okay, we've totally got this. Let me pick your clothes for you, and then you can practice your pitch on me. It's going to be killer. But I only have an hour to work this miracle because I've got myself a hot dinner date."

"Thank you. I owe you."

"Least I can do. You're the one who gave me Jason's number. He said he's had a crush on me forever." She gave me a huge smile. "You can do this, Ana. You know you can. You can make a hell of an app. You may not be able to land a plane, but you *can* land this account. Get it?"

"*God*, Heidi," I groaned. "Yes, I get it." I didn't love the comparison. I *had* to land this because it was the only shot Apollo IT would get.

Chapter 13

I ARRIVED AT THE FAMILY SPORTS CENTER IN CENTENNIAL WAY EAR-lier than I'd intended to. Traffic hadn't been bad, and I'd been unable to sleep most of the night before anyway. When I had, I'd dreamed of beating Melvin over the head with a hockey stick. Not healthy and, although satisfying, not practical. I shook off the thought and glanced up at the structure in front of me. Heidi was right; this place was massive. I'd driven past it a million times as a kid, and a few friends had had birthday parties here, but not being in the sports world, I'd never given it any thought. But now...now things were different.

I had enough time to wallow in my anger before getting my game face on. I was wearing Heidi's creation: dress pants, wedges, and a tailored sweater. All my hair was wound into a low bun that had been sprayed to a stonelike texture. I could definitely pass as an adult, but not as a skydiving, knife-wielding EBUG who expressed his time in "a war" through art. You couldn't have everything.

I willed my blood pressure to stay down as I entered the building. I thought longingly of going to the arcade (video games were a great de-stressor) but followed the directions to the meeting room. It was on the west side of the complex, located on the second floor.

Could I do this? I could totally do this. Deep breaths. I opened the glass-paneled door at the west end labeled HOCKEY OPERATIONS and walked up to a receptionist's desk. She looked a lot like me, or me on a regular day. Fresh-faced, bright, and probably worth more than several of her bosses put together.

"I'm here to see S.J. Sharpe. I'm a little early."

She looked me up and down and then met my eyes. "Name?" she asked.

Here we go. "Indiana Aaron."

"I'm sorry, did you say—"

"Yes, Indiana Aaron. I have a meeting with S.J. Sharpe."

She blinked but kept her face neutral. "Yes, of course. S.J. is just finishing something up. I'll let the team know you're here, but it might still be a while."

"I understand," I said. "I'm happy to wait until they're ready." I felt a little ill. Truth was, I wasn't going to be sure I could pull this off until I'd actually done it.

She made a note and tapped her pen against her desk. "You might be more comfortable waiting in the second-floor lounge. The elevators are just over there." She pointed down the hall. "By the way, there's a bathroom right when you get off. You might want to freshen up first."

Yikes. My hair must be a disaster. I thanked her, then headed to the elevators and punched the up button for the next floor. I shoved my self-doubt down deep, but one thought kept resurfacing: If my own colleagues wouldn't value me for who I was, how was a random stuffy old man going to appreciate my talents? I could feel myself getting angry again, and I let it fuel me as the elevator doors opened and I stepped through them into my future. A tall imposing man wearing a custom suit with the build of an athlete strode toward me, and my courage drained completely. I ducked into the bathroom. No way was I going to talk to him before I'd fixed whatever was wrong with my appearance.

The bathroom was plush, with silver fixtures and lots of off-white colors. There was a fainting couch in one corner (I hoped *I* wouldn't need it), mirrors along one wall, and several individual stalls.

I went to the sinks and checked my hair. It hadn't moved at all. Everything else looked normal, too. No lipstick on my teeth, no raccoon eyes. So why had the receptionist suggested I "freshen up"? I turned on the cold water and splashed just a little on my cheeks. It calmed my nerves, but I had on way too much makeup to appreciate the full effect.

A toilet flushed, and an older woman came out of one of the stalls. She had shoulder-length dark hair and was wearing cream slacks with a matching sleeveless sweater. She was messing with her phone and cursing under her breath.

She gave me a wan smile as she joined me at the sinks and threw the phone in her purse. "Useless piece of junk," she muttered.

"What's wrong?"

She shoved her bag away from her and looked herself over critically in the mirror as she washed her hands. "The phone never connects to the network here, and I don't receive messages in the building. Sometimes I just want to throw it against the wall."

"Mind if I take a look at it?"

"Go ahead. It might as well be a paperweight." She dug the phone back out, unlocked it, and passed it over.

I thumbed past the lock screen, then rummaged around in the settings. "Just a few little tweaks should get you going," I murmured as I clicked a couple of different toggle switches. I handed it back. "You shouldn't have any more issues," I said.

She blinked at me, then looked down at the phone. She quickly scrolled through a few apps and then pulled up her messages. "You fixed it. How did you do that? And so fast?"

"I work in IT. Technology is my thing."

"Well, I'm impressed. I've been struggling with that forever." She put the phone away, then pulled a lip gloss from her bag and reapplied it, meeting my eyes in the mirror. "Thanks. Are you here to see the Avs practice?"

"No," I answered and checked my own reflection again. "Unlike tech, sports are *not* my thing. I'm a coder. If it's electronic, I'm interested. If it involves using my triceps or quads or whatever, I'm not."

She leaned against the sink and looked at me fully. "Then why would you be *here?*" she asked, sounding amused. "This place is literally called the Family Sports Center."

I let out a breath. How did the meme go? That there were no more supportive people in the world than women you met in the bathroom. So I took a chance.

"I'm here for a meeting with S.J. Sporting," I confessed. "They're looking to do a collaboration with the Avs and revamp their app and web services. I have a lot of ideas that will get attention from the media. The only problem is…my boss is trying to take credit so he doesn't have to give me the promotion he promised, so I'm giving the pitch without him."

"Come again?"

"He changed the meeting time and told me I wasn't needed any longer. He wants to take full credit, and he didn't do *anything*," I said bitterly. "His phone actually *is* a paperweight."

She crossed her arms over her chest. "What's your name?"

"Indiana," I said. "You?"

"I'm Sara," she said. "It's nice to meet you, Indiana." She seemed almost amused by the whole situation.

"You, too. And please call me 'Ana.'"

"You know," she said thoughtfully, "I don't know anything about coding, but you could practice your pitch on me, if you think it would help. What do you think is the right way to launch a new online presence?"

I lit up (again) at the thought of sharing my thoughts. It was so nice to be listened to instead of dismissed. "Well, S.J. Sporting is collaborating with the Avs, right? That means merchandise exclusives, clothing, etc. being sold by one company, along with actual hockey equipment with the Avs trademark. An app that showcased that would have to be streamlined and uncomplicated, so the regular user would have to do as little as possible. Have you ever heard of *Pokémon Go*?"

She laughed brightly. "I have a ten-year-old, so yeah. We catch Weedles and Caterpies all over the stadium. He's obsessed with the bug ones."

"What about an S.J. *Pokémon Go* type of experience? You're chasing products, though, not Weedles. If the customer sees something they like, like a jersey or a bag with a logo, they open the app and point it at the object. Then the app takes you to where you can buy it. If it's not an S.J. product, it'll take you to the nearest equivalent that S.J. makes. Then it'll show them the price, a link to buy directly online, and even, location-specific, the aisle of the store where they can find it if they prefer in-store shopping. The analytics could show a lot of valuable information about what S.J. customers like and what they don't. And the app could also have a place to rewatch highlights of the Avs games. It could be a special feature for the Avs, which increases revenue for both S.J. and the NHL, but it would include, eventually, other teams and other sports altogether." I let out a breath and looked down at my shoes. "That's the basic version of my pitch, anyway. I'm sorry, I don't even know you, and I've involved you in my drama."

She winked at me. "What's the saying about drunk girls in the bathroom?"

I nodded. "Very true, but we're both unfortunately sober."

She gestured for me to follow her as she stepped toward the door. "I have a few mimosas that can fix that. And I need to know more—what you're describing sounds really complicated."

"Actually, it's not, for the consumer, anyway. It's as easy as taking a selfie. I'd love to take you up on that drink, but I really should go find S.J. Sharpe. I need to hurry if I'm going to make the meeting."

"Just follow me," she said and led me down the hall to a meeting room. She went to the wet bar at the back of the room along the row of windows and poured two stemmed glasses of orange liquid. She brought one back over to me. "Cheers," she said.

I looked at the drink and then back at her. "Who are you?" I asked.

"Sara Jean."

I felt cold adrenaline flood my entire body. "As in SJ, Sara Jean?" I asked in a whisper.

"Yeah," she said and looked a little sheepish. "I should have told you earlier. It's just that people are so much freer and more authentic when they don't know who I am. You never would have told me any of that, would you?"

I shook my head, tamping back the panic. "No, sir," I said quietly.

She suppressed a grin and gestured for me to sit at a high table in the corner of the conference room against the windows. The mountains were in the backdrop. I did as she asked, then took a long sip, actually a gulp, from my mimosa. I'd really stepped in it this time.

At that moment, there was a knock on the door.

"Come in," Sara called.

I glanced at the clock—11:00 a.m. on the dot. A handful of men in suits came in, and Sara waved them to the chairs around the conference table. "You're all on time. Ms. Aaron from Apollo IT is getting ready to show us what she has in mind for our web collaboration with the Avs." She turned to me and smiled conspiratorially. "Whenever you're ready, Ms. Aaron."

I cleared my throat and stood. "Thank you, Ms. Sharpe." I turned to address the room, opening a projection app I'd made on my phone to broadcast the visuals onto the wall at the end of the room. Then I took a deep breath and began the practiced formal description of how the web and app interfaces would change the face of S.J. Sporting in the online world.

After the presentation, Sara had a quick meeting with the men while I took another trip to the bathroom to freshen up (really, just to give them time to talk about me). When I got back to the meeting room, they were gone, and it was just Sara and me again.

"Your proposal was very impressive, Indiana. We're excited about the growth potential, too." She leaned forward conspiratorially. "But I have to know, how did you find out your boss was going to steal your idea?"

"Long story. Point is, he's the worst. And I don't even have recourse because of another…small issue."

"And what's that?"

"He thinks I'm a guy. In my defense, it was his idea, not mine."

She let out a startled laugh. "What would lead him to that conclusion?" She looked me up and down.

"My name." I sighed. "I sort of called him out once in an email, and he addressed me as 'Mr.' when he responded. I work remotely, so we haven't met in person. I should have fessed up right away, but there was a fire, and then a baby, and, oh god, the plane—" I stopped cold. My nerves had me chattering, and this potential client didn't need more details. "The point is, I can't tell you how hard it is to get respect in the tech world when you're a woman. Actually, I'm sure I don't need to tell you—you've probably experienced it in the sporting world. I imagine it's just as bad, if not worse."

"Do you know why I use initials in my name?" she asked.

I shrugged. "I could guess."

"I do it for the same reason that J. K. Rowling, S. E. Hinton, and J.D. Robb did. The same reason George Sand, George Eliot, and the Brontë sisters changed their names. To combat the misogyny. When you're the CEO of a sporting company, they expect, well, Elon Musk or Jeff Bezos. A guy who really wants to be a cowboy and shakes hands too tightly. Or"— she gestured at me—"Indiana Jones."

I let out a breath and felt the tension leave my shoulders. "You really do get it."

"I really do," she said. "People can't separate the persona from the product. We're terrible at it, and it makes everything harder for people like us, people who are *unexpected*, in our industries."

"I actually struggle with that a lot," I said thoughtfully. "The identity shouldn't affect the product. Who the artist is, their look, their backstory should have no bearing on the value of what they produce. But it does. And it's frustrating because part of me agrees that, in some cases, it does matter, but I can't figure out *why* it does. I, of all people, should know better."

Sara nodded and put her chin in her hand.

In that moment, it felt like all pretense was gone, just the way I liked it. "You remember Marla Olmstead, that three-year-old painter who was supposed to be the next Pollack?" I asked.

"Refresh my memory," Sara said and leaned back comfortably in her chair.

I was relaxed for the first time since I'd learned what Melvin had planned to do. "In the early aughts, Marla's dad, who was an amateur painter, set her down in front of her own canvas to distract her. Or so the story goes. And she started making these amazing pieces of art. Like, huge abstract blobs that people loved. They said she was a reincarnation of Rembrandt, which made no sense since their styles were nothing alike, but whatever, and she had all these showings in New York. She—well, her family—made a ton of money. Then *60 Minutes* came along and tried to film her painting, and they couldn't do it. The family said it was because she didn't perform well under pressure."

Sara laughed at that.

"But no matter what they tried, they couldn't film her doing more than pushing paint into muddy puddles like all kids do. So the question is, should the early paintings belong in the Metropolitan Museum of Art *because* they were painted by a three-year-old? Or should they not, because they may have been painted by her father? Does that make them not 'good enough' now because he's a dude in his forties who works the night shift at Frito Lay? And what if she did paint them, but as she got older, her work lost its appeal because it became less abstract? Does that detract from the value?"

She sat forward. "I remember when that scandal broke. Everyone loves it when someone pulls one over on the art community. They don't get a lot of sympathy because they have millions to burn, so when they're duped, it's more amusing than sad. They have to take the word of critics as to what has value. But I see your point. Is the art good or bad? Why does the rest matter?"

"I hate that it does." I groaned. "That's how I got into this mess."

"Maybe it's because we crave 'authenticity,'" Sara suggested. "Maybe we let some less polished things slide because of what we believe the artist has had to overcome, like James Frey's *A Million Little Pieces* or J. T. LeRoy. Or a three-year-old who makes amazing blobs."

"That's actually a really good point," I said. I took a long swallow of the mimosa. It was so freaking good. "If J. T. LeRoy isn't a fifteen-year-old 'lot lizard' with AIDS but instead a woman in her thirties who couldn't get published otherwise, it's 'inauthentic.' But authenticity as a concept is problematic and kind of sucks."

"It totally does," she agreed. "But we'll give a lot more to a fifteen-year-old sex worker with AIDS than we will a grown woman who went to college."

"And then there's me," I said.

"If Melvin met you like this"—she gestured at me—"would he take you seriously?"

I snorted. "He *has* met me like this, and before I could tell him the truth, he drank my coffee, then told me to run along while the big boys talked."

She shook her head in exasperation. "How is it we basically live in the future and still have to deal with this shit?"

"Right?" I asked, leaning back. "He likes my work. Obviously, because he's trying to take credit for it. He thinks I'm talented. But he only gave me the opportunity to create the pitch in the first place because he thinks I'm like James Bond. That I can ski down mountains with a severely shaken martini in one hand. That I read *Walden* while I chop wood in the forest to live off the land."

"Why would he think—"

"Uh, not really important. The real me watches *90 Day Fiancé* under a blanket with a box of Mallomars."

"I love that show," Sara said. "Maybe my high school teacher wouldn't agree, but it's way more entertaining than Thoreau."

"A hundred percent. But mostly because Thoreau was a fraud, like me. His mommy brought him sandwiches at Walden Pond and did his laundry. At least reality television doesn't take itself so seriously."

"So you're really in a bind, aren't you? You've made the pitch, but what happens when he finds out?"

I sagged a little against the chair. She was right. Without Patrick and Heidi here boosting me up, the whole thing was seeming more and more impossible. "Yeah. I guess I am. But I had to give it a shot. All I've ever wanted was a creative director position. If I could just get a foot in the door, maybe I could help change the industry. I could try to pave the way for women in the field who are struggling the same way I am. I think women should support women." I blushed a little. "I'll get off my soapbox now."

I felt my phone vibrate in my bag. I reached in to see the screen and winced. Several missed texts and an actual call from Melvin.

Sara leaned over my shoulder. "Those from the boss?" she asked.

"Yep," I said. "We've never actually talked on the phone."

"Is he coming here?"

I opened the messages from Melvin. Indiana—I flew in today and heard you were at the Family Sports Center. I need to speak with you immediately. I've been in the arena watching you play goalie.

Shit. He was here. Now. How had he known? In my panic, I took a second to feel sorry for the poor guy who was down on the ice wearing a hockey mask while Melvin ogled him from the stands and blew up my phone.

Sara leaned over my shoulder. "That reminds me. I have to ask, when we set up this meeting initially, I was told Indiana Aaron was an EBUG for the Avs and had extensive parasailing experience."

I groaned. "*Why?*" I muttered to myself under my breath before turning back to Sara. "Apparently, I *am* an emergency goalie because my boss is watching me practice right now."

"But how—"

"Indiana Aaron has become sort of a legend. I'm not any of those things, Sara. I'm just a coder. But Melvin's not lying to you, at least about that. He really believes those things. This persona has a life of its own."

"Sounds like someone's created a monster."

"Believe me, it was a joint effort. This wasn't just me being a sweaty Frankenstein, feverishly making a guy in a laboratory. It was a gossipy game of telephone in an office."

She sat back, thoughtful. "I have a little test I like to run on potential collaborators. How about we go down to the arena, and you shoot Melvin a text letting him know I'm there." I must have blanched because she quickly shook her head. "Trust me."

"If he recognizes me, he really might kill me," I said. "Like literally. And I'd be dead. And my poor dad—"

"Relax. If what you've been saying is true, he won't."

"Oh god, what if he kills that random goalie?"

She grabbed a badge out of one of the drawers next to the table and handed it over. "This is a VIP pass for the executive box. Go up there and hang out for a bit. Feel free to watch the stadium. He won't see you, but you'll be able to see him."

I took the badge and tamped down the fear rush that flooded my body. Then I drafted a message to Melvin. Was practicing with the team. S.J. is waiting for you in the arena.

Sara nodded. "Perfect."

I hit *send* and followed her to the elevator, again trying to keep the mimosa from coming back up. Even though I felt a little bit like a baby bear hiding behind its mama, I was still terrified. I ran scenarios like programs in my head, but every one of them came back bad for me.

The elevator doors opened, and the first thing I saw was the receptionist at her desk. She flashed me a smile that I tried to return.

Sara and I walked down the hall together, past a bunch of training rooms and sports equipment areas before coming to the practice ice. Just before she opened the door, she leaned down quickly. "What's Melvin look like?"

"Teddy Roosevelt," I said immediately.

She nodded and gestured for me to take the back stairs to the VIP box before she went into the arena.

I clumped up the back steps in my wedges with my heart in my throat. Luckily, when I got to the box, it was deserted. I sat in one of the seats that gave me a good view of the arena below. What I saw took my breath away.

Not because ice golf is amazing. It took my breath away because the lobby in front of the ice was filled with well-dressed men. They were almost all athletically built, wearing suits and shoes that cost more than my rent. They were talking in small groups, and booming masculine laughter rang out repeatedly.

It took me a hot minute to find Melvin from my perch, since the room was crowded and everyone was so tall. Melvin looked as little as I usually felt, which wasn't his fault, given the crowd was made up of athletes and former athletes.

Then I turned my attention to Sara, who casually made a lap around the room, clearly spotted Melvin, then took a seat in a plush chair at the edge of the lobby.

What was she doing? I stared for a moment before it dawned on me. It didn't calm the dread, though.

Sara sat still and watched. Sometimes she nodded to someone she knew, but she didn't talk to anyone. She just watched.

Melvin went from group to group asking for Mr. Sharpe. Over and over. With each new cluster of dudes, he walked over and said, "Hey!" with a grand gesture, shaking hands and pounding their backs. At one point, a man said, "Sharpe? Over there," and pointed in Sara's general direction. And Melvin rushed off to that corner of the room, never glancing at Sara.

"She's waiting to see how long it takes him to make his way over," I mumbled to myself as I peered over the ledge.

After about twenty minutes, the fear began to calm, but the anger started to ramp up again. Melvin hadn't glanced at Sara once. There were a few other women in the room, of course, but he hadn't glanced at them either. Sara seemed to wait a few more minutes before she got up and walked past him. "Are you looking for someone?" I heard her ask loudly.

"I am, but it isn't you," he retorted irritably. She nodded thoughtfully, then glanced up to the box where I was hiding before leaving the arena.

A few minutes later, I heard the door open behind me. "Your story checks out," Sara said. "I think he'd try to drink my coffee, too." She took a seat next to me.

"Yeah," I sighed. "He really is the worst."

"On a brighter note, though, I'm going to give you the account."

"What?" I yelped.

She nodded. "If you can pull this off, S.J. Sporting will have the corner on the entire market. This could open us up to other teams and leagues across the country."

I wiggled in my seat. "Thank you, Sara. I appreciate this opportunity. If I'm still employed tomorrow, I'd be happy to work with you."

"You will be. I have one condition. I work with you. Not with him."

That one might not go over well. "How about we don't specify that in writing just yet." Sara opened her mouth, but I held up my hand. "We'll work together, promise. I'd just rather not make Melvin any madder than I have to at the moment. Is that okay?"

She nodded. "I understand office politics can be tricky sometimes." She pulled out her phone and fired off a quick email to Melvin, cc'ing the head of Apollo IT and me.

Mr. Hammer:

Our meeting tomorrow is cancelled. I ran into Indiana Aaron and have been thoroughly impressed by the interface proposal. We will be going ahead with Apollo IT for this project and are drafting up a contract for approval.

Best,

S.J. Sharpe

S.J. Sporting

I winced but smiled quickly when Sara looked back over.

"Let's go back to my office to draw up the paperwork."

"You might need to speak with Shane Dalton about the contract. He handles the finances for the Artemis team. He's actually in Denver today, so let me drop him a quick note..." I opened my texts.

Hey Shane, looks like Artemis is going to get the S.J. Sporting account! S.J. is going to need your help getting the paperwork in order.

There was an unusually long pause before the jumping gray dots indicated Shane's response. You'll have to ask someone else. Seems I'm no longer working with Artemis. And maybe no longer working at Apollo after today.

I gasped. What?

Melvin thinks I came to Denver early to tell Indiana's daughter he was going to steal his idea. He flew in today and headed straight for the meeting. A heads-up would have been nice, Ana.

I swallowed hard. This one was on me. I'm so sorry, Shane.

It's fine. Enjoy your success.

I turned back to Sara, hoping she didn't notice how suddenly shiny my eyes were. "On second thought, I'll help with the paperwork for now, then we can pass it to the legal team later."

"Great." She smiled. "Looking forward to taking the tech world by storm with you, Ana."

I smiled back at her the best I could. "Me, too."

Chapter 14

THE DRIVE HOME SUCKED. YES, I'D GOTTEN THE S.J. ACCOUNT, BUT AT what cost? Shane's job? My job was one thing, but the possibility of him losing his hadn't even been on my radar. My success was never supposed to be at someone else's expense—especially not Shane's. I should have at least shared my plans with him, but it wouldn't have changed anything. Melvin had me blocked on all sides.

Speaking of Melvin, about an hour after I got home, a text came through. You have a lot of nerve taking that meeting without me. I won't forget this. Consider yourself on notice.

I rolled my eyes and flopped back onto my couch, staring at the ceiling. He'd told me to consider myself on notice once before. And, incidentally, that had been what started this whole mess. I sat back up. Well, this time *he* was on notice, too. I should have taken the high road and not responded, but I was feeling petty. And angry. You cut me out after all the hard work I'd put in and the promises you'd made.

There was a pause, during which I imagined him sweating and

stomping and kicking random chair legs. You are obligated to come to me before meeting with any potential client. You're my subordinate. Your work product doesn't belong to you; it belongs to the company.

I did the work, and I need this project in my portfolio, I wrote back. So I landed the biggest account of your career and saved our jobs. Artemis can't execute that interface without my direction and you know it. If you want to keep that account, you can't fire me.

I'm not firing you. Yet. But you will regret the stunt you pulled today.

I threw my phone down next to me on the couch. Great, Indiana was a stuntperson now, too.

There was a soft knock at the door, and I sat up, startled. On high alert again, I went over to look through the peephole, then sagged with relief. I opened the door, and Nancy held out her arms. I fell into them and let her hug me. She rubbed my back soothingly for a few minutes.

"You didn't flick your lights when you got home, so I just wanted to make sure you're okay," she said gently.

"I forgot." I sniffed, the fight thoroughly leaving me. "I'm sorry."

"You're clearly not okay," she said, pulling back to look at my face before settling me back into the hug. "But you will be, honey. Does this have to do with that young man with the radio voice?"

It did, but there was so much more to it than that. Too much to explain to Nancy and not enough energy to do it. So I just nodded and tried to keep my tears in check.

"I figured as much. You know George and I are always here if you need us. Did you know George was the biggest ass when I met him?"

I pulled back and looked at her. "George is so nice."

"He is," she said. Then she thought for a moment. "You know, maybe it was me who was the ass. We've been together for forty years, so sometimes I forget."

Could you really get to a point in a relationship when you couldn't remember which one of you was the ass? That seemed impossible to me.

"Regardless," Nancy said, waving off my thoughts, "one of us sucked, and we figured it out. Forty years later it won't matter which one of you was the ass either. If it's meant to be, it'll work out. Promise."

She grabbed me back into the hug, and I let her hold me for a few more minutes before I pulled away. "Thanks, Nancy. You've given me a lot to think about." *Like, for real. WTF.*

"Anytime, darling." She waved good night and went back upstairs toward her part of the house.

I shut the door with a soft click and pushed my shoulders back. I was done feeling like this, and I wasn't going to let Melvin intimidate me any longer. Or ruin my life. Or Shane's.

———————

I woke up the next morning still on the couch, having slept in my clothes from the day before. My oversprayed hair was practically standing up on its own, and my makeup had run under my eyes. I didn't like the person I saw staring back at me in the mirror.

As always, despite the mess I'd made, the first thing I did was check my email. A few messages from the S.J. Sporting team about setting up some meetings. Nothing from Melvin. There was, however, a message from Evan Smith. Why was he writing to me? Then I read the subject line, and my heart dropped into my stomach.

From: Evan Smith

To: Indiana Aaron

Subject: I know your secret

Hi Indiana,

Meet me at the coffee shop at 8th Street and Main at noon.

Trust me, you'll want to hear what I have to say.

Evan Smith

My secret? Which one? That I'd gone behind Melvin's back? That I wasn't half the man Indiana was? Or that I wasn't a man at all? Whatever he knew, or thought he knew, I could pretty much guarantee I did *not* want to hear it. It was only 8:00 a.m., and I hadn't even had any caffeine yet. I took a deep breath. I could handle him; I just wished I didn't have to.

The email was sent just to me, not to Melvin, so clearly Evan wanted something from *me*, and it wasn't just to get me fired.

I took a long shower, shampooed my hair twice, and let the warm water help center my thoughts. Evan may have deduced that I was female. Or maybe he only knew I hadn't delivered a baby. Or that I hadn't learned obstetrics with the SEALs. Or hadn't had a world-record high jump. Or that I didn't mold my thoughts about *a* war into clay. So there were a few possibilities, but Occam's razor suggested it wasn't any of those things. There wouldn't be a way to hide who I was at the coffee shop, and I was sick of it all. Of keeping the creation alive. Of being in this situation in the first place. Whether Evan was ready or not, he was about to meet the real Indiana Aaron.

But, as a woman who had grown up aware of how I would stack up in an abduction kind of situation, I didn't feel safe meeting Evan alone. Even if Patrick and Heidi and I all had Share My Location turned on in our phone settings.

So I shot a quick text to Patrick. That weird guy Evan wants me to meet him at the coffee shop on 8th at noon. He says he knows my secret.

Which one? Patrick wrote back.

Not 100% sure. Probably that my masculinity is metaphorical and not physical. Would you be willing to meet me there? Like on the down-low. I don't want to be alone with him.

Yes immediately appeared on the screen, and I sighed with relief. I'm bringing Joseph, he added.

Great, it's going to be a party, I thought. Sure. You can sit in the next booth over or something. I appreciate this, Patrick. I hate having to ask.

I know but I'm glad you did.

———

I got to the coffee shop an hour early. It had a relaxing feel to it; the walls were bamboo, and all the fabric on the tables and booths was a soft green. They served coffee out of wide, low mugs with wraparound handles to keep the customer's hands warm, which was a huge plus during Denver's chilly fall weather.

I grabbed the brew of the day and settled into a booth near one of the windows. I wanted to be seated and double caffeinated before Evan got there, in part to see if he knew who I was or if he'd ignore me like he'd always done before.

About a half hour later, Patrick and Joseph showed up, both wearing impeccable suits and looking very much out of place with the shop's casual vibe. They practically tripped over each other getting to the counter to order their drinks. They each independently turned to me to give me a thumbs-up several times.

Given his size, Joseph was even more conspicuous than Patrick, if that was possible. The two of them together would never blend in. Once they'd paid for their drinks, they walked over to the booth behind me. They didn't speak to me. Patrick just winked, and they sat next to each other on the same side of their booth so their backs were up against mine.

"Psst," Patrick whispered out of the side of his mouth. "Doing okay?"

I sighed. "Do you have to sit on the same side of the booth? It makes you stick out even more than you already do. You look like a couple of FBI agents."

Joseph slid his arm around Patrick's shoulders. "We're just a young couple in love. Couples do that," he said. "Nothing to see here."

"Do they?" I asked skeptically.

"Patrick and I sit on the same side of the booth all the time."

I supposed that was sweet, under other circumstances.

"So, wut ur de deets?" Patrick whispered out of the side of his mouth again. It took me a moment to decipher.

"What are my details? Is that what you asked?" I said loudly.

Patrick slunk down in the booth and nodded, adding a loud "shhhh."

"Yesterday sucked. Melvin tried to cut me out of my own project, and he ruined my romantic dinner with the sharks. But I won the S.J. account and saved his ass, so naturally he's pissed because who doesn't hate a win-win, right?"

"Oooh, you did? That's awesome, Ana." Patrick turned around fully, his stealth mode momentarily forgotten. "I'm so proud of you. Sorry about Melvin, though. He's an ass. And before I forget, did you say 'romantic dinner with sharks'? What role did the sharks play, Ana? I need this broken down for me."

I rolled my eyes. "I don't date sharks, Patrick. Focus. But I did get the account."

He pumped his fists in the air. "Yeah, you did!"

I smiled at his enthusiasm despite myself. "Thanks. I think Melvin might have sent Mini Melvin to scare me, but who knows?"

Joseph turned to Patrick. "Melvin has a Mini-Me?"

"Yeah, his name is Evan," Patrick explained and turned to me. "So why does he want to see you?"

I shrugged. "Evan writes emails like he grew up watching too many soap operas, so I'm not a hundred percent sure, but he seems to think I have a dark side, and he came off as vaguely threatening to me. So thank you for coming. I owe you both."

Joseph seemed far less worried about being seen speaking to me than Patrick. "We got you, Ana. I will gladly intimidate the hell out of anyone who messes with you."

I softened. "Thank you. I don't think either of you will need to get involved, but I'm pretty sure you'd scare Evan far more than I would." I looked down at myself and wondered briefly what it would be like to be built like Joseph. To be able to walk at night without fear. To intimidate others just by existing. To reach the top shelf. But there was always a flip side. Patrick had told me people often picked fights with Joseph when they went out together because he was so big. Drunk guys saw him as a challenge. He also always tried to cross to the other side of the street when he saw a woman walking alone because she might feel threatened by him, even though Joseph was extremely gentle, raised orchids in his spare time, and would never intentionally hurt anyone. But he had to live with the consequences of people thinking he would just because of how he looked.

The door to the shop opened, and a rush of crisp air came in. There he was. The latest thorn in my side. Evan's eyes scanned the room before they lit on me, and his lip curled in a sneer. So he had figured it out. Damn it. He made his way over and lowered himself into the booth before sprawling spread-eagle across his side. Black denim jacket, black T-shirt, and black jeans, with all black Converse shoes. *The nineties called*, I thought snarkily but didn't say. The nineties were still the height of fashion.

"Hello, *In-di-ana*," he said, drawing out the word in a kind of gross way. I immediately wanted to take my name out of his mouth for good. "You're the girl who took my coffee order before that fire."

"I didn't take your coffee order. You just kind of babbled it at me."

"And you never delivered."

"Because one, I'm not your coffee bitch, and two, I was putting out the actual *fire*." I heard Patrick choke and sputter a little, followed by several loud thumps, presumably Joseph beating on his back. "Can I help you, Evan?" I sighed.

"So you're not even going to deny it?" he asked.

"Deny what?"

"That you're the famous Indiana Aaron? Don't bother because I already know the truth."

I felt Patrick shift again behind me but ignored him. "Famous? Not so much. But I have a birth certificate and a driver's license, so what exactly is this great secret of mine that you've discovered?"

Evan scoffed. "You let everyone think you were an athlete. A man's man. A hero. And look at you." He gestured at me and laughed derisively.

I straightened my spine. I wasn't going to let him diminish me. "No, I'm not any of those things. And neither are you. But I'm the best coder at Apollo, and you know it."

His eyes narrowed at me, but then he sat up straight and spread his hands on the table. "There are people who would like to know that you're not who you say you are."

"I'm exactly who I say I am. I never did anything to hide who I was." And I hadn't. My HR records were the same; my online presence, though almost nonexistent, hadn't changed. I had literally done nothing but lean into an idea that had never been mine. "My credentials—" I began, but Evan held up a hand.

"Melvin Hammer, for instance."

I nodded. "I assume that's why you're here. He sent you to find out information about me."

"Yes, he did. He flew me out to Denver to see what dirt I could dig up on you. And I found a lot of dirt."

I put my fingers on my temples and rubbed. "You didn't need to fly out here to find out I was female, which is not *dirt*, by the way. It's a misconception that *he* made. Just check the company records. Or use Google. You're being so dramatic. I bet Melvin was every bit as dramatic when you told him."

"I haven't told him."

That stopped me. "Why not?"

"Because I have a proposition for you."

Patrick's foot caught mine under the table, and I yelped, then cleared my throat. "You have a what now?"

"I won't tell Melvin what I found out. On one condition."

"Whatever it is, the answer is probably no."

"Then I'll go to Melvin right now." He started to stand.

"I want to hear what the proposition is," Patrick whispered from the other booth.

I rolled my eyes. "Okay, what's the proposition? Just out of curiosity."

He immediately sat back down. "I'm here on behalf of Artemis."

I blinked. Whatever I'd been expecting, it wasn't that. "What do you mean?"

"You know what they're saying, right? That if this deal with S.J. Sporting goes south, our entire team will be cut."

"Yeah, I've heard that a few times," I said. "But things with Melvin and me are bad right now, and he's going to fire me."

"Probably, but not until the interface is done. Please"—he almost choked on the word—"stick around that long. We need you. We all talked it over. We all agreed that if we follow Melvin, we'll crash and burn. So we want to follow you instead. Well, they do. I'd rather walk adjacent. I'm not a follower."

What? Had I misheard? "So you're not here because you found out I'm female?"

"Technically, that's why I'm here, at least at the coffee shop. But I'm not stupid, and neither is the rest of the team. When he told us he was spending sleepless nights coming up with this great proposal, we all knew it was bullshit. So we assumed you were the one not sleeping. Were we right?"

I nodded, surprised. But then this group, or at least Evan, had known Melvin a lot longer than I had.

"We're going to let Melvin think he's getting away with it. We all need this to succeed, and the easiest way to deal with him is to keep him in the dark."

"And the Artemis team doesn't care that I'm not a rugged uber-masculine man?"

"I have no idea. I didn't tell them."

"What? Why not?"

"I thought there was the off chance you'd let me be Indiana."

There was a gasp from the booth behind me, and then it moved a little with Patrick's silent laughter.

I squeezed the bridge of my nose. I was for sure in the Upside Down. "You can't be Indiana Aaron," I said. "There is no vacancy here. *I'm* Indiana." God, he reminded me of Heidi. "He's not a separate person, despite how it seems. So no, you can't be me."

"But no one's met you in person, except me. So in order to win the S.J. account, I could show up and be manly." He averted his eyes, like he couldn't believe what he was asking but was also stoked by the possibility I might agree. "I could give the pitch. Just so we don't lose the account because you're not masculine, and obviously, it's a man's world. At least in sports."

I took a moment to digest the absurdity he was spewing. He didn't know Melvin had moved the pitch up, and that I'd moved it up again and gotten the account. The booth had stopped quivering behind me, and I wondered if Patrick and Joseph were just as confused as I was.

"So you think if I gave the pitch, they wouldn't want it?"

"Look at you," he said as he leaned back, spreading his arms across the top of the booth.

"Look at you!" I cried. I fought the urge to reach across the table and smack him. "You may be a dude, but you and I would both scream at the same decibel if the Avs started taking shots at us on the ice."

His face reddened, and he looked down at his arms, still spread across the table. "It was worth asking," he muttered.

I silently counted to ten and held my tongue as best I could. "The answer is no. How do you think the team will react when they meet me?"

"I think keeping our jobs outweighs any weirdness they might have about the fact you have boobs." I opened my mouth and then closed it again, but Evan plunged on. "We have a Zoom meeting coming up this afternoon, but all invites are going to personal email addresses. Can you give me yours?"

I wrote it on a napkin and handed it to him.

He put it in his pocket. "We're keeping the Hammer out of this. You can tell the team everything at the meeting."

He got up and swaggered to the door of the shop. Before he opened it, he turned around and gave me a kind of finger-guns salute.

Patrick turned around in the booth immediately. "'Evan and the Audacity of This Bitch!' That should be the title of today. I don't know how you didn't roundhouse kick him in the neck, Ana. You've really grown as a person."

"If I were growing that much as a person, I'd be ten feet tall by now," I grumbled as he and Joseph grabbed their drinks and settled into the bench across from me. "But the team wants to put their trust in me, which is actually really cool."

Joseph nodded. "But I still don't trust that guy."

"Are you going to go to the Zoom meeting?" Patrick asked. "It's like you hold the weight of their whole lives in your hands. Like your fish, only they're grown men."

"Yeah, I have to. They're depending on me, Patrick."

He took a sip of his fancy mocha, and then his eyes lit up. "It's just like *The Fellowship of the Ring!*"

I ignored that. "Also, Evan's wrong—I gave my presentation for the S.J. account in person and succeeded. So the less altruistic side of me thinks it'd be hilarious if I let him swagger on up to the S.J. Sporting offices and say he was Indiana Aaron. But I'm not going to let that happen," I said hastily, seeing the expression of distaste on Joseph's face.

"Now I have all morning to stress about revealing my true self to the team this afternoon," I said.

Patrick quickly made a slashing motion with his hand. "Ixnay on the 'true self' thing. They're not ready. Just show them your face. Keep the internal dialogue to yourself."

I swatted him. "It's not that snarky in here." I pointed to my head.

"Are you kidding? The amount of bitterness and sass in there would kill a lesser person."

"*Anyway,*" I said, giving him a look, "there's something I'd like to get your opinion on." I quickly filled them in on what had happened with Shane over the past couple of days.

"I don't know how to fix it. I don't even know if he still works at Apollo. I keep wondering if there's anything *I* can do to help him keep his job, but I think I'd probably just make things worse if I tried. I bet he doesn't ever want to see me again."

"Have you asked him?" Joseph asked.

"No, I haven't texted. I'm sure I'm the last person he wants to hear from."

"You might be, but there's only one way to find out."

"Don't you think I should, like, give him a day? Give him a little time to miss me?"

Patrick shrugged and put his arm around Joseph's shoulders. "I think giving it a couple of days is probably a good idea. It'll give him time to calm down and get perspective. Let him sigh and get misty-eyed every time he sees a guppy, or a picture of Harrison Ford, or seafood, or I guess, now, sharks. Or whatever it is that makes him think of you."

"You can make your own decisions, Ana," Joseph broke in, "but if he were me, and if you were Patrick, I'd want to hear from you as soon as possible. That's all."

I nodded, mulling it over. Our relationship wasn't as secure as theirs, obviously, so it was probably best to wait until I had things under control. I didn't want Shane to suffer any more because of my actions. It really hurt not to be able to help his situation. Even if I knew it was Melvin's fault and not mine, it still stung. If I came up with another (let's face it, harebrained) idea on how to handle everything, I would want Shane as far away from it as possible. I just hoped, when this was all over, he wouldn't hate me.

Chapter 15

It was almost showtime. I grabbed some reinforcements—a box of Mallomars—out of my pantry (thank goodness for the colder weather, since they weren't available in the summer; I had to stock up each year before spring) and ate a few, determined to de-stress. At noon I'd be revealing my true self to my coworkers. I watched Hopper and his descendants explore their tank and tried to lose my anxiety in their fascinating little world. The babies were growing up more and more every day. Some had purple stripes, a few were turning yellow, and about a third of them had fire-red tails. None were blue like Hopper. Who knew how many different daddies they might have had. My research indicated that they reached maturity at about two months old and could get pregnant as early as a few weeks old. Yikes.

I let the cookie's chocolate coating melt in my mouth as I watched the guppies, trying again to relax, repeating Heidi's mantra—*You got this!*—in my head, and trying not to imagine my entire apartment overrun with the trillions of descendants they might have. After a few minutes, I had to admit the relaxing thing wasn't working. Being high-strung meant I never really knew what it was like to have my muscles loosen up. My shoulders were perpetually up at my ears. I was great at trading one source of worry for another.

I turned away from the tank and reread a message that had come through earlier on my personal email, with a link to a Zoom meeting called "OPERATION DIANA." I shook my head. Diana was the Roman name for Artemis. This crew was not exactly stealthy. Twenty minutes to go.

When it was finally time, I logged in, fighting my nerves, and kept my camera off. Slowly, names and accompanying little boxes appeared on the screen. *Bruce Atkins has joined the call. Evan Smith has joined the call. Allen Parks has joined the call.* It continued until all the boxes were visible along the side of the screen. Evan flipped his camera on, his forehead looking disproportionately large. "Hey, guys. Operation Diana is in effect. I've talked with Indiana, who's on the call here. I laid out everything we agreed on, so if there's anything you'd like to say, here's your chance."

Mike Mowery also turned his camera on. I remembered him from the bar. Red hair, beard, young-looking. He'd given Evan some sass that evening. "Yo, Indy. Melvin came to us with some sort of interface design he wants us to create, but it doesn't make any sense. We can't figure out what he wants. That guy's a mess."

Bruce Atkins broke in, and his image shifted to the center of the screen. I knew his name well because he had Venmoed me money for a drink when the whole misunderstanding started. That seemed like so long ago. "It obviously wasn't his idea, and he doesn't understand it, so we figured he stole it from you and cut you out."

I sat back, still saying nothing. I hadn't given any of them nearly enough credit. They were smart, observant, and stuck in a difficult situation, just like I was.

Allen Parks cleared his throat, which moved him to center screen. "We want to make the interface *you* designed. That's the only way we can stay employed. The pitch is next week. We can keep Melvin off your back so you can present your real idea to S.J. Sporting. If he presents it, we're toast. We can keep him occupied while we get it made." He blew out a breath, and I realized I wasn't the only one who was nervous. "What do you say?"

They didn't know I'd won the pitch already. My fingers hovered over the keyboard. The moment of truth. I typed a message into the chat window. I'm on board. But first, there's something you should know. I took a deep, fortifying breath, then flipped my camera on.

My face became the center screen for the first time, well, ever, with the Artemis team. I could see myself in the upper corner, looking impossibly young, with curls everywhere and freckles and eyes too large for my face. Across the bottom of my image was my name: Indiana Aaron.

I cleared my throat. "Hi, everyone," I said.

There was silence. Finally, Mike broke it. "Can you go get your dad?"

"Wait a second," Bruce said. "I recognize you. We saw you at the bar when we all came to Denver, didn't we? Oh! And we saw you hiding *behind* the bar when Melvin played Waffle Wars. You're Indiana? You were Indiana then, too, weren't you?"

"I'm Indiana Aaron. I always have been," I said, with as much authority as I could muster. "But you can call me 'Ana.'"

Again, another long pause. Then what sounded like a disappointed sigh from Allen. "For real?"

"Yes, for real," I said.

"I kind of had a crush on Indiana," Allen said. "He sounded so cool."

"You and the rest of the world. I'm not a pilot, or a lion tamer, or a race car driver. None of which have anything to do with my job. I'm a coder, and I let Melvin and the rest of you believe what you wanted. Is this going to be a problem?"

They all shook their heads politely.

"Absolutely not," Bruce said. "Frankly, I'm far less intimidated than I was before. Not because you're a girl," he added hastily, "but because Indiana was, like, *too* perfect. Even a little bit scary."

"*Yes*," Mike added emphatically. "Nobody's that cool. It was unnerving. Not that you're not cool," he said to me, looking embarrassed. "I just mean—"

"It's okay," I told them. "I understand what you meant. And I feel the same way. Indiana is a lot to live up to. But I'm Ana, and I put together the interface idea for S.J. Sporting. And you were right; Melvin tried to steal my idea and cut me out."

"I knew it!" Bruce yelled, pointing at me. "I called it. Everyone owes me a beer."

"But I was able to meet with S.J. before Melvin could, and I secured the account for Artemis."

"Yesssssss," Evan cried and sprang out of his seat. "You didn't tell me that! That makes things so much easier!"

"Wooooooo!" Allen whooped. "You rock, Ana!"

A lump welled in my throat, and I swallowed hard. *This* was what I'd been missing and craving. Comradery, support, being part of a team in more than name only.

"What about the pottery?" Allen asked tentatively. "Someone keeps outbidding me on one of Indiana's pieces about his time in a war. Is that real?"

I blinked at him. "I made the pottery, Allen. But it doesn't reflect my time in a war. I wasn't in a war. And neither was Indiana—" I stopped. What was the point in policing a fictional narrative? It was weird how people, as accepting as the team might be of me personally, refused to completely let go of the idea of Indiana, even, apparently, me. And someone was outbidding him? What was wrong with people?

"So what comes next?" Mike asked.

"Well, obviously Melvin is going to fire me," I said. "I think he'll wait until after the project is complete because he needs me, but he's frozen me out, so I'm not totally sure. I debated just peacing out—"

"No!" Mike exclaimed. "Please don't. We can't make this without you. And I need this job. Violet and I are trying IVF, and it's so freaking expensive, and I can't afford to lose this job."

"I can't either," Allen added. "I just hired an at-home hospice nurse for my mom. She really doesn't want to go to a home."

"That's super sad," Bruce threw in. "I want to keep my job because I want a sweet car."

Boy, they knew how to tug at the heartstrings. Except Bruce. "I'm going to stay on and see this project through," I told them. "I need this on my résumé, and I would hate to leave you all in that situation. The only potential issue is Melvin."

"He sent me to Denver to find out what I could about the famous Indiana Aaron," Evan said. "And I found her." He laughed.

"And Melvin doesn't know Indiana's really his own daughter?" Bruce asked.

Like, what?

Evan grinned. "Nope."

They all laughed this time, and even I joined in because it wasn't malicious; it was joy in having secret information that Melvin didn't share.

"How about you explain exactly how this interface is supposed to work, and we can start creating it. You said there's a contract in place?" Allen asked. "Maybe we should get Mr. Radio Voice to help then. He would know the numbers better than we do."

I immediately knew who he meant. There was only one guy who had a smooth, low voice worthy of podcasting in our group. "You mean Shane Dalton," I said.

"That's him," Allen said. "He does all our accounting. And wait, weren't you two, like, together or something? You looked pretty close when we were at those work events."

I took another moment to appreciate how much they'd been paying attention. "Shane's been removed from the project. Because of Melvin. Maybe even from Apollo IT altogether. I don't know."

"You don't know? Isn't he your boyfriend?" Mike.

"It's complicated." I looked down. I hadn't really imagined having this conversation with coworkers.

"Awww, Indy—I mean Ana—you can't let Melvin ruin your life. If you two are meant to be, don't let anything stand in your way. If I had let outside circumstances—" Mike started.

Bruce interrupted quickly. "Don't let him start. He'll tell you his whole life story and how he met Violet, and then he'll cry, and we'll be here all day."

Mike didn't even bother to look offended. "I hope you find love someday, Bruce. That's my greatest wish for you."

"I hate to cut into this," I said, and all attention turned back to me. "We have one month to construct and deliver. A lot of it is already complete, but I would love the help." I'd never imagined having the rest of the team work with me on this. It had seemed too risky to include them when I was in that constant balancing act.

"Great," Evan said. "Leave Melvin to me. I'll keep him off your back, and we'll just pretend to report to him."

"That works for now," I said, "but again, I'll be damned if I'm letting Melvin take credit for my idea or for all our hard work."

"Fuck no," Bruce yelled. "We're taking that drunk monkey down."

I blinked. They continued to surprise me.

Evan started talking, which moved Bruce's face back down to the line of boxes along the bottom of the screen. "You know the annual company event in Vegas each year? The higher-ups were talking today, and since this account will be such a big win for Apollo, there's going to be a launch party at the event once the interface is complete. Melvin made himself keynote speaker, but all of us on Artemis agreed it should be you. But don't worry about that. We're on it."

That thought filled me both with warmth and a little bit of fear. I really had no idea what these guys were capable of.

"Um. Okay. I'm going to send over the proposal that was presented to S.J. Sporting and the notes I have to go along with it. I'll also show you what's been completed thus far. We can meet again tomorrow morning to go over who will do what. Are you in?" Leading a team was all about finding the best person for each part of the project.

"Ana to the rescue!" Allen said and grinned. "I think I need to reword my original message: All hail the queen!"

"I'm fine with *king*," I said. "All right, let's log off, and I'll get some info to you all right away."

"Hey, Indy," Mike said before I could switch my camera off. "Talk to Shane. True love is worth the heartache."

I narrowed my eyes at him. "How do you know it's true love?"

"I…don't? But what if it is!" he exclaimed.

Evan cut Mike off and said, "Keep an eye on your email, guys." Then he shut down the meeting, and my screen went black. I sat back in my chair and turned in my chair to tell Hopper what had happened. Which was pathetic because Hopper could hear the whole thing, and he didn't give a shit. But Shane would have. Blowing out a breath, I went to sit on the couch and took my phone out of my pocket.

Hey, I texted.

A few minutes later, Shane texted back. Hey.

I really am sorry.

It's fine. I'm on probation with Apollo, but I still have a job. Hope you're well.

I squeezed my eyes tight and screwed up my courage, then typed the words I might regret. I miss you. I threw the phone on the cushion and pulled a blanket up over my head. When the phone buzzed, it was a few seconds before I could look.

Yeah. Miss you too.

Well, that was something? I guess? It wasn't the declaration I'd been looking for, but it wasn't *You jerk, you almost got me fired*, so at least it could be worse.

———

After I'd sent all the materials over to "Operation Diana" (so stupid), I got a message on my group chat with Patrick and Heidi. Patrick was dying to come over, so I told him they were both welcome whenever. It was just under twenty minutes before there was pounding on the door.

When I opened it, not only were Heidi and Patrick there, but so were Jason and Joseph. Everyone crowded into my apartment, all talking loudly.

"And now she has these little helpers," Patrick was saying.

"Not the way I expected this whole thing to go, if we're being honest," Jason replied.

"Me neither!" Heidi exclaimed. "And c'mere, Jason, you have to see all of Ana's little babies." She led him over to the tank, while he gave me a big grin over her shoulder. Hopper greeted them enthusiastically as I turned to Patrick and Joseph. "Looks like we're having a party. Or something."

Patrick nodded happily. "I'll order the takeout. We all want a rundown of how things went." Patrick put in a huge order, while Jason and Joseph pretended to share Heidi's enthusiasm for the baby fish.

When the order arrived (dim sum and dumplings), everyone grabbed floor pillows and sat around the coffee table. Then I filled them in on my coffee meeting with Evan. It took longer than it needed to, punctuated here and there by Patrick adding comments like, "And then he said he wanted to be Indiana, and she said, 'Shut your damn mouth, son!'" which I had to correct. Afterward, I told them about Operation Diana and how my team had come through for me in a touching and unexpected way.

Jason shook his head. "Melvin's always been a bit of a dick, but I didn't expect him to take things that far. Though, technically, all the work you do at Apollo belongs to Apollo."

"That's true," I allowed. "It belongs to Apollo IT but not to Melvin. I need this for future employment. What he's done is unethical, dishonest, opportunistic—"

"I agree," Jason said. "And who knows how many times he's gotten away with this in the past."

"And it's not even all that uncommon," Joseph threw in. Then he looked self-conscious. "I'm assuming. I know I'm only a personal trainer, but taking the ideas of your employees and presenting them as your own seems to be common."

Patrick touched his shoulder gently. "You're not 'only' a personal trainer. You're gainfully employed with a difficult and rewarding job that really helps people." Joseph gave him a sweet smile that made my heart feel like it would burst. "And it may be common, but I think Ana and her fellowship are taking a good first step to stopping it."

"*Dude*," I said. "We're not a fellowship, and we're not destroying some guy's ring."

"But you're embarking on a journey together to preserve your way of life?" he asked.

"I guess you could put it that way, but it's a little dramatic."

"Do you call the interface 'my precious'?" Jason asked.

I turned to him. "*Et tu, Brute?*"

He grinned. "Are you the last hope for Middle Earth?"

Patrick looked back and forth between us, clearly ecstatic.

"I'm going to throat punch all of you," I muttered.

Jason snickered at me, then cleared his throat. "So, I'm assuming you've heard about the change in plans for the annual event in Las Vegas?"

"Evan mentioned something about it, but I don't know a lot of details,"

I said. "Melvin made himself keynote speaker and made the deal with S.J. Sporting the highlight?" The yearly company meeting in Vegas had always struck me as completely useless. I'd never gone before, so this would be my first, and likely last, opportunity.

"All of Apollo IT employees are invited. The S.J. Sporting interface will be the main draw and the keynote event, but there will be other tech advancement presentations, too."

"Great. Well, I guess that's the night I quit then," I said.

"No!" Heidi cried. "I still don't like that."

"Melvin's going to fire me either way. I was insubordinate, I went behind his back, and I'm not going to take on extra responsibility without the title or the salary that goes with it. So I'm going to make the best interface the world has ever seen, with the help of *The Fellowship of the Ring*. Then I'm gonna get a better job somewhere else."

"I wanna be Stryder," Patrick muttered under his breath at me.

"You can't be; you're not on the team," I told him.

"Melvin's kinda like Golem, trying to steal your stuff," Jason interjected, and I stared at him again.

"I really didn't expect this of you."

He grinned at me. "Teasing you has always been fun. I'm just glad you're starting to realize it's teasing."

"I used to think you were kind of a jerk," I admitted.

"But now you realize I'm hilarious instead."

I inclined my head as Heidi looked at him, doe-eyed. "Maybe I was shortsighted," I told him.

Patrick suddenly gasped. "You're Frodo," he said, turning to me.

"What?" I yelped. "Am not."

"Well, you're sure as hell not Gandolf. Frodo is kind of the leader of the little guys, and you're so—"

"You better not be about to compare my size to a hobbit. My parents had me tested."

"Frodo is an adorable nickname for you," Joseph said kindly, smiling at me. "Plus, you're the last hope. It fits."

I slumped my forehead onto the coffee table. "I hate you all," I mumbled.

"We would all hate to see you leave Apollo, Frodo," Patrick said. "But I get why you feel this way. Plus, someone as tart as you probably only has about two years at any given job before you burn all your bridges anyway."

I sighed. "Once again, you speak truth I don't wish to hear, Patrick. Did you watch reruns of *90210* growing up?" I asked the group. Joseph and Heidi nodded enthusiastically, while Patrick looked at me with distaste.

"What's that?" Jason asked.

"Just when I started to think you were cool." I sighed. "An iconic '90s TV show. Anyway, when Dylan was on drugs, Brandon told him he was going to burn all his bridges. Dylan said, 'May the bridges I burn light the way.'"

"Ooooh, I remember that one!" Joseph said. "I really wanted those two to get together."

"Yeah, well, that's kind of been my life's motto ever since," I confessed.

Patrick dropped his head in his hands. "That's literally the worst life motto I've ever heard. How're you even serious right now?"

I sat up straight, defensive. "I'll have you know that I have an actual, physical plastic trophy acknowledging my ability to say what everyone else is thinking. There are worse role models than Luke Perry."

"RIP," Joseph whispered and crossed himself.

Patrick groaned. "Yeah, but your role model is *not* Luke Perry—it's Dylan McKay, a drugged-out high schooler who was practically in his forties even as a teenager and couldn't even decide between Kelly and Brenda."

Unexpected joy bubbled up in my chest. "You watched it. You were a fan."

Patrick's cheeks turned a shade I'd never seen them before. "Did not. I read *The Lord of the Rings* and other great literature. I didn't watch crappy teen shows."

"He knows about the love triangle," Heidi said happily. "He's definitely a fan. We should all meet back here this weekend for a marathon!" She turned to Jason. "You're in for such a treat. You're going to love it."

"Nope," I said. No way was I getting roped into hosting a ten-season marathon of *Beverly Hills, 90210*, of all things. "The Fellowship and I have work to do."

Chapter 16

As the new project manager, I wanted to play to the strength of my team. I went back through all the old spreadsheets Artemis had kept since the beginning to see where everyone's talents lay. When I had a good understanding of which part of the S.J. Sporting project I should give to which person, I sent out detailed instructions and set up a new meeting time.

A few hours later, I got a video chat request from Mike. I froze for a moment, then reminded myself that my secret was out, at least with Diana. I clicked *accept*, and Mike's red beard filled my screen.

"Anal Yo," he said. "I got your email, and I got an idea I wanna run past you, cool?"

"Sure," I said. "What've you got?"

"So you have me doing this web piece, right? Nice choice, by the way, because I kick ass at this stuff."

I grinned. "I know you do. That's why I chose you for it."

He grinned. "Well, you know the product landing page? We should have a chatbot feature that incorporates the user's location and connects to the wireless app interface. Wouldn't that be cool?" His face disappeared as he shared his screen with me. "This is what you sent me for instructions...." He showed me a page and took me through the steps. "But if we change the programming just a bit, it'd look like this." He flipped the screen to a new image. "Then users can navigate *this* way."

I watched his screen, paying close attention.

"Um, Ana?" he asked. He sounded nervous. "You're being quiet. Do you hate it?"

I startled out of my reverie. "Not at all, Mike. I think this is amazing. We should go with your idea. It'll improve the product. Well done."

His face came back on-screen, and his smile was wide. "Really? Okay! Cool! Awesome. Okay. I'm going to get to work on completing it right now!"

I laughed at his enthusiasm. "Thanks for bringing this to me. We're going to be a great team."

"Yeah, we are!" he exclaimed. "Peace out, Ana. Bye!"

Was this what it was like in the boys' club, minus the fabled, stereotypical locker room talk? Because it was pretty great. I could get used to being in a boys' club like this.

Because of the exchange with Mike, I made a point to send a message to each team member individually, reminding them that if they had any ideas to run past me, or any additions to make, I would love to hear them. It didn't take long before the others took me up on it, too.

Turned out we had a really smart group. Allen, Bruce, even Evan, wrote back with minor tweaks here and there that improved the product. Even though I knew this whole situation meant leaving Apollo IT, I couldn't help but be incredibly proud of them. And sorry that we wouldn't have the opportunity to work together again in the future. C'est la vie. There was no point in being sad about it. If I found this camaraderie once, I could find it again. I pushed away the thought that it had taken so long, and so many lies, and finally a common enemy to find it in the first place. It would be okay, I told myself again. If there was anything I was good at, it was finding an enemy.

————————

Later that afternoon, I met Sara Jean for coffee. She picked a swanky little upscale place I'd never been to before, and my cold brew was served in a little porcelain cup. "I feel so fancy," I murmured as I took a tiny sip.

"Cheers." She held up her own tiny cup. "I can't wait to see what you have for me."

I opened my laptop. "I hope you like it as much as we do. I have an amazing team, and we've put our heart and soul into this." I had a gorgeous portfolio to show her, courtesy of Allen. I took her through all we'd done so far and showed her what we had yet to implement.

"It's perfect," she said, and I could see her getting excited. "I can't wait to show the board, and the Avs are going to be thrilled."

"Everyone will be so happy to hear that. We have a few more tweaks and testing to do before it's debuted at the Apollo IT company retreat in Las Vegas. Provided you don't have any changes, it's set to go live that same week."

"Great. We've been working on how we're going to advertise, so that dovetails nicely." Then she leaned forward in her chair. "So how are things going with your little situation?"

"It's interesting. Turns out I underestimated my team. I assumed that, since Melvin treated me, and you for that matter, like we weren't important, they would have the same reaction. But they didn't. At all."

"You told them who you really are?"

"I did, and they didn't even blink. They want to make the best product for you, and they don't seem to care at all what I look like, so long as I can help them do it."

She smiled at me knowingly. "And that's why I do my little test. When you find people eager to look past appearances, you're more likely to get the respect you deserve and cultivate a good working relationship."

"I'm very lucky to have had this opportunity to work with them and with you. When the project is over, though, I'm going to part ways with Apollo IT."

"I take it you haven't worked things out with Mr. Hammer?"

"No. And I don't intend to. Even if he didn't take advantage of his employees, there's no room on his team for an unapologetic feminist."

"I'm sorry to hear that, but believe me, I understand," she said, taking another sip. "I've had lunch with the CEO of Apollo since we struck a deal, so if you'd like me to say anything on your behalf—"

"Thank you but no," I said, then regretted cutting her off. But oh my god, no. I needed to fight my own battles. She'd already given me an incredible gift by trusting me with her company, but I could speak for myself. "If there's anything he needs to know, I'll make sure to tell him. Has Melvin emailed you at all?"

She shook her head. "He stopped by the practice arena a couple of times, but like before, he never came by to say hello."

I rolled my eyes even as she laughed.

"This may sound condescending, and I don't mean it to be, but I'm proud of you, Ana."

I looked at her, feeling the lump in my throat again. "Thank you, Sara. That means a lot."

"You should be proud of yourself, too, you know."

"I am. And even if Apollo isn't my home going forward, I'm thankful that we got to meet."

"As am I," she said warmly. "And maybe, at the end of the day, don't let Melvin steal all the praise."

"I've wrestled with that. But as long as I have you and my team as a reference, I'll find another job. And Melvin can say whatever he likes."

She smirked at me around the rim of her cup. "That's very mature of you. But *maturity* isn't always the most fun."

"Don't tempt me," I warned. "I'm working on creating a new life motto." *One that doesn't reference a soulful drug addict from a '90s television show.*

———————

Nancy sat on my living room couch, squinting at the aquarium. "You want me to do what?" she asked.

I was already starting to wonder if I'd made a bad choice in seeking her out. "I want you to feed my fish while I'm gone. It'll only be a few days. I wish I didn't have to go on this work trip at all," I grumbled. Vegas might sound like fun, but it represented the end of so many things, instead of hanging out with Elvis impersonators and gambling.

"Okay. Feed the fish. What if they die?"

I looked at her in horror. "I really hope they don't!"

"Well, I hope not, too, sweetie, but I have bad luck, and, you know, they're fish. That's what they do."

"I really don't like that line of thinking," I muttered as I directed her attention back to the list I'd written out. "Keep the lid on. They like to jump. They eat one pinch of flakes a day."

"Surely they need more than that, honey. Nobody can live on a pinch a day."

"One pinch! Their stomachs are the size of their eyeballs and look how tiny they are." I squinted against the glass and gestured for Nancy to do the same. "See? If you feed them too much, they get constipated, and then you have to give them shelled peas to clean them out, which can upset the water parameters—"

"How about I just give them peas instead of flakes? Cut out the in-between. Do they like zucchini, too? George makes a great casserole. It's got some peas in it, too, I think."

My head was starting to hurt. I picked up the list and held it in front of her face. "Stick to the list. Please. Their light is on a timer, so don't worry about turning it on or off. And, I know how this sounds"—I closed my eyes—"but please don't watch them poop. They get embarrassed, which can also lead to constipation. They're basically just swimming around waiting for their digestive tracks to freeze."

"Got it. No eye contact during pooping." She nodded resolutely, then looked unsure. "What if they make eye contact with me first?"

"Look away!" I said, exasperated. "Treat them like they're people. Nobody likes to stare into someone's eyes while they relieve themselves."

"If they're people, they need to address the suicidal ideation that leads to jumping."

God, she was right. "I can't currently help them with that, since we have a language barrier, but I can look into it when I'm back from my trip." At this point I wasn't sure who was the weird one, me or Nancy. Still probably Nancy? "They like to be sung to, but you don't need to worry about that; I'll leave the radio on," I said.

"Honey, I don't think these little ones have ears."

Hm. I'd have to google that later, too. "Maybe not, but they can feel the vibrations, and they like it." I swore Hopper and his babies really did like my concerts. I was confident of that.

"Okay, I'll make sure they get their lullabies," Nancy said. "I'll follow the list. But make sure you leave it here, or I'll forget." She inspired so much confidence. Then she turned to me, a serious look on her face, and patted the spot next to her on the sofa. Uh-oh. I sat down. "George and I just want to make sure you're okay. You haven't seemed as happy as we'd like to see you."

"Yeah," I said softly. "I'm okay. Sorry to worry you."

She rubbed my back, and tears pricked my eyes. I was lucky to have a landlord who wanted to be like a mom to me. Even if she was likely to dump George's famous casserole into my tank while dead-ass staring them in the eyes as they tried to relax enough to poop. "Thanks, Nancy. Now, I'm only going to be gone for three days, but make sure to call me if you have any questions or you're worried about anything. I'm sure it'll all go fine."

She nodded. "They probably won't all die. There's about a hundred in there, right? I'm sure most of them will still be there when you get home," she said, patting my hand.

Great. "Thanks again. I should go say goodbye to my dad."

When I got to Aspen Skies, Dad and Margaret were in the garden, as usual, though the temperature was dropping. She'd wrapped a blanket around his legs, and they were sitting very close, sipping hot chocolate.

"Hey!" I called as I made my way over. I tightened my scarf against the chill. "I just wanted to come by and give you a hug before my work trip," I said.

"Where are you going?" Margaret asked, smiling at me.

"Las Vegas. It's a required thing, and I'm probably going to have to find a new job after this anyway."

My dad leaned over to give me a hug. "Why? You okay, honey?"

"Yeah, I'm fine. Remember how I told you about the boys' club? I just think it's probably best for me to move on."

"Do you want to talk about it?"

I shook my head. "I really just wanted to catch you before the trip to say goodbye. I'll be back in a couple of days, though. Nancy is watching your great-grandfish."

"I expect to hear all about that."

I laughed. "I'm sure you will. I just hope it isn't too much responsibility for her."

"Well, they're just—"

"If you say, 'They're just fish,' I'm going to smack you," I warned.

He held up his hands, laughing. "Okay," he relented. "Tell me about your trip. Where in Vegas are you staying?"

I gave him the details, explained the convention, and told him where I'd be staying.

"Have you ever been to Vegas, Mags?" Dad asked her.

"Nope," she said. "Sounds like a pretty interesting place, though."

They stared into each other's eyes, and I started to feel like I was interrupting something.

"Um, I was just stopping by before I leave, but I'm going to take the hint now, and I'll come by when I get back, okay?" I told them.

Dad looked up at me. "No, it's okay, stay."

I snorted at him. "Y'all are having a moment, and I don't want to intrude."

"Really," Margaret said warmly, "we most certainly are not."

Dad winked at her, then turned to me. "How's that young man you brought by a while back?"

"Um, I assume he's fine?" I said, keeping my tone light. I wasn't in the mood to talk about it.

"I'm sorry I missed meeting him," Margaret added. "Your dad told me all about him."

"He said he was taking you to the aquarium! I told him that was the way to your heart, for sure. So did it work? Did he worm his way in there?" Dad asked.

"To the aquarium? Yes. He wormed his way right in through the door."

"You know what I meant, Indi—"

I quickly stood and put my hands up. "I know, but I'm not up to talking about that right now. Sorry. You two have fun. I'll see you later." I leaned down and kissed Dad on the top of his head. "Love you."

"Love you, too," he said. "Didn't mean to offend."

"It's okay." I leaned over and gave Margaret a hug, too. "I'll call when I'm back."

"Does what happens in Vegas really stay in Vegas?" Dad asked suddenly.

"No," I answered. "Liminal spaces aren't really a thing."

"Excellent," he answered happily.

Weird.

Chapter 17

I GOT TO THE DENVER INTERNATIONAL AIRPORT EARLY THE NEXT
morning to meet Heidi and Patrick. Out of all the airports I'd been to,
none of them were quite as unique as DIA. It was a point of pride for
a lot of us native to Denver, but there was no denying the place was
unapologetically weird. When I found them, Heidi was wearing Mardi
Gras beads and sunglasses, even at the airport, but Patrick was in his usual
perfect suit and tie.

"Why are you dressed like that?" I asked Heidi.

"Because vacay!" She beamed.

"But it's Vegas, not New Orle—wait, aren't you not allowed to go back
to New Orleans?"

"I'm *allowed*. In fact, I think they would prefer it because of the warrant
out for my arrest." She sniffed.

Patrick's head swiveled in an almost complete circle. "Come again?"

Heidi turned away and mumbled, "I can go back. I just might not be
able to *come* back afterward."

"Does this have something to do with how you got those beads?" I asked.

"These?" She held up the glittering plastic strands around her neck. "I got these at CVS. So, no, smarty-pants, it doesn't."

"When are you going to tell us what happened there?" I complained as we made our way to the check-in.

"It's not a big deal," she said breezily. "I'm wearing beads to be festive, and maybe I dressed this way to hide from the gargoyles. This airport is so freaking creepy, literally all the 'artwork' is staring at me."

"Hurry up, let's go," Patrick said out of the corner of his mouth as I put my luggage on the conveyer belt at the security check.

"What's your problem?" I asked. I'd only had one cup of coffee so far, and airports always required at least two before I felt awake enough to deal with them, especially DIA. "You're not scared of the airport, too, are you?"

Heidi pulled down her glasses and rolled her eyes. "He thinks there are monsters that live in the tunnels," she said, then pushed the glasses back up on her nose.

"Shut up," he hissed.

"I need way more caffeine before we talk about monsters or pervy gargoyles," I said. "It's just an airport."

"It can't be just an airport with that atrocity outside," he said, vaguely gesturing toward the entrance.

"Surely you don't think Blucifer and the tunnels are connected?" I asked. I saw a Starbucks just past the gate and felt my mouth water. I had to admit, though, Patrick was right about the massive, unnecessarily blue statue of a mustang that Denverites had nicknamed Blucifer. Back in 2008, for unknown reasons, the airport had installed the sculpture outside the entrance to welcome travelers. Or to scare off children. He was creepy as all get-out, not to mention anatomically correct. Since he was over thirty feet tall, you really got an eyeful if you found yourself standing near the hooves. The worst part were the eyes. They were red and glowing, and you could even see them from the highway.

"Well, that horse killed his creator, so tell me what *you* think," Patrick said, his gaze shifty.

"That's just a rumor," Heidi groaned. "That horse didn't kill his maker."

"I hate to burst your bubble, Heidi, but that one's actually true. I fact-checked it. When the creator was sculpting the horse, it fell on him and severed an artery. Killed him. So everybody just put it back together, installed those dead eyes, and put it on display. As you do."

"Ewwww," she squealed.

"See?" Patrick said as we passed through security and got our bags. "Now tell me there's nothing to be scared of."

I sighed. "Let's get some coffee and then get on the plane so we'll get home faster."

"C'mon," Heidi said as she followed me to the coffee counter, "it's going to be fun! It's Vegas! Jason will be there! There's supposed to be a for-real open bar this time! And Cirque du Soleil! And who knows what else!"

"Yaaaaay," I said weakly. All that sounded expensive. I appreciated her enthusiasm, though. Mandatory work trips tended to suck, but Vegas wasn't as bad a location as some others I'd had to attend. One time, I'd worked at an office that insisted on having yearly meetings at a water park. Embarrassing and weird and not at all conducive to actual working. But then, neither was Vegas.

Patrick let out a big breath when we finally boarded the plane.

"Happy to be out of the airport?" I asked.

"If monsters are really living in those underground bunkers, then I think we're safer in the air," he said, his mouth tight.

"You can't really believe that stuff," I argued. "Bilbo would be disappointed. The real enemies are the orcs, remember?"

Despite himself, Patrick's eyes lit up, and he launched into a long explanation of the differences between orcs and other Tolkien creatures. Happy to have relaxed him a little, I promptly tuned him out. The two-hour flight was uneventful, and I tried to stay positive. Heidi and Patrick chattered around me for most of the flight, but I didn't catch much of it. I was excited to see my team in person and actually be able to hang out with them this time, but was also bummed that everything was coming to an end. And Shane was going to be there, which had my nerves all tied up. Too many unknowns to relax.

I jammed a travel pillow behind my head and reclined my seat. Patrick was patiently telling Heidi that gargoyles had no place in Middle Earth, and their conversation was almost comforting in its absurdity. Between them and the drone of the engine, my eyelids got heavy, and I managed to doze off.

I must have fallen into a dream. Hopper had come to me for help. He appeared to have grown a pair of legs and was tottering around like a T. Rex. He was hard to understand, but he seemed to be telling me that Nancy had sent him on a mission through Middle Earth to find Bilbo, so he'd had no choice but to grow legs and engage in combat along the way.

"Bilbo is fine," I kept telling him, but only bubbles came out when he tried to respond. "You don't have to go to Middle Earth just because Nancy is worried about Bilbo. Has she tried to give you casserole?"

I couldn't make out his response as he pivoted in a circle and almost lost his balance, his blue tail fin brushing his new knees. I tried to help him stay on his feet. "You look a little gross like this, Hopper. I don't like this journey for you—"

Something nudged me, and I woke up sweaty and breathing hard.

"You okay?" Patrick asked. "We're about to land."

"Um, yeah. Just a bad dream."

"Want to talk about it?"

"No, because I don't want you to think I'm weird."

"Ana, I admitted my fear of the airport to you."

"True," I said. But a fish on two back legs like a T. Rex was still too much. "Still, no."

"Okay," he said. "Let's find the hotel, then find the hotel bar!" He pulled his carry-on and mine down from the storage compartment. "Helloooo, Vegas!"

———

After we landed and finally made it out of the airport, we hailed a cab. Heidi slid in next to me. "So, you know how I handled most of the plans for this convention?" she began, then stopped. She'd ditched the glasses but kept the beads, and they glittered in the evening light.

"What is it?" I asked.

"Well, pretty much all of Apollo IT is going to be staying at the Mirage. That means Jason, Melvin, your hobbit friends, and...Shane."

I nodded, squashed between her and Patrick while he instructed the driver on where to take us. "It's sort of like we're on a high school trip, but we're all too old to be doing this."

"Sort of," she said, "except we're totally not." She paused, then rushed on. "Nobody's supposed to share rooms, but I went ahead and put you and me together. And…I might have put Shane's room right next to ours. How does that make you feel?"

My stomach dropped as the cab lurched forward. "I feel fine. Totally normal."

She put a hand on my arm, even though our legs and shoulders were smushed together. "Ana, you can confide in me."

"Well, ditto," I snapped. "You could have told me sooner." The anticipation and anxiety of possibly seeing Shane every time I opened my hotel room door was starting to override all my other emotions.

"I also put Patrick on the other side of him," she mumbled.

"Oh, cool!" Patrick said, his voice higher than normal. "That's a nice surprise, Heidi. Shane is a nice young man."

I narrowed my eyes. "You two planned this."

"What?" Patrick asked innocently. "I plan nothing. I live by the seat of my pants."

"I don't think that's how the saying goes," I said accusatorily.

Heidi blew out a breath, her curtain bangs fluttering around her temples. "I was going to give you a spiel about how there were no rooms left and I didn't have a choice, but that would be a total lie. I booked our rooms first. Maybe that should earn me some points for honesty?" she asked hopefully.

Patrick also leaned in closer, making me suddenly claustrophobic. "How're you feeling about the whole thing with him?"

I blew out a breath. "We've texted a bit, and honestly, it's not like anything happened between us that's all that horrible, except maybe me putting his job in danger. We just haven't known each other long enough to push through this, you know?"

"It'll be fine," Heidi said. "We'll make sure you're looking killer this whole trip. Leave that part to me."

If I were being honest, I could use the help, but I wasn't sure "looking killer" would be enough in this case.

I didn't say anything for the rest of the trip to the hotel. Which was fine since Heidi was practically hanging out the window and squealing at all the lights and architecture and fountains. "This place is so cool!" she yelled. "Everything is neon!"

I turned to Patrick. "What do you think? Would Bilbo like it here?"

He paused, like he was taking my question seriously. "Probably not. Hobbits are humble creatures. But the dwarves would love it. They really like ostentatious displays of wealth."

I bit back a smile. "One day I'm going to have to read that series, aren't I?"

"It's not a *series*, Ana, or even a trilogy. It's one novel consisting of six books—"

"Books? I thought it was just a movie," Heidi said, then squealed as the cab lurched to a stop in front of the hotel. Patrick was red-faced yet had no choice but to let it go for now.

The air was warmer than I'd been used to in Denver but just as dry. We grabbed our bags from the trunk and entered the lobby.

The tropical smell of piña colada hit me, and I breathed in deep. There was a gorgeous atrium full of trees, and when we came around the corner, I almost dropped my bag. "It's beautiful," I whispered. Behind the check-in counter at the hotel was a massive saltwater aquarium. It seemed big enough for all of Apollo IT to swim in.

Heidi grinned. "I knew you would like it. I booked us here to apologize for killing you at brunch. And for playing matchmaker without asking."

Heidi checked us in while I trailed behind and gaped.

"You like the tank?" the man behind the counter asked me.

I nodded, staring at all the fish and coral.

"It's over twenty thousand gallons," he said. "We have at least eighty species in there."

I turned to Heidi as she handed me my key card. "Are there more?"

"Aquariums? Yes." She grinned. "There's one at the restaurant, and there's a pool built right next to a shark tank so you can feel like you're swimming with them, and there's even one tank with a slide that goes through it."

"You're forgiven," I said and threw an arm around her neck.

She laughed. "Whew. I figured since this is our first and last work trip together, we could combine our loves. I love sun and pools the way you do aquariums. Win-win."

Patrick also checked in while I was busy being distracted by the trees, the smells, and all the artificial beauty. Then we got on the elevator to find our floor. Even though the whole area felt fake, so to speak, it was still amazing. A weird sort of Disneyland for adults.

Our room was nice but in no way extravagant. Two queen-size beds, a bathroom, a TV, and a tiny desk in the corner. It was much simpler than what we'd seen of the hotel so far. The awe of our location had started to fade a bit, and I found myself getting pissed off again. The room had still cost a hell of a lot. And yeah, flights to Vegas tended to be cheap, but to put a whole company up at a luxury hotel and rent conference rooms for a self-indulgent convention? All this while telling employees that there wasn't enough money in the budget for promotions or bonuses or raises. I was pretty sure the money they'd spent just on the buffet for the next evening would have been life-changing for me.

Heidi immediately jumped on a bed, then looked at me. "What?"

"Nothing. I'm just in this mess because the company only had enough money to pay Taggert. Remember? Or so they said. And as gorgeous as this place is, wouldn't you rather they just gave each of us the couple of thousand dollars they're spending to keep each of us here for the next few days?"

"No!" Heidi said, bouncing on the mattress. "Sleepover. Girls' night. They can keep their money. We're in Vegas! When will we get another opportunity to do this?"

I felt a grin tugging at my lips. It was hard not to fall for her enthusiasm. Besides, I wasn't going to change Apollo's business practices, and it was getting closer and closer to time for me to move on anyway.

"Okay," I relented. "What's on tap for the evening?"

She grabbed her phone and pulled up a schedule. "Looks like there's a company drinks event at eight tonight, and then we're free until an informal brunch tomorrow morning. So maybe we can explore!"

Hm. I wasn't stoked about the drinks thing, but I really wanted to see my team.

"But first—let me do your hair."

I grabbed a fistful of curls. "Is something wrong with it?" My hair was hard to tame, but it was one of my favorite things about my appearance.

"No," she said unconvincingly. "I'm just known for improving on perfection. And you know, there was that nap you took on the plane."

I let Heidi work her magic, which ended up including some liner, a subtle eyeshadow, and a dark red lip. "Brings out the red in your hair, and it's perfect for fall," she murmured as she worked.

When she finally pronounced me done, we entered the hallway. Heidi was fiddling with her key card when I heard someone clear their throat behind me. I felt like I'd been doused in ice water. Only one person could make a grunt sound good.

Shane. Handsome in a suit jacket and jeans, tousled hair, and black-framed glasses. I'd almost forgotten how attractive he was. Because of me, he hadn't had a reason to come to Denver, and it's hard to casually run into someone when you don't live in the same city.

"Hi," I said, trying to keep my voice calm. "How are you?"

He smiled, and I felt a little of my nervousness ease. "Good, thanks. It's nice to see you, Ana. You look stunning."

A blush rose onto my cheeks and I tried to redirect the blood flow. I was suddenly very glad I'd let Heidi fix me up. "Thank you?"

Behind me, I heard her slowly shuffling off down the hall. I whipped around. "Where are you going?"

She froze like a deer in headlights. She looked back and forth between us, then stage-whispered, "I'm giving you and Shane a little alone time."

"He's right here, Heidi. He can hear you."

She waved at him. "Oh, hello, don't mind me." Then she took off running.

I stared after her helplessly, then turned back to Shane. "So awkward," I mumbled.

"We have an hour or two before we're required to be anywhere. Would you like to find somewhere and talk?"

I looked up at him, struck by how much I'd missed him and how he really was wasted as an accountant and not a voice-over actor. "I'd like that a lot."

He smiled down at me. "I would, too. I got here earlier today, and I found the perfect place."

My stomach rolled over. Maybe Vegas wasn't all about endings. Maybe it could also be about beginnings.

Chapter 18

SHANE WAS RIGHT; HE'D FOUND THE PERFECT PLACE, BUT GETTING there wasn't as easy. I almost got hit by a couple of cars before we ended up at a hotel a little farther down the Strip. I was regretting the heels, embarrassed at how bad I was at playing *Frogger* with cars, and feeling a bit out of breath. Shane led me through the foyer to a set of ornate doors nestled off to the side. "Are you ready?" he whispered.

"Is something on the other side of these doors going to attack us?" I asked.

He looked at me weirdly. "No." Then a pause. "Not that I'm aware of, anyway."

"Then it should be fine," I said and slowly pushed one open.

For the second time that day, words failed me. The room that looked back at me had a domed ceiling with skylights, a gold chandelier, and beautiful trees, with a mosaic pathway surrounded by a koi pond. We were the only ones there, and it was maybe the most romantic place I'd ever seen. If I had to dream up a perfect oasis, this would be it.

"How did you find this place?" I asked, my voice echoing.

He took my hand and led me down the path, where we settled on a little bench that allowed us to take in the entire scene. "I may have done a little research before the trip," he said. He stuffed his hands in his pockets and looked down. Was he nervous, too? "I googled the best water-related attractions in Vegas. This place is supposed to be Vegas's best-kept secret. Or at least the only fish-related one I could find. Your dad said it was the way to your heart, so I figured...."

"You want to find your way to my...heart?" I asked, sounding stupid, even to my own ears.

He pulled a hand out of his pocket and ran it over his knee, then took my hand. "I want to apologize for how I acted. I know you were, and probably still are, in a tough spot with Melvin. And we don't know each other well. When I explained things to my supervisor—"

I opened my mouth, but he put his other hand up. "Only the part about Melvin and me, nothing about you. He'd heard enough about Melvin that he actually transferred me a step up over what I'd been doing before. I like my new assignment a lot."

"I'm so relieved," I said, "but I should have given you a heads-up. I would never want to gamble with your livelihood or in any way impact your career. I hate that it happened, and I was bummed because, since we don't live near each other or anything, we could easily just never see each other again. If that was what you wanted."

"Thing is, I haven't been able to stop thinking about you," he said, meeting my eyes.

"I think about you all the time," I admitted, then wished I could slap myself for being so honest.

He tried to hide a grin. Then he squeezed my hand and leaned back on the bench. "How's Hopper?"

"I hope he's okay. Nancy is watching him. I had a dream on the plane that she'd sent him on a quest, and he'd grown legs, but—" I willed my mouth to close.

"Legs? Like a reverse mermaid?"

"Yes!" I cried. "If you're going to evolve, go the other way."

"Hopper wouldn't do something just because Nancy told him to. I'm confident it was just a dream."

I looked up, fully drinking in his eyes. "You really do get me, don't you?"

He laughed and shrugged. "I don't know for sure, but I think I'm starting to."

I looked down at our entwined hands. "I really wish you didn't live in New York," I said softly.

"Don't worry about that." He leaned in close and idly touched a strand of hair near my temple. "Like I said before, if you hadn't wanted to seduce me, you shouldn't have done that chicken dance when you beat me at *Mario Kart*," he whispered.

I stared at his mouth as he lowered his face and kissed me. All the background noise faded, and my heart squeezed so hard, I thought it would break my chest.

When he finally pulled back, the noise rushed in again, and I felt dizzy, light-headed.

"Ana," he whispered.

"Mm?" I asked. I felt completely wired and relaxed at the same time.

"That security guard is giving us a look. Like this place is for watching fish, not making out like teenagers."

I looked over and saw him, an older man in a guard uniform looking at us with his nostrils flared. I covered my face with my hands. "We should go."

Shane stood and offered me his arm again. "We should probably meet the others for drinks. If you're okay with it, maybe you'd like to come as my date?"

"The Fellowship would make fun of me so hard." I groaned. "Except Mike. But yes, I'd like that."

"Fellowship?" he asked tentatively.

"*Lord of the Rings*. I'll explain on the way over." I took his arm, and he leaned down, putting a soft kiss on the back of my hand. Was swooning really a thing? Because my giddiness was getting the best of my balance.

Our return game of *Frogger* was just as bad as before. There were so many lights, occasional bursts of fire, and massive statues that I had trouble focusing on the road. "Do you play *Animal Crossing*?" I asked Shane distractedly as we passed a Roman-themed casino.

"Of course," he said. "Tom Nook is the devil."

"You're so right," I said and pointed to a replica of the Nike of Samothrace. "It's like all the fake art from Redd's boat ended up here."

He laughed and pulled me away from the street again. "All Vegas is Redd's *Treasure Trawler*."

Once back at the Mirage, we made our way through the lobby, past the mermaid statues (in the correct form, with a tail and no legs) that I must have missed the first time, and toward, of course, a sports bar. It was full of televisions, swanky seating, and even an old Airstream trailer at the back. It was all dark wood and sleek, but like everything else in Vegas, it had a bit of an artificial feel to it.

I couldn't help but laugh. "Indiana would love this place," I said, gesturing to the sign offering over fifty craft beers. "Inauthentic and a bit over-the-top, but still kind of fun. Just how I imagined him," I said.

"It literally advertises itself as a man cave," Shane said.

"Ana!" someone yelled from behind us. I turned around, and at one of the elevated tables, I found my group. Evan, Bruce, Allen, and Mike, each with a beer, were waving frantically at me.

"I'm getting you a beer!" Allen said and took off toward the bar.

"It's so good to see you all," I said.

"You're littler than I thought," Bruce said loudly as Allen arrived a few minutes later with a draft for both Shane and me.

"To Diana!" Mike yelled and held up his drink.

Shane looked confused, but we all drank to the toast.

"Are they the Fellowship?" Shane whispered in my ear. "Are you, like, Gandalf or something?"

I sighed. "No, I'm Frodo."

"But you're not—"

"Keep your logic to yourself."

"I knew it!" Mike yelled, watching us. "I told you, Ana, true love finds a way."

I wanted to hide in the rush of embarrassment that hit me. Clearly, they'd gotten here a bit early and weren't on their first round.

"You better be good to our esteemed leader," Allen said to Shane. Then he hiccupped. "We like her, even if I miss the cliff-diving version sometimes."

"I see quite a bit has changed since we last talked," Shane murmured.

"You could say that," I admitted. Shane and I sat with them, and wonderfully, the conversation was like catching up with old friends. We toasted a few more things, some serious, some silly, like Melvin's gourmet pancakes, my near brush with death while landing a plane, and Evan's idea of getting the truth in the open so we could be a real team. Before I knew it, most of my beer was gone.

We were talking excitedly about the interface, when Mike stood up, ready to make yet another toast. "I've been saving this news, but now that my work fam is all together, I wanted to tell you"—he paused dramatically—"Violet's pregnant!"

"That's amazing!" I cried. I jumped up to hug him, only to find Evan, Bruce, and Allen doing the same. We were all in a sort of squashed hug, slapping him on the back and spilling what was left of the beer. Shane waited until there was room, then shook Mike's hand.

"I hope you don't mind if we have a real doctor deliver the baby, Indiana," Mike said.

I hugged him again, too happy to even swat him. "Fine, as long as you name the baby Indiana."

Once we were all seated again, Bruce went on and on about the car he wanted to buy. Evan wanted to do a little gambling, but Allen was adamant that Evan should make good financial choices.

I sat back, trying to savor the moment. As much as it bothered me that the company had spent the money to send us here, it really was kind of cool to see everyone in this setting and feel a strong connection, which was so valuable to a creative team. My heart swelled. I wanted the best for these guys, and it was going to be so hard to leave them.

While we were talking, my phone buzzed, and when I looked down, I was shocked to see it was my dad. And he wasn't just calling—he was FaceTiming. This couldn't be good.

I clicked *accept*, and his and Margaret's faces appeared on the screen.

"Indiana!" Dad bellowed. He'd never learned you didn't have to yell when you were on speaker or FaceTime.

"Dad? Are you okay?" I asked, trying to drown out the background noise so I could hear him better.

"I'm great!" he screamed. Margaret gave me a thumbs-up over his shoulder.

"Then why are you calling?" I asked. "You never do this."

"Guess where we are?" he said excitedly.

"Uh, Aspen Skies?" I asked.

Shane leaned over, and I could tell the minute they both spotted him. Their eyes lit up. "Hello, young man!" Dad said.

"Hi, Mr. Aaron," Shane answered. "And this is Margaret?"

"Where are you, Dad?" I broke in as Margaret nodded happily.

"We're in Vegas!" they yelled together.

I blinked. Something wasn't computing. "What? Why are you here?"

"Is that your dad?" Bruce asked from across the table. "Hi, Indiana's dad!"

"Hello, random person!" Dad yelled back. "We're here because…wait for it—we're getting married!"

"What?" I yelped. "Why didn't you tell me? Are you near the hotel?"

"A wedding?" Mike asked, already looking like he was about to tear up. "Can I go?"

"Of course you can, whoever you are," Dad bellowed. "You can all come!"

"But wait," I said, still trying to process. "You just met!"

"And we're old as dirt!" he shouted back. "Why wait? We're in love!"

"He makes an excellent point," Evan said. "Why wait when you're old as dirt?"

I could see Margaret smacking Dad. "We just decided to do it," she said. "We want to share a room at Aspen Skies but not in a sinful way." She laughed, and I could tell she didn't give a damn about that. "We just want to be together, and you're already here, so we figured what the hell!"

"When are you doing it?" I asked.

"Now!" they said together.

"Now?" I asked. "Like right now?"

"Yes!" they screamed.

Mike slammed down his beer and stood. "Then what're we doing here?" He came around behind me and put his full face up to the phone. "Indiana's dad, what chapel are you at?"

Dad looked thrilled to see him. "We're at the Graceland Wedding Chapel, of course!"

Mike nodded vigorously. "Of course! That's where Bon Jovi got married." He turned to us. "What're we still doing here? We have a wedding to attend!"

"We're hanging up now. I'm about to kiss my fiancée!" Dad yelled. The screen went black, and Evan, Bruce, and Allen slammed their beers down as well.

"It's time to go!" Evan said.

I looked helplessly at Shane, who nodded at Evan. "He's right. It's time to go."

"My dad's getting married," I said in wonder. "I've wanted him to find someone who makes him happy for as long as I can remember, and it's finally happening." I turned to the group. "You don't all have to go."

"Are you kidding?" Evan said.

"Oh, we're going," Allen said, crossing his arms. "Vegas is for weddings!"

An excited laugh bubbled up in my throat. "I have no idea where this chapel is, but we have to get there!"

Mike put a hand over his heart. His plaid shirt and dark jeans made him look more like a lumberjack than someone about to attend a wedding. "I've had the pleasure of attending more than one wedding at Graceland. I'll get us there safely."

"Okay, hang on just a sec." I pulled out my phone and sent a text to Heidi and Patrick. My dad's here in Vegas and he's getting married!!!

Heidi wrote back quickly. Awesome! I want to go but I'm in a bit of a predicament. No worries! Tell me all about it tomorrow!

Tell him congrats for me! Patrick. I'm in the middle of a boring meeting. Take pictures!

We took off running through the lobby, away from the man cave and out onto the street. The sky was darkening, and the city itself was brightening. Neon lights were everywhere, and combined with the palm trees, they made everything feel a little more magical.

"We're gonna have to take the Deuce!" Mike called. "Follow me!"

Allen got distracted by a fake volcano spewing real fire, but we all managed to stick with Mike, who got us on a bus that apparently looped the Strip throughout the day. It was a good thing, too, because after I'd walked with Shane, my feet were already sore.

After what felt like a zillion stops, we finally reached the chapel. I couldn't believe how tiny it was. The door was open, and through it I could see them. Dad's wheelchair took up a lot of room, but Margaret was sitting on his lap, and I'd never seen him look so happy in his life.

The staff waved us inside, and I ran over to give him a hug. "This is bananas, you know that?" I told them.

"We know," Margaret said happily. "But after you left, we got to talking about how neither of us had been to Vegas and how neither of us had felt like this in a really long time, so…I proposed." She shrugged.

"You proposed to Dad?" I asked, my voice breaking.

He squeezed her tight in his arms. "She did, darlin'. Told me she wanted to marry me. She doesn't have any family left, and I don't have an inheritance for her to steal, so I'm fairly confident this isn't part of a plan to kill me."

She gently smacked the back of his head. "Russell Aaron, you hush."

Margaret looked up at me tentatively. "Is this okay, Indiana? Will you give us your blessing?"

The tears started then, and I threw my arms around them both. "I'm just worried who I'll live with if you get divorced." I sniffed.

Dad poked me in the side and looked past me into the lobby. It was packed. "You've brought so many young men here with you," he said. "Any of you here to marry Indiana?" he boomed.

I hid my face. "*Shut up, Dad*," I hissed.

I could hear Allen sigh behind me. "I would have, but not anymore. No offense, Ana."

I fought back a smile. "None taken, Allen."

"Maybe Shane?" Mike offered helpfully.

I kept my face hidden, suddenly beyond mortified.

"I think we still have some time," Shane said. "We're not old as dirt yet."

An attendant motioned for us to take seats in the chapel. Shane and I grabbed a spot near the front, and the others shuffled into the pews the best they could. The place really was tiny. Dad wheeled himself down the aisle to the flower-covered podium and turned so he was looking back at all of us. A tear slipped down my cheek, and I silently thanked Heidi for her insistence that my makeup be waterproof.

The music swelled, and we all turned to see Margaret walking down the aisle with Elvis at her side. He was crooning "Can't Help Falling in Love" while making finger guns at all of us. Margaret looked radiant in her black dress, and she and my dad couldn't stop staring at each other. When the song ended and they got to the end of the aisle, Elvis kissed Margaret's hand, then went to stand behind the podium. He cleared his throat, and I thought he was going to start officiating. Instead, he abruptly launched into "It's Now or Never."

Hysterical giggles escaped Margaret's lips. Her eyes slid over to Dad, and he started giggling, too. Elvis looked a little annoyed but kept plowing on. By the end of the song, Margaret was doubled over, holding on to Dad's chair, and his head was thrown back in laughter.

Elvis cleared his throat loudly, and I tried not to look at the deep V of his costume that went all the way to his belly button, exposing quite a bit of fluffy body hair. "Now, do you, Russell Aaron, take Margaret Sheridan, to be your wedded wife?"

"I sure as hell do," he said, his eyes twinkling at her.

Elvis rolled his eyes. "And do you, Margaret Sheridan, take Russell Aaron to be your wedded husband?"

"Damn straight," she responded, then broke into giggles again.

Elvis sighed, like he was above all this. "I now pronounce you husband and wife. You may kiss each other, if you want."

Margaret threw her arms around my dad, and they kissed. I had to look away but jumped when I heard the honk behind me. Mike was sobbing openly, and an attendant was shoving a box of tissues at him.

Shane squeezed my hand. "This complete weirdness might be the most romantic thing I've ever seen," he whispered.

"Right?" I said, sniffling.

Margaret slipped into Dad's lap and looked over at me, trying to compose herself. "We did pay for him to sing two songs," she said, wheezing.

"And I did," Elvis grouched, which brought a fresh set of giggles.

"Hey, has anyone seen Allen?" I asked, looking at the pews.

A few seconds later, he came around the corner wearing a pair of aviator sunglasses with what looked like strips of carpet hanging from the arms. "They have a gift shop!" he exclaimed. "Do you like my sideburns?"

I stood. "Heidi definitely needs a pair of those."

We all crowded into the gift shop, and I grabbed a pair of the glasses, then balked at the price. They were extremely proud of their carpet shades, for real. Dad must have seen me hesitate because he smacked me on the arm. "You don't need to worry about money so much anymore, darlin'," he said. "Maggie and I are going to move into a suite together at Aspen Skies. We already cleared the whole thing with Rita. Once we split the cost, it's going to be cheaper for both of us. Buy yourself a pair of Elvis glasses, damn it."

I laughed even as I teared up again because my dad was literally telling me I could afford to buy a handful of fake sideburn sunglasses because of his new living arrangement. We ended up buying every pair they had.

I didn't usually go in for a cinematic effect, but I would have loved to have seen a slow-mo shot of the eight of us swaggering out of the chapel, all wearing those stupid sunglasses like the total badasses we were.

Once outside, I turned to Dad. "Where are you staying?"

"Well, I've never been to Egypt, so Mags suggested we stay at the Luxor."

I put my hand on his shoulder. "Dad, the Luxor hotel is still in Vegas. It doesn't magically transport you to a different country."

"It does, too," he retorted. "There's a sphinx out front and everything. That's how you know you're in Egypt."

I leaned down. "Dad, how can we afford this? I mean, Apollo paid for me to come here, but—"

"Mags is paying, not me," he whispered back. "She's got a nest egg stashed away, so you should really be worried about *me* trying to off *her*." He grinned.

I grabbed Margaret and gave her an extra hug. "Thank you for loving my dad so much."

"He didn't give me much choice, sweetheart."

Mike, ever prepared, pulled a map out of his back pocket. "Looks like your hotel is a few miles down past ours. But the bus is wheelchair accessible. I'm assuming you all would like some time alone?" He waggled his eyebrows at them, and I pretended to barf.

Dad laughed. "Yes, we would! I would like to take my bride back to our room."

Mike helped get them on the next bus that was coming by, and we all crowded in with them. I leaned against Shane, feeling overwhelmed. Again. He put his arm around my waist tightly, and I took a deep breath. When we got to our stop, we left my dad and Margaret on the bus headed to the Luxor.

"I want to see you both tomorrow!" I told them as we waved goodbye. This trip was turning out to be nothing like I'd expected. And the day wasn't over. Next stop: the hotel.

Chapter 19

Back at the Mirage, Shane and I walked around the grounds as I filled him in on everything that had happened with Indiana and Ana since I'd seen him last. It was hard to believe the day had started with me staring into the eyes of the demonic horse at the Denver airport. I was pretty drained, and after checking in with Patrick and Heidi over text, I went back to our room and crashed. Heidi came in some time around 2:00 a.m. She woke me out of a dead sleep tripping over things and giggling. I made her drink some water and gave her a couple of Tylenol before tucking her in. She was going to be pretty hungover the next day.

Turns out she wasn't the only one. When Heidi and I finally got up, showered, and dressed, it was already around 10:00 a.m. I asked her several times to tell me about her night, but she was tight-lipped, saying only that she'd had a great time with Jason. I couldn't get any more details out of her.

I banged on Patrick's door. He answered, looking shockingly well rested. "You have no right to look that good this early in the morning," I muttered.

"It's after ten but thank you. Shane's already gone for breakfast. He told me to tell you he'd meet you there." His eyes slid to Heidi behind me. "She looks like she went through the spin cycle," he whispered, then raised his voice. "Are you really wearing your slippers to breakfast?"

Heidi looked down as if she were surprised to see them. "Um. Yes. I am," she said. Her blond hair stuck up off her head, and what was left of her eyeliner was smeared.

"Did you have a good night last night?" I asked Patrick. "What did you do?"

"They had me in tons of meetings yesterday. Afterward I just watched a movie and crashed. Joseph and I come here once a year or so, and turns out it's not as much fun without him. But it looks like it's fun for you guys; my besties are falling in love."

I leaned in to give him a hug, a little embarrassed. "We missed you at the wedding. I got to meet Elvis when he married my dad and Margaret."

I filled them in on the night before as we got on the elevator. Fortunately, Patrick knew where we were going in this maze of a hotel. When we walked into the conference room Apollo had rented for the brunch, it was clear the crowd looked decidedly worse than it had the night before. Small groups of people were milling about, but most were sitting, their heads in their hands, untouched orange juice and scrambled eggs in front of them.

I quickly spotted my group and headed over. They were sitting at a corner table by themselves, except for a couple of men I hadn't met who sat slightly outside their circle. I nodded to them, then turned to the guys. "Good morning!"

"Please don't talk so loudly," Allen murmured and touched his temple.

Mike was doubled over in his seat. "Everything is still blurry," he mumbled.

"How late did you all stay up after I went to bed?" I asked.

"Late," Evan answered. "Or early, if you're Bruce."

Bruce looked up and grinned. He had a slightly crazed look on his face. "I haven't gone to bed yet."

Yikes on bikes.

I grabbed a plate of eggs and toast and settled in next to them. A few minutes later, Jason and Shane joined us from the buffet table. Shane looked gorgeous, as always, but Jason...Jason looked the same way Heidi did. His suit was rumpled, his shirt slightly untucked, and he had what looked like pillow creases on his face.

"What did you and Heidi do last night?" I asked him.

He blinked. "Whatever it was, we definitely didn't get arrested."

"I'm sorry, what?" I yelped.

"We had a busy night, but one thing we did *not* do," he said again, "was get arrested."

Shane shrugged at me as they both sat at the table. "That's all I got out of him, too," he said.

I had clearly slept through so much. I glanced over to see Patrick helping Heidi load her plate. Once I got her alone, I'd make her tell me everything—or at least what she could remember.

Evan turned to me, looking a bit green but alert. "Today's the day."

I nodded and took a sip of coffee, then winced. For a swanky hotel, the coffee sucked. I'd seen a little bistro on the Strip last night, so maybe after this was over, Shane and I could grab a cup... I sighed, then gave Evan my full attention. I couldn't avoid it forever.

"Yeah. Today's the day. Honestly, I wish it weren't. I've wanted to get this over with forever, but yesterday was such a blast. I'm going to miss Apollo. And especially all of you."

"There's still the possibility Melvin won't fire you," Evan said, but he sounded unconvincing.

"No, there isn't," I said, shoveling a forkful of eggs in my mouth. "And even if he didn't, I want out. He trusted me as a coder because I have a manly name. When he met me in person, he called me a little girl. Then he reneged on his promise for a promotion and tried to take credit for my idea. This is not someone I want to work for or with. And no offense to your car dreams," I said to Bruce, who didn't seem at all focused on the conversation, "but last night you all met the reason why I needed that promotion. Keeping my dad in assisted living has taken every spare penny I have. Not that Melvin knows about that, and it shouldn't matter either way. He should promote me because, with all your help, we made a product that's going to change the way people interact with consumerism from now on."

"Wait, are you all talking about the S.J. Sporting interface?" one of the men sitting near us asked. I'd seen him somewhere but couldn't place him.

Evan froze. "Um. No?"

I rolled my eyes. "Yes, we are," I told him. "You said it yourself, Evan: this whole thing ends today."

"I don't mean to interrupt," the guy said, "I was just curious because that product is the reason we're all here, and from what I've seen, it's amazing."

"It is," I said and gestured to my team. "We made something amazing."

Shane leaned over. "Maybe Evan's right. You love Artemis, and you've worked really hard. If the higher-ups know about Melvin, maybe you won't have to go."

"I don't love Artemis. I love Diana," I said. "And the higher-ups haven't inspired a ton of confidence with their leadership choices. Just saying. Besides, I've become kind of close with Sara Jean. She's so refreshing to work with. I have a feeling if I wanted a job with her at SJ, she'd find a spot for me. Point is, I think I have a future in coding, but not at Apollo."

"Sara Jean, as in SJ?" the man asked.

"Yeah," I answered, then narrowed my eyes at him. "Who are you, anyway?"

"David," he answered. "I work on the"—he hesitated—"the Poseidon team."

Hm. Hadn't heard of that one, but when Apollo IT found a theme, they clearly stuck to it. I turned back to the group. "Melvin gives his speech tonight; then I give my resignation. But you all will keep in touch, right?"

They nodded and began talking all at once. Mike and Bruce wanted to meet my dad and Margaret for coffee before the big meeting, and Evan and Allen wanted to look over the final presentation they'd prepared for Melvin before it was showtime.

There were a couple of events scheduled for the afternoon, but I didn't really feel the need to show up. Fortunately, neither did Shane. I leaned into him at the breakfast table, and he rested his chin on top of my head. Bliss. He might live across the country, but for now, we were together and our issues were in the past, where they belonged.

That afternoon, Shane and I ditched the "mandatory" events and checked out the shark reef at the Mandalay Bay Resort. He said it was a way to make up for losing our romantic dinner in the shark tunnel. I squealed the whole time and pestered him with uncomfortable facts about sharks until it was time to go back to the hotel to get ready for the evening keynote event. I asked if there was anything he wanted to do, like see some German shepherds (dogs or people, whichever he preferred), but he politely declined.

Once back at the hotel, Heidi remained tight-lipped about her evening the night before, but she chattered happily at me as she did my hair and makeup, delivering on her promise to make me look "killer" for the duration of the trip. It was amazing how having my outfit, hair, and makeup on point could boost my confidence.

———

When it was finally time for the big event, Heidi and I met Patrick, Shane, and Jason at the entrance of the Montego Ballroom. There were people milling about everywhere, so I grabbed on to my friends so as not to lose them. We snagged a table off to the side, and I looked around for my team in the crowd. Then I saw Mike at the back of the room with (seriously?) my dad and Margaret.

"I'll be right back," I told my group, then took off to speak with them.

"Dad! Margaret! What're you doing here?" I asked.

They looked so happy that I decided then and there, everything that had led to this moment for them was worth it.

"Mike invited us to your swanky event," Dad said. "We thought it would be fun!"

"You're on your honeymoon," I insisted. "There's no way you want to attend a navel-gazing tech event instead of exploring the city."

"And each other," Mike said and high-fived my dad.

"Never do that again." I groaned.

"Russell, behave," Margaret said to him. "You're embarrassing your daughter. We're not going to stay long, Indiana. We're really just stopping by. Russell and Mike have been having a great time talking about life and sports and Violet's pregnancy. We might hit the slot machines later or find a garden to look at the stars. Don't worry about us."

"I'm so, so happy for you," I said and hugged them. Little Ana would have been over the moon to know that, sometime in the future, Dad would find love again. He'd put it all on hold for me and because he'd loved my mom so much. But hearts don't get full; they grow. Dad could love my mom, Margaret, and me with everything he had. It wasn't either/or.

———

The evening was full of speeches perfect for tuning out. The only time I geeked out was when other teams presented some of the things they'd been working on, and turns out there were some cool ideas floating around Apollo. So far I'd been lucky to avoid seeing Melvin at all. I wondered where he'd been hiding himself, then realized I didn't care.

Finally, it was time for the keynote address. Melvin swaggered to the stage, his too-small suit bunching at the elbows and knees. I settled into a chair at the edge of the room, grabbing a flute of champagne from a waiter who went by. I took a big sip and idly wondered if someone in Melvin's circle was shrinking his clothes. What might he have done to make someone want to do that? After this, I could send over my resignation letter and call it a day. I fought the childish urge to repeat everything he said in a condescending voice as he took the microphone.

"Thank you all for being here! It is my distinct honor to demonstrate for you the new interface that has been created through the Artemis partnership with S.J. Sporting, with a special nod to our friends at the Colorado Avalanche!"

Cheering from the audience. Looked like a lot of cold stick fighting fans worked at Apollo IT. I took another sip from my champagne. Carbonation really did improve everything. I idly wondered if carbonated coffee would be any good. If it were, Starbucks would probably already be selling it.

"This web-app interface allows for the ultimate consumer experience. It makes shopping as easy as taking a selfie. I remember when the idea came to me…"

"Blah, blah, blah," I said snarkily under my breath and went back to thinking about what other things I could carbonize. Was that a word? Could you put it in milkshakes? I grabbed one of those short pencils with the hotel logo on it from the center of the table and a comment card from the stack next to it. I started making a list of all the things I could carbonate. Maybe this was my true calling. Or maybe I shouldn't have started drinking a second glass.

Melvin continued his presentation, jabbing his laser pointer this way and that, to talk about his ingeniousness and how his leadership had inspired his team. Good thing there weren't any cats in attendance. For Melvin, anyway. I would have been stoked if there were cats in attendance. The PowerPoint was projected onto the wall behind him, larger-than-life, full of charts and graphs. He went on and on about what a great working relationship he had with SJ, and I thought I might pull a muscle from rolling my eyes so hard.

I was deep in thought when a collective gasp pulled my attention back to the stage. The slide changed, and there I was. The actual me, not Harrison Ford. A mass of auburn curls, gray eyes, and freckles for days. I sat up straight, sputtering a little from swallowing the champagne wrong.

Melvin recognized the commotion at the same time I did and turned around to see the screen behind him. He froze. "Who is that?" he asked. "Why is she on my PowerPoint?"

"That's the real creator of the S.J. Sporting interface, Melvin," Evan said, coming around from the side of the stage.

"Evan." Melvin narrowed his eyes. "What're you trying to pull here?"

Evan shrugged and held his hands wide. "Just giving credit where credit is due."

"Is this because of Indiana?" Melvin snarled. He looked out at the crowd. "Indiana, get your ass out here once and for all."

Yes, sir. I started to stand but got the heel of my shoe hooked around the bottom of the chair. I stumbled a bit, and before I could right myself, I heard a loud voice on my right. "I am Indiana."

I squinted over to find Mike, bashful, standing with his hands folded behind his back, still next to my dad, his red beard straightened and shiny for the occasion.

"I am Indiana," a smaller, higher voice said, one I immediately recognized to be Allen. He was also standing with his hands behind his back, looking dapper in his little suit.

"I'm Indy," Bruce boomed from the other side of the room. He didn't look like he'd found time to fit in a nap since the morning. A laugh escaped my throat. They all looked so serious, and somehow silly, and oh, so sweet. But this was totally unnecessary—nobody needed to Spartacus themselves on my account. Suddenly, I remembered Evan saying at our first Diana meeting that they had Melvin under control. Was this what he had meant?

Flustered, Melvin stomped his foot on the ground and gritted his teeth. "Indiana is now officially fired. Stop interrupting my presentation, or I'll have you all fired as well." He turned back to the PowerPoint and hit the button to go to the next slide.

Damn it, I didn't even get the opportunity to quit. But when the next slide came up, the giggles hit. It was a picture of Evan, Bruce, Mike, Allen, and me, with Elvis in the middle. He had his sequined bat wings spread wide, and Bruce was lifting me so I fit in the frame with the rest of them. We were all laughing in the image. All it was missing was an *Operation Diana 4 Eva* in the bottom corner.

Evan casually strolled onto the stage and took the microphone out of Melvin's stunned hand. "Artemis worked very hard to put this project together. We had an amazing project manager, one who deserves the real credit here."

Melvin moved to take the microphone back, but Evan held it out of a stunned Melvin's hand. "Indiana Aaron, not Melvin Hammer, designed, constructed, and implemented this project. And it was an honor working with her."

Gasps from the crowd. I'd untangled my heel a while back but was now regretting the two champagnes I'd had to make the evening palatable. This would be an amazing time to be sober.

"Indiana? I think Apollo would like to meet you. Officially."

"Yep, coming," I said.

People swiveled their heads in my direction, but I heard a lot of mumbled, "Who said that?" and "Do you see anybody?" God damn it. I had on my highest heels. I pushed my way through the crowd and joined Evan at the podium. He handed me the microphone with triumph, and I fought a sudden rush of adrenaline and dread. But I wasn't Pope Joan. There wasn't a potty seat for me here, and even if it felt like it sometimes, this wasn't the Middle Ages. "A little warning would have been nice," I whispered to him.

"Then you might not have come," he said.

"Eh, I still would have," I said to him, then turned to the crowd. "I'm Indiana Aaron," I said. There were several collective gasps, and Melvin put his hand on his heart, but I plowed through. Now or never.

"I know I'm not who you were expecting," I said. "I never set out to deceive anyone, but I didn't correct a misconception, which kind of snowballed to where we are now."

"Were you ever in a war?" someone yelled from the crowd.

"No! What war would that even be?" I asked, exasperated. "I think Indiana was a parasailer at one point, not a paratrooper. Honestly, I don't really know the difference," I admitted. "Or—" I cut myself off. I was helping everyone miss the point.

"I am Indiana Aaron," I said again. "I'm an employee at Apollo, and I've had the honor of working on the Artemis team for the duration of the S.J. Sporting project. I'm so proud of the work we've done and the team we've built."

I grinned at the fist pumps Mike and Bruce threw in the air from their seats. "I've been looking for that type of comradery and teamwork for my entire work life. But I didn't find it because I was lucky. I found it because of that misconception.

"I was given an opportunity to have more creative power on the team because Melvin Hammer"—he jumped at the sound of his name—"thought I was a male go-getter instead of an outspoken female. If he had known what I looked like, he never would have given me the opportunity."

His eyes slid away from mine, and I thought I saw some semblance of shame there. "Would, too," he muttered.

I snorted into the microphone, instantly regretting the way the sound reverberated. I covered it with my hand and leaned his way. "You're full of crap, Melvin, you know that? You dismissed me out of hand." Then I turned back to the crowd. "This isn't the eighteen hundreds, but for women in the workplace, especially in male-dominated fields like this one, it can feel like it. It's still a man's world. It's harder to get respect, we don't make as much money, we aren't promoted, and we're just as often mistaken as the girl who takes the coffee orders."

Evan's eyes met mine, and he, too, looked down.

"Preach!" yelled a female voice from the crowd.

"I'm gonna!" I raised my champagne glass in her direction.

"Have any of you heard of Laura Mulvey?" I asked the crowd. Looking around, I saw a sea of blank faces and had to kick myself. I was talking to a tech crowd composed mainly of men. The likelihood that they'd taken a film theory class or a women's studies course in college was close to nil. "Anyway, Laura Mulvey wrote a life-changing piece, *Visual Pleasure and Narrative Cinema*. You all should totally read it. She changed the world. And she did it by putting into words a feeling I'd had since I was a kid and couldn't articulate. Mulvey's main idea is that, when you watch a movie, you're encouraged to identify with the main male character. The movie is shot through his eyes. When the woman comes on-screen, the story stops, the wind machine starts, the slow jazz plays, and she blinks like her lashes are stuck to her eyeballs." I rolled my eyes. "It even happens in children's cartoons—kids who *have no idea what they're looking at*. That girl bunny from *Bambi* who seduces Thumper, or the girl dog in *Lady and the Tramp*, or, God, the girl character in any cartoon. I could literally go on forever. But I won't," I added.

"We're asked to see what the man sees, to *be* James Bond and therefore win the Bond Girl. She's a reward; her only job is to be rescued. And these women don't historically have a ton to offer in terms of intellectual prowess. Their purpose is to look pretty and get rescued. And we, as viewers, get to be the hero. Even with"—I looked down, my throat suddenly dry— "Indiana Jones." I focused back on the audience. "That's why we love it so much—we get to *be* Indiana when we watch the movies. To get the girl, to be the hero he is.

"Speaking as someone who has had the 'pleasure'"—I smiled wryly— "of being Indiana over the past few months, it's not all it's cracked up to be. These messages work their magic on women, too—we're taught to see other women as competition, to value ourselves based on our appearance, and to defer to men. We all learn not to look to women for ideas or innovation, not to see them as equals." Probably not what Evan had been expecting when he handed me the mic, but once I started, I had no desire to stop.

"Things are changing, but it's glacial. As you grow up, it's on you to see through these messages and to take responsibility for your own biases— and not to take those biases into your work life. Because office culture is full of that. Anyway," I said, addressing the rest of them, "this leads to my own small problem. I have an opinion about everything. That makes me bossy, insubordinate, and emotional. It makes my counterpart, the manly

Indiana, assertive, a risk-taker, and an innovator." I was so far up on my soapbox now, no one could pull me down. But again, they were the ones who'd called me up here, so they were trapped now. "But despite all that, I would never want to be a man." My eyes found Margaret in the crowd, and she lifted her glass to me.

I could feel Melvin getting restless and more upset, so I tried to wrap it up before he tried to wrestle the mic away. "And what does that look like for women? It means we still make less money, don't get the same respect, and are passed over for less-qualified white boys like Taggert who 'drive a hard bargain.' No offense, Taggert," I yelled into the crowd.

"None taken! We all owe you our lives anyway."

I grinned. "I saved you that day, my dude. I only got the opportunity I did because my name inspires the image of a rugged manly man." I peered into the crowd. "Thanks for that, Dad. I guess."

"You were almost Melanie!" he yelled from the back of the crowd.

"So, to wrap up my point, this was all a misunderstanding. But I turned it into an amazing accomplishment that I am so proud of due to the help of Evan Smith, Allen Parks, Bruce Atkins, and Mike Mowery, who didn't care if I was male or female. And our inspiring client, S.J. Sharpe.

"And no thanks to you, Melvin," I said.

He was opening and closing his mouth like he still couldn't find the words.

"Melvin Hammer was not involved with the creation or implementation of this project. And maybe it's time we stop promoting him and throwing him from department to department until he floats. Just sayin'." I paused for a second, then looked out into the darkness until I found Shane's face.

"I don't regret the way this all went down, but I do regret that it hurt my friend Shane Dalton. I'm very thankful that you've forgiven me. And I'd love it if you would go out on another date with me. That's all."

I gave the mic to Evan and jumped down from the stage but had a last-minute thought and scrambled back up. I pulled the mic, still in Evan's hand, over to my face and added, "And by the way, I quit." Then I jumped back down and went off to find my table.

I didn't get too far before there was another voice, one I vaguely recognized, calling me back to the stage. I grumbled under my breath because I didn't want to go back, but I turned around anyway and found the guy from this morning (David, was it?) holding the microphone and looking from me to Melvin expectantly.

Uh-oh. Team Poseidon had seemed a bit cliché, given the Greek god theme Apollo had going on, but you never knew. I climbed back up on the stage and crossed my arms. "What?" I asked.

Instead, David turned to Melvin. "You've worked closely with S.J. on this project, correct?"

Melvin nodded, but his eyes were wider than usual. I wondered if he was sweating. I wasn't. At this point, I couldn't care less what these people thought of me.

"What does S.J. stand for?" David asked Melvin, then put the mic in his face.

"Um…Sharpe? Sharpe…Jabs?" he whispered.

"Sharp Jabs," David repeated. "Is that your final answer?"

"No?" Melvin said.

"What does S.J. Sharpe look like?"

"Uh, he's athletic, graying hair, a little like me, actually," Melvin said, gaining steam as he spoke.

David turned to me. "What does S.J. stand for?"

"Sharp Jabs," I deadpanned, then couldn't control the giggles.

David narrowed his eyes at me.

"Sorry, that's way funnier than it should be. Who names their kid Jabs?" I tried to tamp down the giggles. "Her name is Sara Jean. She uses initials to combat misogyny in the workforce. Like, you know, when she might have to deal with people like Melvin. She tried to introduce herself to him, but he dismissed her. Sound familiar?" I asked the audience.

Quite a few visible nods.

"So you never met S.J. in person," David said to Melvin.

"Oh, he did," I interjected. "And he didn't make a very good impression. By the way, who are you?" I asked.

"I'm David Olsen, CEO of Apollo IT."

I felt like someone had splashed cold water over me. Saying "Sharp Jabs" was no longer as funny as it had been. "I really wish you'd introduced yourself earlier," I muttered to him off mic.

"You wouldn't have been as honest if I had, would you?" he murmured back.

"Eh, probably still would have."

"I think, under the circumstances, Indiana should continue the presentation. I know you're all very interested to know exactly how this interface works and what went into making the dream a reality." David handed the microphone to me and leaned over. "But maybe less long-winded this time?" he muttered. Then he made eye contact with Melvin. "You're fired."

Melvin sputtered and grabbed at David's shoulder. "You and I should go somewhere and talk. I can explain everything. This young lady—"

I looked at the mic in my hand, a little stunned, and turned back to the crowd. "Get up here, Mike, Allen, and Bruce," I said. "Well, maybe not Bruce." He wasn't looking so good. They made their way through the crowd and joined Evan and me onstage. Then I happily took the audience through the innovation and hard work that had led to the product, giving credit at each point where credit was due.

Chapter 20

THAT EVENING, I FOUND MYSELF SITTING AT THE EDGE OF A FOUNTAIN outside the ballroom, my shoes off, feeling a little tipsy and content. Shane had draped his suit jacket over my shoulders, which I loved, and I leaned into him as I relaxed. Nothing about this trip had gone as expected, and now that it was coming to an end, I didn't want it to end. I knew Hopper needed me back at home, but—

I sat up straight, suddenly feeling very sober.

"You okay?" Shane asked. He'd been leaning his chin on top of my head, and I'd accidentally clicked his teeth together.

"Uh, yeah, just need to see how Hopper and the Hopperites are holding up."

Hi Nancy—just checking in. How are things with the fish? I held my breath, praying she didn't tell me she'd drowned them in George's casserole.

They seem fine, honey, she wrote back.

I let out a huge sigh of relief. "They seem fine," I repeated to Shane.

"Good," he murmured and settled me back against him. I was getting comfortable when the next text came through.

They don't like country music, though.

I gasped. Not country! They like progressive rock, Nancy. We talked about this.

I thought we could expand their music tastes. I got a pair of binoculars. If I sit behind your couch and keep the lights off, I can watch them poop without them noticing.

Shane leaned down to read the messages over my shoulder, then sat back. "I just decided that I don't want to know."

I smiled and sent Nancy another quick message. Thank you for caring for them. Remember, just a pinch.

I pinch them all the time, we're fine here, everyone's having fun. Then she sent me a kissy face emoji. Maybe it was time to get back to Denver after all.

"Excuse me," someone interrupted, and I jumped, almost knocking my phone into the fountain. I looked up to see David Olsen, CEO or Poseidon team member, depending on which story you believed. "Can I speak with you for a moment?"

Shane squeezed my shoulder and stood. "I'll go check on Heidi and Jason," he said, then left.

David sat next to me at the fountain. "Quite an evening, huh?" he said.

"Yep," I responded.

"I wish you and the rest of the Artemis team had felt like you could come to me with your concerns about Melvin."

"Permission to speak freely, sir?" I asked.

He grinned. "Granted."

"For reasons I can't understand, Apollo IT has continued to promote and celebrate Melvin Hammer. You pass him from department to department and deny opportunities to the rest of us. How did he get that status? Because you guys play cricket or grasshopper or whatever on the weekends? You have a group of extremely talented programmers who felt the need to go underground to create an amazing product without Melvin messing it up. The hoops we had to jump through to actually do our jobs… I mean no disrespect—"

He opened his mouth, but I kept going. "Really, I don't. But you're complicit in Melvin's reign of terror. You shouldn't have to ask why no one felt comfortable coming to you."

He sat for a minute, and I saw a few unreadable emotions pass over his face. "You're right. We've passed him around, hoping to find the right place for him, and that wasn't the right decision for the company or the people working under him. Your candor makes you valuable to Apollo IT. And I think your innovation can help make it a better place to work. Would you consider withdrawing your resignation?"

I blinked. It hadn't occurred to me that I might end up with the option of staying at Apollo IT. Part of me was drawn to the idea, if it meant I could keep my team. But then I looked at the opulence around us, paid for by the potential future salaries of Apollo's workers. "I don't think so. Your company promises no raises for hard work, no promotions for innovation, no room for growth. There's a hiring and promotion freeze unless you're Melvin or Taggert. In the end, there wasn't even room for the manly Indiana Aaron."

David shifted his weight uncomfortably on the fountain edge. "A lot of the conversations we've had with employees are about managing expectations. It's less about the idea that there will never be opportunities in the future and more about how to foster contentment with one's current situation."

Spoken truly as someone who'd never had their feelings "managed" by a superior. But was Apollo any different than any other office? Didn't every office have a Melvin Hammer, in some form or another? If I went somewhere else, would I have to start all over as the girl in the wrong room? At least here, I'd blown that stereotype all to hell, and I had the ear of the CEO.

"I might consider staying, on several conditions. I would get to keep my team, Evan Smith, Allen Parks, Mike Mowery, and Bruce Atkins. And we would be known as Diana, not Artemis, going forward. And as the creative director of Diana, I would require a salary on par with what other creative directors make at Apollo IT. There also need to be step increases and incentives for the team members to keep them motivated to give their best. I'm sure I have some other conditions as well, but I'm a little tipsy, and it's been a long day."

David leaned forward and put his elbows on his knees, seeming to think for a few seconds. Then he nodded. "You drive a hard bargain, Indiana. I'll have some conversations with the CFO, and then you and I can sit down and look at some potential offers."

I nodded. "I'm open to hearing what you come up with. I'm going to require my lawyer to attend and review all documents before I consider an actual offer." Margaret was about to become my legal counsel, even though she didn't know it.

David stood. "I'll get the ball rolling on Monday. Does that work?"

I nodded, then realized I was still barefoot. I tucked my feet under my legs. "I look forward to hearing from you."

He walked away, and warmth spread through my chest. Maybe it was just the champagne, but I doubted it. If this didn't fall through, I could pull myself and Dad out of the financial hole we'd been in. Maybe I could keep the Fellowship. Things might actually be comfortable. And I might finally have the recognition I'd craved for so long.

Regardless of the outcome with Apollo, I'd found a side of myself I hadn't known I had. Not one that looked like Indiana Jones, but a woman who'd proven to the world just how capable she was.

Epilogue

"Are you excited?" I asked, bouncing up and down on my knees on Shane's sofa. Odin bounced along with me, like he had springs in his feet.

"Not as excited as you two are, but yes," he replied. "I've lived in New York for so long that it's kind of weird to leave." He pulled some books off his bookshelf and put them in a cardboard box.

"But it's not forever. David said you could split your time—six months here, six months there. Seems like the best of both worlds. Then, when you decide you can't live without me, the Hopperites, and Denver in general, you'll stay there indefinitely."

Shane leaned down and gave me a soft kiss. "David said you could do the six and six, too, if you wanted, so I wouldn't have to live without you at all."

"I know," I said. "In the end he really came through. But I love Denver. And I couldn't miss the monthly poker nights with my dad, Margaret, and the Fellowship." I sat on the couch, and Odin immediately licked my face.

"Plus, with Heidi and Jason getting married, they'll need us around to help them stay out of trouble."

"Doubt we can help with that," he said over his shoulder. He moved a few more things on his bookcase, and something caught my eye.

"Wait a second," I said and quickly came up behind him.

He used his bigger frame to block my view. "Go sit down. You'll get Odin all excited again."

"Lemme see what you're hiding!" I exclaimed.

"No." He folded his arms across his chest.

I tried to push him out of the way, but he was solid as a rock. Odin immediately got in between us, not sure who to protect. Then he started howling. With a big sigh, Shane admitted defeat and moved out of the way.

On the shelf was a lopsided, cracked, poorly fired statue that looked vaguely like a cat, complete with a plaque that read "SUSPICION" BY INDIANA AARON.

"No way," I breathed.

Shane shrugged and looked away.

"You bought that piece of pottery? You paid like five hundred bucks for junk I made? You must be, like, hopelessly in love with me to waste your money like that. And you must be totally embarrassed that I found out."

His ears turned pink, but he looked me dead in the eyes. "I don't disagree with what you just said. And if that little punk Allen hadn't kept outbidding me, it wouldn't have gone that far." Then he offered me a shy grin, and my heart flipped over. "It was for a good cause, though. A donation to the pottery studio you love so much."

I stood on my tiptoes and put my arms around his neck, suddenly ashamed for teasing him. "I'm sorry, I don't mean to make fun. It's just, why would *anyone* want that in their house?"

"If things go the way I'm hoping they do, it'll be in *our* house one day."

Warmth bubbled up inside me. "When it is, you're going to be so sad when Odin knocks it on the floor one day and shatters it. He can't help it; he's only got one eye."

"Then you can make more. New Emotions for your series."

"I'm thinking *Nausea* would be a good one to make next. And you know, if we ever *do* have a house together, one wall will have to be an aquarium."

He went back to packing books. "I'm well aware. I've already done some calculations about how much water weighs and what floor it would have to be on."

I stared at his back as he worked, idly stroking Odin's fur. I never would have guessed that something as simple as a name and a misunderstanding, compounded by my choice in friends, could have ended like this. It had been an adventure, but I was so glad to be me again. Occasionally, I missed being an obstetrically trained cowboy who'd fought in a war, but in the end, I'd much rather be a kick-ass coder with a talented team to manage.

I pulled out my phone, opened my email app, and started a new message to Team Diana. To the Fellowship of the Ring, I began. It's Frodo. We have work to do.

Check out this excerpt from
Anastasia Ryan's debut novel

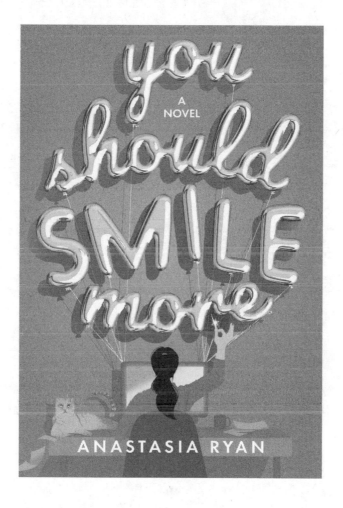

Chapter 1

"WE DON'T LIKE YOUR FACE." XAVIER ADAMS STARED UNBLINKINGLY at me from across the conference table.

What? Surely he hadn't said what I thought he'd said. "You called me in here because you don't like my face?"

"It's been brought to our attention, and we've started taking notice," Xavier replied. "Both your face and your expressions aren't acceptable in the workplace and especially not at Directis." Xavier leaned back in his chair and made aggressive eye contact.

I reached up and touched my cheek. It wasn't a *bad* face. I was pretty attached to it. "I don't understand," I managed.

I looked him over. He wasn't exactly someone to be offering advice about appearances. I knew he was tapping his bare feet against the floor from the slapping sound they made against the hardwood. And the fact that he never wore shoes. His graying hair was swept back from his forehead as if he wanted people to think he was outdoorsy in a rugged yet high-end sort of way. He owned the company, which I suppose gave him a lot of latitude. He'd only noticed me in passing before, offering unsolicited advice about herbal teas in the break room or mansplaining why women aren't as good at high-endurance sports as men. I honestly hadn't thought he knew my name until he called me into the conference room. To complain about my face. A man who never wore shoes.

On my first day, he'd whizzed past my desk barefoot, his dress pants rolled up to the ankles. "That guy forgot his shoes," I had whispered to the person sitting next to me.

"That's Xavier Adams. He's the boss. Bare feet connect him to nature and ground his circle of energy," she'd whispered back. "He has a pallet of grass under his desk that he rubs his feet in while he's working. It keeps him centered."

"Hm. I think shoes are always a good idea at work," I'd mumbled back.

I couldn't remember her name. She was gone less than two weeks later.

Across from me at the conference table, Xavier was flanked on either side by a member of the HR department, Gary, who was portly and unassuming, and Xavier's second-in-command, Bobbert. Management called him *Bob*, and his employees called him *Robert*, so I'd taken to referring to him as *Bobbert* in my head. He was an overgrown frat boy in a suit. He always had a smarmy smile and winked at everyone. Once, I'd thought he was flirting with me, but then he'd turned and winked at Gary in just the same way.

"We've called you in here," Xavier explained, adjusting his Christophe Claret watch, "because we're going to terminate you."

"Like Liam Neeson style?" My heart stopped for a second.

"Your services here are no longer needed," he clarified.

I let out a breath. In that split second, I'd taken mental stock of the room. Xavier was about five four, and I was pretty sure I could take him. I had at least a couple of inches on him, and one good stomp on his naked toes would probably stop him cold. Gary seemed unlikely to participate. Bobbert gave me pause, though. He looked slippery.

"I'm being fired?" I glanced over at Gary, who was staring at the ceiling and chewing on his lip. He didn't look at me. Bobbert was now doubled over, sweating profusely. He looked like he was about to vomit. I focused again on Xavier's face, trying to tamp down my panic. I was a good employee. I'd worked for Directis—"Telemarketing with a Personal Touch!"—for almost two years. Not that you had to be great to be a telemarketer, but I was. I hadn't done anything wrong. "For my expressions?" I asked. "Over the phone?"

"Your face makes it clear you don't think very highly of the management here. Quite frankly, it gives the impression that you have a dark soul. You can gather your things, and Gary will walk you out."

He was right about the first part. I *did* think everyone in management was useless. Xavier's pretentiousness was really annoying. A few days after my coworker had told me about his pallet of grass, I'd dropped off a document in Xavier's office. He hadn't been there, so I'd taken my chance and gotten down on my hands and knees to see under his desk. The "grass" had looked kind of shiny and short. Who watered it? Where was its light source? So many questions. My heart beating fast, I'd leaned over and touched a blade. It had felt like plastic. *There's no way this dude has a square of Astroturf under his desk*, I'd thought. For weeks after, when I was falling asleep, I couldn't help thinking about Xavier and his feet and his Astroturf. Did being a CEO automatically make you weird? Could fake grass connect you to anything?

I didn't like Bobbert either. His hands were always wet, and he laughed loudly at his own jokes. But I hadn't said that out loud, had I? At least not to anyone except my closest friends, when no one else was around. Had my resting bitch face awakened? And even so, shouldn't they just give me a warning?

But the other part? WTF? "I have a dark soul?" I asked. "I foster kittens for the Humane Society."

"Dark soul. Walk her out, Gary." He slid a piece of paper toward me with my name, Vanessa Blair, handwritten across on top. A box labeled INSUBORDINATION was checked. I almost laughed out loud, despite the panic flooding through me. The number of people throughout my life who had probably wanted to call me out for insubordination...and I'd made it to twenty-eight before it had actually happened. Because of my face.

"How in the world do you know what kind of soul I have? And how is this relevant to my job performance?"

"As I just explained, your face." He looked at me as if I were a small child for asking.

An ill-timed snort escaped me. This was beyond ridiculous, and yet they all looked perfectly serious. I opened my mouth to request the real reason they were firing me, but Xavier shook his head and said, "Go!"

Gary, the HR guy, who had been silent the whole time, got up and opened the door. He still wouldn't look at me. Bobbert shrank farther down in his seat. I followed Gary out of the conference room, my legs shaky, making eye contact with my coworker Jane as I walked past. "Fired," I mouthed to her as I went to pack up my mountain of coffee mugs and fancy pens in an empty box that had appeared on my desk during my absence.

"*What?*" she mouthed back. "No way. What for?"

I shrugged, still reeling from the unreality of it all. I said, "I don't like his feet, and he doesn't like my face."

"Are you all high?" Jane asked, wide-eyed.

Gary walked me toward the door as I heard Xavier say behind me, "Jane, please come in the conference room to meet with me, Bob, and Gary."

Shit. Jane too? What was wrong with *her* face?

Gary escorted me all the way to my car. A slight rain had begun to fall. Balancing my belongings on my hip, I fumbled in my handbag for my keys but couldn't find them. I dug through all the sample lipsticks and old receipts, searching as hard as I could. Gary turned around to go back inside. I set my stuff on the curb in a heap and slumped beside it, letting the rain ruin my makeup as I looked up at the clouds and waited for Jane. The September air was colder than it had been earlier, and the concrete curb felt like a block of ice through my dress pants. I shivered. I was pretty sure I'd left my jacket inside somewhere. I wasn't going back in for it, even if now I wouldn't have the money for a new one. I had five mouths to feed at home. All of them kittens.

It took Jane less than five minutes to show up with her box. "Those dudes are *all* high," she proclaimed, flipping Gary off as he hurried back inside. She dumped her stuff in the trunk of her car and turned to me, fuming. "I hate them all."

"What just happened?" I asked numbly.

"Beats me." She closed the trunk and turned to face me. "I have to take off before I punch them."

"Something rotten is going on in there—"

"It's probably just Xavier's feet. I'll text you later."

After I found my keys, I drove around aimlessly for a while, not knowing where to go, before finally heading home. I kept waiting for the tears to come, but my eyes stayed dry. I felt like I was falling, like the ground itself had been pulled out from under me. No one says, *I want to be a telemarketer when I grow up*, but a job is a job, and it kept me in my apartment with a car and food and soap. Without it, I could end up on the street, just me and the kittens, who would inevitably wander away. The only thing keeping them with me were four walls and no thumbs. I would be totally alone. Maybe I'd end up living under the bridge down the street, slowly going insane, admonishing myself for even having a face.

When I stepped inside my apartment, I kept the lights off and stumbled down the hall into the living room. At least it was warm in there. For now. I lay down in the middle of the floor and stared at the ceiling, trying to figure out why I wasn't crying yet. Because I hated working there? I had, but it was more than that. It was the injustice of it all and the sneaking suspicion that my firing didn't make any sense, not with my production numbers. I'd be hard to replace. So would Jane. Whatever the reason, I was now on a path to paranoid homelessness, to ending up as barefoot as my new archenemy. The apartment was small, only one bedroom, but it was mine, and it had a washer and dryer in the unit. That wasn't common, and I'd paid extra for it when I'd signed the lease. Everything felt like it was slipping away.

The kittens tiptoed over one by one and had begun to purr when one started to settle its fluffy calico rump on my face. I sat up, gagging on the fur and the indignity, when there was a pounding on the door.

"I've been meaning to talk to you about your face," a familiar voice yelled as I made my way to the door. Jane was standing on the other side, her eyeliner winged out and her blond hair in a messy bun. She shifted against the doorframe, and I saw Trisha, another one of our coworkers, behind her. Jane was tall, and her frame had hidden Trisha completely. I hadn't expected her, too. I wasn't as close with her since we had never hung out outside of work before. She gave me a little wave as I moved aside to let them in.

Jane headed down the hall to the living room and squinted. "Why's it so dark in here?" She turned on the light and settled onto the couch, propping her knee-high boots on the armrest. A kitten bolted, and I cringed a little. That couch was one of the only furnishings in my apartment I'd bought for myself: it had been either that or take my mother's floral sectional sofa. I'd chosen a modern, sleek couch that didn't attract cat hair. I guessed, at this point, it didn't matter if Jane's dirty shoes were all over the armrest since it wasn't like she could do more damage than the mud under the bridge. I was taking the damn thing with me when I got evicted.

"I'm practicing living without electricity," I said.

Trisha settled onto the corner of the love seat, diagonally from the couch, trying not to dislodge two kittens playing on the cushion. The love seat was a hand-me-down from my dad's corner of the basement and was now showing signs of kitten claws. I decided I'd leave it here when I became a squatter under the bridge.

"What excuse did they give you?" I asked.

"Smirking and laughing will not be tolerated in an office setting," Jane answered, using air quotes. "Not Trisha, though. She had to kiss Xavier's feet to keep her job."

I gasped. "You kissed his naked feet?" Bile rose in my throat.

"She means metaphorically," Trisha corrected. "I had to write a thousand-word memo of apology for my behavior and choice of work friends." She glanced up at Jane and me then averted her eyes apologetically.

I could tell Trisha had been crying. I liked her a lot, and she'd always had more tact than me. But seriously? "You're not going to do it, are you? He's just trying to humiliate you. All of us."

"She already did," Jane answered. "He made her send it to the entire office. 'Dear Unbalanced Poser Who Calls His Office a Dojo, I'm sorry I thought Vanessa and Jane were cool and hung out with them. I've learned from this and thought very hard about the kind of person I want to be.'"

"I think they want me to be some kind of Barbie," Trisha said. "Do they make Chinese Barbies?"

I looked back and forth between them, horrified. "No," I breathed. "I mean, yes, they make Chinese Barbies, but no, you can't become one."

Jane had dubbed a particular clique in the office *the Barbies*. There was Brunette Barbie, Bitter Barbie, Bad Barbie, Burned-Out Barbie… They dressed well, drank over lunch, and frequently used happy hour to talk about their wild nights out on the weekends. They all had the same smile (except Burned-Out Barbie, who never seemed too "with it"). Their faces had traded in and out as some left the company and new ones were hired, and I hadn't spent much time getting to know them. Or anyone, really, except Jane.

"What was I supposed to do?" Trisha asked, a little defensively. "I need this job."

I tried to check myself. Trisha was a single mom, and she adored her daughter, Claire. I understood but hated how Xavier was playing god with people's self-worth and livelihood.

"Rumor is we could have stayed, too, if we'd begged," Jane told me. She picked up a kitten and tried to settle it on her lap. The kitten let out a loud yowl and bit her index finger. Jane and I locked eyes for a minute while she nursed her finger and I considered her words. A mutual understanding passed between us. We didn't beg for anything. Except maybe food, if we ended up under the bridge.

A lot of good our pride did us, though. We were the two who would have to check the YES box after *Have you ever been fired?* on any application going forward. Next question: *Reason? Face.*

I shook my head. "Can I get you anything?" I asked them.

"Yeah. We got fired today. On a Thursday. Calls for shots," Jane responded as she leaned back and closed her eyes. A kitten got stuck between her and the back of the couch and squeaked. "Seriously, Nessa? These little floofs are everywhere."

"I know," I said apologetically. "It feels like so many more than five."

"There are at least seven," Jane said.

"Maybe six?" Trisha added.

"No, no," I told them. "Definitely only five. They're all calicos, so it just looks like more. I named them Unus, Duo, Tres, Quattuor, and Quinque. One through five in Latin. Thank God there weren't six. Sex the kitten is *not* okay."

I went to the kitchen to see if I had any alcohol. "Sex kittens always get adopted first!" Jane yelled from the living room.

I grabbed an unopened bottle of peppermint schnapps someone had left at my apartment a while back. I twisted off the cap and grabbed three glasses from the cabinet over the refrigerator. I wasn't a big drinker, so I didn't have a large selection. I brought the bottle and glasses back into the room.

"Which one is which?" Trisha asked.

I shrugged. "They all have long white fur with black and orange spots, you know? I have a checklist somewhere that specifies all their markings, but the only one that stands out to me is that one," I said, indicating the kitten that had gotten stuck behind Jane. "She has a beauty mark on her cheek."

Jane looked behind her on the couch. "She looks like Marilyn Monroe! But, you know, furry. Could've named that one *Sex*. Just saying."

I ignored her. "That's Duo. But the others all look the same. When I first got them, I tried labeling them with a Sharpie, but they just licked it off."

"You drew on them with a marker?" Jane asked, horrified.

"Just a little number inside one of their ears. That's what they do at the shelter," I replied. "That's another thing that sucked about Directis. They made it so hard to volunteer. I'm supposed to handle the promotional stuff for the animals, like the posters and advertisements, and I've barely been keeping up by working on them late at night. Which cuts into, you know, sleep." I swallowed. "I guess not now, though."

"Do they take people at the shelter?" Jane asked.

"That's not how human adoption works," Trisha told her.

Jane grabbed the schnapps from my hands and took a long swig straight from the bottle. She ignored the glasses I'd brought and passed the bottle to Trisha, who reluctantly took it with two fingers. "Uh, no, I'm good. Being sanitary is kind of my thing."

"Take a sip, Trisha. We had a bad day today," Jane said.

Trisha relented and took a long drag from the bottle. She looked a little sick. "Tastes like toothpaste. Gross." My stomach turned a little watching her. Trisha started to hand the bottle back to Jane but seemed to think better of it and took another long drink. "Actually, it reminds me of the mint baijiu cocktails my dad makes. Except for the aftertaste."

Jane squinted at her. "I used to work at a bar, but I've never heard of baijiu."

"It's like Chinese vodka," Trisha said. "My parents still prefer it over wine."

"My parents grew up in Illinois," Jane said. She reached back for the schnapps. "Wow, you just downed like half the bottle, Trish." She looked at Trisha with respect. "Nice."

She gave Jane an uncharacteristically large grin. "Claire's with my mom tonight, so bottoms up."

"I'm sorry this happened to you two," I told them. I swept two of the kittens off the couch and settled next to Jane. Trisha passed the bottle to me, and I also took a long swig and immediately gagged a little.

"It's not your fault," Trisha murmured as she held her hand out again for the bottle, and I gave it to her.

"But it is. I showed management I didn't respect them through my offensive face." I had staved off the tears all day, but I felt them prick my eyes as I leaned back into the cushions.

"Well, I got fired because I laugh inappropriately," Jane offered. She'd finally managed to get a kitten to settle on her thigh.

"And I got almost fired because I hang out with you two and need to think 'long and hard about whether or not I want to be a bad person or try to redeem myself,'" Trisha told us.

I hadn't known it was possible to feel worse. "This is all my fault," I moaned. "My dark soul is destroying your lives. I'm taking both of you with me to hell."

"We might be going to hell, but it won't be for this," Jane said sympathetically and took the bottle back. Some blond strands had slipped out of her messy bun. "Did you know we're just like that guy on the news who ran a drug ring out of the hotel he worked at? He was fired. We were fired. We're now in the same category as that guy." She let out a deep breath. "Do you think everyone there hates us now?"

"I doubt it," I said. "Xavier makes it hard to be on his side, you know?"

Jane looked up at the ceiling. "I just hope Marcus doesn't hate us. I don't care what anyone thinks but Marcus." Then she looked down at her hands.

"I'm sure Marcus doesn't think differently of you," I said softly. Marcus was the receptionist in the office. He was a few years younger than Jane, wore black hipster glasses, and had the tiniest man bun imaginable. She'd carried a torch for him since he'd been hired eight months ago.

Trisha let out a small hiccup. "You have a great face, Vanessa. Xavier is just jealous he's less beautiful-er than you are."

Jane and I looked at each other. Apparently, it didn't take long to get Trisha a little tipsy. Trisha reached for the bottle again, but Jane held it back.

"Maybe a break for you," Jane told her. "And if Xavier is firing people because they have better faces than him, that whole building is about to be out on their asses."

"That can't be why, though, right?" I asked. "There has to be some other reason."

"Who the hell knows," Jane said.

Trisha sighed loudly and dropped her head forward. Her long hair covered her face. "If I didn't have a kid, I wouldn't have written that memo, you know. Claire is counting on me. She's only four. I didn't do the best job picking her dad, so even if it means kissing the ass, or the ass feet, of someone like Xavier, I've gotta do what I've gotta do to take care of her."

My heart squeezed. "Trisha, we totally get it. Nobody's faulting you. I mean, Jane still lives with her parents. All our circumstances are different."

Jane flopped backward and dislodged the kitten from her leg. "Yep, and I totally lied to my mom and dad about all this. I told them our account got cut. So what're we gonna do? Like, I could waitress, but I can barely tolerate talking to people over the phone, let alone in person. Some of us weren't meant for customer service."

"Give me the bottle of toothpaste," I said. "I need some liquid courage to text my mom." I took the schnapps from her and had another sip. It was starting to taste a lot better. And I was definitely feeling warmer.

I pulled out my phone and sent a quick text to my mom. I got fired today.

OMG, are you okay? she texted back.

They were mean to me and Jane and they fired us and it sucked, I wrote back. I felt a rush of relief that I didn't have to lie to her like Jane did with her parents. My mom always took my side. Even if she still treated me like I was twelve.

I put the phone down on the coffee table. "I wish I could make Xavier feel as bad as he made us feel. You want to fire me, fine, but the insults weren't necessary. Someone needs to make Xavier understand that."

Trisha slid from her spot on the love seat onto the floor before leaning her back against the faux-leather armrest. The kittens all made a beeline for her and started clawing at her pants. "I think I'm seeing double," she said solemnly as she ruffled a little calico's ear. "There's like a zillion cats in my lap. Hand me that bottle, Nessa."

I passed it over and thought about Xavier and Bobbert and Gary. "Calling three women into the conference room, one by one, criticizing us, not even letting us respond, then walking us out? It's just not right." As much as I hated being fired, I almost felt sorrier for Trisha, who had to go back in the morning. It all sucked, but Trisha was in for continuing humiliation. And so was anyone else who worked for Xavier if someone didn't stop him.

"They're horrible people," Jane said. "All of them. Bobbert was huddled in the corner like he was going to pass out. It's not like *he* was getting fired. Calm yourself and take a seat, Bobbert." She grabbed the bottle back from Trisha. "Once, when my cousin was tending bar, his boss made him work a lot of mandatory overtime. He got one of those little devices that makes noise like a smoke detector running out of batteries. He hid it behind the mini fridge under the bar and set it to go off every fifteen minutes. That thing went off for two weeks. They had to shut the restaurant down. I think they opened again once the batteries ran out, but they never found it."

"That's so badass. I wanna marry your cousin." My eyelids were getting heavy. "We should get one of those things for Xavier's office."

Trisha had slumped into a prone position on the floor, and the cats were pouncing and playing with her sweater. "Totally," she said. "We should do that." Her voice was really faint like she was about to fall asleep. "Is this what heaven is like? Kittens everywhere?"

"Maybe a listening device instead," I said. "It's just as small. Or, even better, a two-way transmitter. Then we could whisper creepy things or cause disruptions at the worst possible time." I grinned. My body felt nice and relaxed.

"Well, it's not like we have anything better to do," Jane grouched.

"You're not wrong," I told her. "We could probably learn all sorts of weird stuff about them. Like, how often do they talk about their feet in there?"

"Bare feet are a magnet for germs," Jane added. "I mean, you can literally get herpes from going barefoot."

"Oh my god, gross," I said.

From her spot under the kittens, Trisha piped up, "Wire the office. Herpes. Check."

"Wiring the office, okay, but no herpes," I protested.

"Maybe herpes," Jane said. She leaned over on the couch and sympathetically rubbed my back. "We could always share a street corner," she suggested.

"I've got my eye on a spot under the bridge, but there's room for two. Not that it counts as a roof, exactly."

"You'll have to keep these kittens on a leash, though, because they're going to peace out as soon as they have the chance," Jane said.

"So true," I agreed and tipped up the bottle to get the last drop. "My whole life I've been a little insubordinate, but that's the first time I've seen it in writing."

"Saaaaaame," Jane groaned.

Trisha hiccupped. "Saaaame," she added, eyes closed.

"There really is something shady going on over there. I want to know what it is," I said as I lazily grabbed a kitten from Trisha's pile.

We were all quiet for a moment until Trisha spoke again. "I've got this." Her slurred voice rose sleepily from her place on the floor. "We consult Sun Tzu. You cool with that?"

It didn't seem to me like any of us "got this." And was Sun Tzu that guy who wrote a war manual a million years ago? "Sure, Trisha," I told her and closed my eyes. Whatever was happening at Directis would have to wait until tomorrow.

Chapter 2

All warfare is based on deception. /

—SUN TZU, *THE ART OF WAR*

I BLINKED BLEARILY. IT WAS FRIDAY MORNING, MY FIRST OFFICIAL day without a job. I'd forgotten to turn off my daily phone alarm, which had sounded at 6:00 a.m. like normal. The beeping pounded in perfect rhythm with my lingering headache. Jane and Trisha had stayed until after 2:00 a.m. the night before. It had taken us that long to sober Trisha up so she could drive. While it had been cathartic, I was going to pay for it today with a hangover. Trisha had to go back this morning, though, and see Xavier. Except for the whole paycheck thing, she had it way worse. As for me, I intended to allow myself a weekend of self-care (otherwise known as *wallowing*) before facing my new situation head on.

I checked my phone and sighed. Twelve missed texts from my mom. I vaguely remembered texting her I'd been fired. I'd have to deal with her at some point, but I didn't feel like talking about it now.

I settled into a morning of pajamas and not showering. I ate peanut butter straight from the jar and kept my TV tuned to the true crime channel. My living calico blanket made me too comfortable to move.

This whole situation had hit me harder than I realized. I was usually pretty confident in myself, but now I felt like keeping a scarf over my face and my personality to myself. After a particularly upsetting episode of *Double Crossed in Dumpsters*, I vowed never to go out in public again.

I'd just started a new episode of *Swampy Deaths* when my email dinged. I pulled my phone up to scan the new messages, and my heart stopped.

From: Gary Gallard

Time: 8:42:03 AM EST

To: Vanessa Blair

Subject: Separation from Directis

Ms. Blair,

Your employment has been terminated. We are willing to provide you with three extra days of wages, to which you are not entitled, if you sign the attached severance agreement. This message also serves to remind you that you are not eligible for unemployment, as you were fired due to misconduct.

Regards,

Gary Gallard

Human Resources

ggallard@directis.com

Huh. I thought an employee only got severance when they were laid off. I didn't know anything about being fired, so maybe I was off base. Regardless, my bullshit meter went off.

I clicked on the attached PDF and skimmed through it. It had a surprising number of *therefore*s and *subsequently nonetheless*es mixed in randomly. Basically, it amounted to a request for me to admit wrongdoing, not sue the company, and not seek unemployment benefits.

All in exchange for three days' pay. My eyes narrowed. Talk about dangling a baby carrot. I wasn't going to sue the company. But to admit to wrongdoing? Hell no. Not in any universe.

I was chewing on my lip and mulling over the email when I heard a key turn in the lock. The kittens scattered. "Vanessa!" my mom called from the hall. "You don't have to let me in. I have a key!" As if I hadn't given it to her.

I sighed. "Hey, Mom," I yelled back. Goddammit. I should have responded to her texts; then maybe I could have wallowed in peace. I shoved the jar of peanut butter behind a couch cushion.

She walked into the living room, wearing her typical uniform of a crisp white button-down shirt, rolled at the sleeves, jeans, and a large beaded necklace. She set a brown paper bag on the coffee table. Her eyes, so much like mine, were filled with concern and a hint of disgust. I looked down at myself. There were smears of peanut butter on my pajama shirt that had attracted little tufts of cat fur.

"Honey, I'm worried about you. You never wrote me back. What happened?"

"They don't like my face," I said, not looking up and willing myself not to cry.

"Oh, darling, what on earth are you saying?" My mom perched on the edge of the couch and lifted my chin. "You have the best face in the entire world."

I rolled my eyes and pulled away. "You're such a mom," I said.

"Did someone actually say that to you?"

I nodded, and fresh waves of shame rolled over me. "Xavier Adams did. He also said I don't respect management and that I have a dark soul."

"Where were you working? Thunderdome?" she exclaimed and pulled me into a hug. "I don't want you respecting anyone who would say something like that."

I nodded as she stroked my hair. "Is it okay if we don't talk about it?" I asked.

"Don't let these people make you doubt yourself. They're terrible, and they shouldn't have fired you, and I bet not a single one of them graduated from college with a four-point-oh average like you did, even if you majored in something useless."

"Mom—"

"I want to know their names, all of them, so I can call their mothers," she said. We'd moved north when I was a kid, but Mom had never really lost her accent or her Southern ways.

"No, totally not necessary, Mom," I told her. "I appreciate the support, but please stay out of it."

"I'm just saying, their mothers need to be made aware of the situation. What was the name of the main guy you said was mean to you? Excalibur? Excalibur Lincoln?"

I stopped for a moment and thought about her logic, which was usually a little off-center from mine. Where had she come up with that? Maybe a name with an *x* and a former president? I was *not* telling her his real name again, so I just nodded. "Yes, Mom, his name is Excalibur Lincoln."

"Well, I'm going to give Mr. Lincoln a piece of my mind. Then I'm calling Mr. Lincoln's mother and letting her know how Excalibur has been behaving." She reached over and smoothed my hair from my face. "I just want my baby to be happy. I raised you to be a strong woman, and your strength is written all over that beautiful face of yours. At least when you have minimal hygiene standards. You intimidated the heck out of Excalibur. That's why he fired you."

I leaned against her and let her stroke my hair. It was nice to be comforted. "I brought you a casserole, too, sweetie," she said. "And some snickerdoodles. I'd offer to let you move in with us, but you know your dad is allergic to cats. Is there anything else I can do for you? What about Jane? I can call her mother, too, and see what we can do for Jane."

"Thanks. And don't call Jane's mom." Why did she always want to talk to everyone's mom?

"I want to help. This is just a bump in the road." She pulled me into a hug. "It's not the same as Auntie Beatrice."

I stiffened and pulled out of the hug. "It's absolutely not!"

"That's what I just said. But maybe we could still learn a few things from her, if you get what I'm saying." She gave me a look.

Aunt Beatrice was my father's sister. She had been in trouble with the law a few times, and I hadn't seen much of her growing up. She'd committed arson and had been in prison for as long as I could remember.

"Different type of fire, Mom. Getting let go from a job isn't a gateway drug to actual fire. I'm not going to end up in jail with a string of burned-down houses behind me."

"I know you're not. I just said it wasn't the same."

"And you know Dad doesn't like it when we talk about Auntie Bea," I told her.

She put up her hands. "You're related to them; I'm not." She looked over my shoulder at the television, and her eyes lit up. "Oooh! *Swampy Deaths*! Are they having a marathon?" She grabbed the remote off the coffee table and checked the guide. "Yes! Time for a day of true crime with my ride-or-die." She winked at me.

Suddenly, I wanted to be anywhere but here. "I should probably spend the day looking for jobs. You know, be productive and stuff instead of watching reality TV."

I'd gotten my love of true crime from my mom, but she always took things a step too far, imagining perpetrators that didn't exist, insisting the police hadn't dug deep enough. She squinted at the screen. "I understand, sweetie. I've seen this one anyway. The husband did it." She looked at me conspiratorially. "It's always the husband, am I right?"

I shrugged. "I mean, yeah. Usually."

"Take the rest of the day to relax, sweetheart. Then you really should shower. And promise me you'll file for unemployment. It can hold you over until your next job."

"Yeah…about that. Directis just emailed me a legal document. It's jargony, but I think they're asking me to sign away my right to unemployment in exchange for three days' pay. I also have to admit I did something wrong, which I didn't. But I need money, and—"

My mother gasped. "Vanessa Leigh, don't you dare. Your integrity is not for sale. They really ought to be ashamed of themselves." She patted my arm. "If it were six months' pay, then…maybe we could fudge the integrity thing. But three days? That's not even a Coach purse; it's a wristlet. Don't sign anything." She leaned over and kissed my forehead. "So you promise you'll file?"

I nodded.

"Say it, Vanessa."

"I promise I'll file for unemployment."

Mom smiled. "That's my girl." She stood. "Okay, sweetie. I'll put the casserole in the fridge. It's your favorite: Alfredo and noodles. The cookies will be on the counter. I'm on my way to bridge club with the girls, but I'll check in on you again tomorrow. And don't you worry at all about Excalibur. It's under control."

I winced again. Awesome.

After she left, I shot Jane a quick text. Did you get an email from Gary?

Yeah, she texted back. Already signed that shit and sent it back. I need the money and I wasn't going to sue anyway.

I'd promised my mother I'd check out unemployment benefits, but maybe if I was super lucky, I wouldn't have to. I loved what I did for the animal shelter, and if I could get paid for it, it'd be a win-win. I grabbed my cell and dialed their number. It couldn't hurt.

When someone picked up, I cleared my throat. "Is Danielle around?" I asked. She was the shelter director. We weren't close, but I liked her, and we worked together on events.

"She's in the back with the new intakes," the voice answered. "Did you have a message?"

"My name is Vanessa Blair. I was checking to see if there were any staff positions available," I said. "I volunteer already and would love a more permanent—"

A sigh stopped me midsentence. "We don't have any openings. Not enough funding. I'll let her know you called, though. Thanks."

The phone clicked off. It had been a long shot, but it still bummed me out. Time to go online and try for another long shot—unemployment benefits. I didn't know anything about them, if I was eligible, or what to expect, but the weight of my situation was starting to bear down on me. I had a rent payment due in a couple weeks, and $47.86 in my bank account. But I'd be damned if I let my indefinite number of furry dependents starve because I'd looked Xavier in the face. At least I had one more check coming, though I wasn't sure how much it would be.

I pulled up my laptop and opened the Job and Family Services page. It was surprisingly straightforward. I lowered the sound on *Swampy Deaths*. It was just getting good. They'd found a body in (where else?) the swamp.

The first portion was all personal and demographic information, which was easy. Strangely enough, Directis wasn't showing up in the computer system under the list of employers, so I manually entered all the information I knew and checked the box for DISCHARGED under reason for unemployment. "I'm not going to let them make me feel like a criminal," I muttered.

A red box appeared in the middle of the screen, with the words NOTICE OF ELIGIBILITY ISSUE in bold. Awesome. *Here comes the fun part.* I clicked on the link in the box, and a separate questionnaire appeared on the screen.

What was the reason for discharge? My fingers hovered over the keys, but I typed it out. *I was told my face was unacceptable in the workplace.*

Did your actions violate any company policy? I doubted the handbook said anything about expressions, so I checked the NO box.

Had you received a prior warning for this conduct? Another no.

Were you aware you could be discharged for such an offense? A resounding no.

I finished the application, which included signing up for job matches, and hit SUBMIT.

The job market for my skills wasn't exactly popping. After college, I'd spent a year as an intern at a classical museum and then a couple years editing intra-industry travel reports, which was as thrilling as it sounded. When the economy took a dive, people stopped traveling, and the company I worked for closed.

I'd sent out my résumé to every place that was hiring, and Directis had been the only one that had called back. Telemarketing had kind of been my only option at the time. Turns out a degree in Latin wasn't the key to financial success. My education had emphasized other things, like *homo doctus in se semper divitias habet.* A learned person always has wealth inside himself. I certainly hoped so because it looked like that was the only wealth I'd have to live on for a while.

I put the laptop away and glanced up. The police on the screen were arresting the husband. I grabbed the remote and flipped off the television. Maybe I could take the weekend to figure out what I actually wanted to do with my life. Did revenge count as an occupation? How much did it pay?

Acknowledgments

As always, thank you to my own Fellowship: Jeff, Chance, Judy, Larry, and Miellyn. The plotting sessions and constant support were invaluable, and I'm forever grateful. And thank you to Jennifer Wills, my agent and cheerleader, and to Deb Werksman, the best editor around.

About the Author

Anastasia Ryan writes about what she loves best: humor, coffee, and cats. She has several useless degrees and fills her time listening to true-crime podcasts. Her debut novel, *You Should Smile More*, focused on what happens when your resting bitch face is wide awake…at work. *Not Bad for a Girl* is her second thoughtfully funny look at the absurdities of our modern workplace.

Instagram:@byanastasiaryan